Agent
OF THE
Heart

ALEXA ASTON

OLIVERHEBERBOOKS

Jace Tanner studied the computer screen in front of him, reviewing the marketing plan Penny Hiller had put together for Tevin Wakeland, one of their biggest clients. Tevin was the starting quarterback for the Detroit Lions and had recently signed with Touchdown Talent Management, the sports agency Jace had founded with Mark Walton five years ago. TTM had just helped Tevin land the highest-paying contract for an NFL quarterback, and they were now looking into various marketing opportunities for the twenty-five-year-old out of LSU.

He texted Penny to come see him, and she arrived at his office in less than two minutes, along with Steve Butler, TTM's graphics guy and social media expert.

Rising, Jace motioned them to the table in the corner of his downtown Dallas office. The entire wall was made of glass, and the view was nothing less than spectacular. The three took seats.

"The shoe contract and athleisure wear endorsements are solid fits for Tevin," he began. "But I like the new additions.

The airline and the watch company have potential. What Tevin will really like is the opportunity to partner with the city of Detroit on municipal playgrounds and the natatorium. This is a guy who likes to give back to his community. Detroit has embraced him these last three years, and he wants to show them some love."

He let Penny run through the details of the product endorsements and signed off on that. The contracts would go to Mark now since he was the lawyer. Jace was more the face of TTM, charming clients and pulling in new business, as well as overseeing all aspects other than contracts. Even those he read through and tweaked with Mark before they presented them to their clients. After interning, working for two other sports management companies, and then founding TTM, he had plenty of experience in reading contracts and contributing salient points to them.

Then the three of them brainstormed ideas regarding Tevin's partnering with the city. Not only would the quarter-back become the face of the community in Detroit, his charity would fund the bulk of the city's playgrounds and pools. This was one athlete who put his money where his mouth was. Tevin would earn millions from his new deal, but he would also sink millions back into Detroit's youth.

"When can we meet with Tevin?" asked Steve.

"I'll get back to you on that," Jace said. "But he's very happy with what you've done with his Instagram, and he really likes the new website design for his charity."

Steve looked pleased. "Good to know."

"While I have you here, let's chat briefly about DeMarcus Green."

Penny grinned. "TTM landing DeMarcus as a client was a real coup, Jace. DeMarcus is bound to go number one in the April NFL draft."

"It's all about guiding champions from the field to the spotlight," he said, parroting TTM's tagline. "Good work. Get with Mark on the contracts, Penny. I want to go in with a solid idea of what DeMarcus will accept."

"How soon do you want these done?"

"Yesterday," he replied, his standard answer since sports management was all about timing.

The pair left, and Elena Arturo entered his office. He'd convinced her to leave the previous agency they both worked for and help him start up TTM. She was bright, attractive, and detail-oriented. She also kept him on track. All roads to Jace went through Elena, and she was the best watchdog he could have looking after him.

"You have someone here to see you. Erasmus Crawford. No appointment, but he said it's urgent."

An odd feeling washed over him. Jace had hired the private investigator over six months ago. He had no website. No internet presence at all. His referrals all came from discreet, word-of-mouth referrals. Crawford had worked for the biggest movers and shakers in Dallas, as well as the richest ones. He charged outrageous prices, ones which his clients were all too willing to pay, all in the name of maintaining privacy. A person came to a guy like Crawford because they wanted no trace of what they wanted done.

In Jace's case, he'd asked Crawford to find his older brother. When a client had mentioned Crawford, Jace was all over it, meeting with the PI and giving him next to nothing to go on. Jace and Eli had been separated when he was three and Eli maybe a couple of years older. He hadn't even known his original last name to give Crawford. All he had were brief flashes of his older brother trying to protect him. Sharing food with him. Sleeping inside a closet to hide from someone who would hit them. He'd guessed his brother's name was Eli, simply because he could remember saying *E-Wi.*

That was all Crawford had to go on. Jace's adopted parents were dead. They'd only told him he was adopted after he had graduated from high school. The Texas birth certificate they had was the one given to them after the adoption, reflecting they were Jace's parents. He knew he was adopted in Texas and hoped the same had happened to Eli. Jace made a point of remaining in Texas to go to college and even after graduation, he passed up better work opportunities in New York and L.A. to remain in Texas, all because he wanted to stay in case he ever found Eli. He'd looked on his own for years, finding next to nothing, before calling in Erasmus Crawford, who hadn't even sent him a single text in all these months.

"Have him come in," he told Elena. "What do I have coming up?"

"Nothing until after lunch. A one o'clock call." She named the client.

"Have all the paperwork ready to go."

She gave him one of her patented Elena looks. "The folder is sitting on your desk, Jace. Everything's summarized for you."

"As always, thanks. No calls while Crawford is here. Thanks."

Elena left. Jace wondered if he should stand. The sudden nerves racing through him were unlike anything he'd ever felt. His gut told him that Crawford had found Eli. Or whatever his name was now. Jace's parents had changed his name to Jason. They'd had a son named Jason who'd drowned, and his adopted mom hadn't been able to have any more children. Even as a small boy, he'd rejected being called Jason, preferring to shorten it to Jace. After he stumbled across old pictures and learned of the first Jason Tanner, it had creeped him out that he had been given the dead boy's same name.

He had respected his parents' wishes, though, and not looked for his brother until after their deaths in a plane crash after his junior year of college.

His assistant appeared again, ushering the investigator into Jace's office, asking, "Anything to drink, Mr. Crawford?"

"Just Crawford. I go by it. Erasmus was my grandfather. I beat up a lot of kids on the playground for making fun of it. Then I simplified things and just went by my last name starting in third grade."

"Even your teachers called you Crawford?" Elena asked.

"*Especially* my teachers. I'd have a little talk with them at the beginning of each school year, and they addressed me as Crawford."

Elena rewarded the PI with a smile. "Good for you, Crawford. Drink?"

He waved her away. "Nah. I'm good." He made his way toward Jace as Elena closed the door, a manila folder in his hand, piquing Jace's curiosity.

Standing, he offered his hand. "Take a seat, Crawford. It's nice to finally hear from you."

Crawford shrugged. "I told you I'd be in contact when I had something. Well, I finally do." He opened the manila folder and picked up a picture, passing it to Jace. "Eli Carson."

Hearing the name Carson set off a bell inside him. There was a familiarity to it. He turned his attention to the photo, staring at it a long time, little tingles zipping through him. It was a formal portrait, probably one off some website for whatever company Eli worked at.

"I should say Dr. Eli Carson," Crawford continued. "Six feet even. Medium brown hair. Dark brown eyes. Runs daily." He passed a second picture to Jace, one which was full body length. "You can tell he's got a runner's body. Lean. Hungry."

He looked at it and then back at the first photo, trying to recall the small boy his brother had been, wondering if he could see any of that boy in this grown man.

"Tell me everything you've learned, including why you think this is my brother."

"I guarantee he is. I snagged a coffee cup he drank from. Ran the DNA. He's a definite match for you, Mr. Tanner."

"Jace," he corrected absent-mindedly, still gazing intently at the photo. "You said Carson. That pulls at a memory. I think that was my name. Before the adoption." He paused. "That means Eli was never adopted."

"Right," the PI confirmed. "Eli Carter went into the system at age five. Wanted to stay with his three-year-old brother, but that request was not honored. Your mother was an addict. Lost her parental rights. No father ever in the picture."

"Alcohol or drugs?"

"Both."

Jace barely touched alcohol and had never tried drugs. Something in the back of his mind had told him he was given up because one or both parents were addicts. He was too driven to let some addiction get in his way.

"What else?"

"He skipped a couple of grades in elementary school and then skipped another one. Graduated high school at fourteen. Rice at seventeen. Med school at twenty. Board certified in family medicine. He's worked in the ER of a large Houston hospital for seven years. Promoted to head of ER several years ago."

"Have you talked to anyone at that hospital?" he asked eagerly.

"I did. Dr. Carson is well liked by staff and patients alike. He's dedicated. Knowledgeable. A little on the quiet side but can take command of a situation when necessary."

"Any family?"

"None."

They had that in common. Jace worked long hours, rarely taking any time off. Vacation wasn't in his vocabulary. Sure, he dated. It was important at times to have a beautiful woman on his arm at different events he attended, but he had never been seriously involved with any woman. Something had started to nag at him recently, and he knew he wanted more than the business life he led. It was what had urged him to seek out Eli.

And a little voice kept whispering in his ear how much he'd like a wife and family.

"You haven't spoken to Eli, though, have you?"

"No. Your instructions were clear on that, Jace. Find your brother. Find out all I could about him." He passed the manila folder to Jace. "Everything I've learned is in here. I followed him around for a few days to see what his habits are like. From all appearances, he's a good guy. I think you'll hit it off if you contact him."

Jace flipped through the file, looking at Crawford's notes. Checking the DNA test. Skimming interviews with several people.

"I know you asked those you spoke with to keep things confidential, but someone is bound to say something to him."

"True. Which is why you should talk to him. I've listed his cell phone number so you can do that."

He couldn't call. Already, he knew he was going to be tongue-tied around his big brother. And to have to tell Eli that he got adopted when Eli had spent years in foster care would be a hard pill for his brother to swallow. He might not want anything to do with Jace.

But he could go see him. Talk face-to-face.

Standing, he offered his hand. "Thank you, Crawford. You've done a really thorough job. You had very little to go on, and yet you found Eli."

"I told you I would do it. It just took time." The investigator stood and took Jace's hand, shaking it. "You'll be receiving my bill. If you have a heart attack when you see the number owed, tell that pretty admin to pay it before you kick the bucket."

He laughed. "I'll do that."

After Crawford left, Jace got on his computer. He looked up the Houston hospital where Eli worked. He was right. The staff picture was the one Crawford had first showed him. A restless feeling passed over him, causing him to make an instant decision.

Buzzing Elena, she came in. "What's up?"

"Book me on the next available flight to Houston."

Without asking what he was up to, she asked, "And your return?"

"Open. I'll probably fly back tonight."

She looked at her watch. "I'll have your car service pick you up downstairs. Head to Love Field. I'll text you your details."

He left the office before he lost his courage. By the time he got downstairs, his car and driver were waiting for him.

"No luggage, Mr. Tanner?"

"Not this trip."

Before they reached the airport, Elena sent him his flight number and time. He checked in and went through security and to his gate. While he waited for his plane to arrive and its passengers to disembark, he spent his time on his phone, answering emails. Elena had sent one, outlining the meetings she'd rescheduled for the rest of the day. She'd also cancelled all his meetings for tomorrow on the off-chance he wouldn't make it back tonight. His admin was worth every penny he paid her—and then some.

After he boarded, he turned off his cell and closed his eyes. Jace had the uncanny ability to fall asleep anywhere. He napped for the forty-five minutes they were in the air and awoke refreshed. When he reached the front entrance, Jace spied his name on a card a driver was holding.

"I'm Jace Tanner."

"Right this way, Mr. Tanner."

Once in the car, he gave the driver the name of the hospital.

"We should be there in about forty minutes, Mr. Tanner, barring any traffic accidents."

"It's Houston," he said. "There'll be accidents. I've never been here when there weren't any."

He worked his phone again, wondering how sports agents in the previous generation had been able to do their jobs without a cell phone.

Lost in thought, it startled him when the driver announced, "This is it, Mr. Tanner."

Looking up, he saw they were pulling up to the front of the hospital. "Take me around to the ER."

The driver did as he requested, and they weaved their way through construction in the parking lot to get there.

"Thank you," he said.

"Ms. Arturo told me to wait for you, wherever I took you, whether it was ten minutes or ten hours."

Nodding, Jace said, "Thank you. I'm not sure how long I'll be inside."

"I'll be here when you're done."

When he entered the emergency room, he could feel the electric buzz. Everyone was in hurry-up mode, something he understood. He headed to the desk. Ahead of him was a crying boy, about three, holding his arm. His mother held the boy, and she was crying, too. Other patients were waiting in chairs, some looking worse for the wear.

The doors opened, and two paramedics rushed in, wheeling a stretcher. A doctor in a white coat met them as one EMT quickly gave a status report on the incoming patient. Within seconds, the patient was wheeled away.

Others in scrubs and white coats were moving from place to place, taking care of the injured. He could feel the rush of excitement and wondered if that was what Eli might be addicted to. Then again, he could simply be an excellent physician who preferred practicing emergency medicine.

The mother and son in front of him were led away, and the receptionist turned to him.

"How may I help you?" she asked.

"Nothing is wrong with me," he assured her. "I just need to see Dr. Eli Carson if he's available."

She looked at him sympathetically. "I'm sorry. Dr. Carson is no longer with us."

"What?"

He had just gotten Crawford's report. How could his brother's job status have changed in a few hours' time?

"Dr. Carson left for another job opportunity," she informed him. "His final shift was last night. Frankly, I think it'll be good for him. Dr. Carson was universally loved, but he also burned the candle at both ends, if you know what I mean. I think he was headed for burnout. A lot of ER physicians experience it."

"Can you tell me where he's gone?"

She frowned. "I'm not really sure I should—"

"He's my brother," Jace blurted out. "I haven't seen him since we were kids. Our mom had to give us up, and we were separated. I just now tracked him down. To here."

Jace had never given out as much personal information about himself as he did in those few seconds. Apparently, what he shared worked.

"Dr. Carson has taken a job as the medical director of a new regional hospital in Montague County. I don't know the name, but it's supposed to open in the next few months. I'm sure you can find it online."

"Thank you."

He wandered back outside, stunned by what he'd just learned. To have come this far and be so close to reuniting with Eli.

His car pulled up, and the driver got out, opening the rear door for Jace. "Where to, Mr. Tanner?"

"The airport."

First, he texted Elena and asked her to book him a return flight ASAP. Next, he began searching for the new hospital. He found a Hogan Health medical facility in Montague County was scheduled to open in early June, and the town was called Hawthorne. Pulling up a map of cities in North Texas, he found Hawthorne was located between Gainesville and Decatur, right on the southeastern edge of Montague County. Probably eighty miles or so from his office in downtown Dallas. With traffic—and no direct interstate—it could be anywhere from ninety minutes to two hours away.

Jace closed his eyes. Maybe doing a face-to-face with Eli wasn't the way to go. He couldn't be rash about this and blow his one chance to get to know his brother after so many years apart. Maybe he could go to Hawthorne and observe Eli. Meet him in some casual way.

He decided to put Erasmus Crawford back on the job and texted him to call him right away.

Seconds later, his phone rang.

"He wasn't there," Jace said. "He just left for a new job. Yesterday was his last day at the ER."

"Where is he? What do you need?"

He shared the name of the new hospital and its location. "Find out everything you can about him. What he's doing. Where he's living. I mean everything. And then come to my office."

"I assume this is a rush job."

"You assume correctly."

Jace ended the connection. He would be more circumspect this second time. Find out as much as he could about Eli and his new place of employment.

But now that he knew his brother was alive and in Texas, nothing was going to stop him from reuniting with all he had left of his family.

CHAPTER

One

KANSAS CITY—SEPTEMBER

Darby Montgomery disembarked from the plane and bypassed the luggage carousels. Having her luggage lost twice over her many years of traveling had convinced her to be a carryon-only passenger. She rolled her suitcase beside her now, backpack slung over one shoulder. As she walked, she opened her rideshare app and scheduled a pickup. Thankfully, a driver was near and retrieved her within three minutes.

During the ride to her office, she scrolled through her emails, answering a few of them. She also texted Mitch Gary, whom she'd been seeing casually for several months now, letting him know she was back in town and asking if he'd like to get together tonight for drinks or dinner.

Dating had been difficult ever since she'd graduated from college a decade ago. For nine of those years, Darby had traveled extensively, often gone on weekends. A guy would ask her out. They would go and have a great time. And then she'd be tied up, teaching cheer clinics across the country for the next three weekends. By the time she was free to see him again, he had already moved on. Because of that, she hadn't been really serious with anyone.

Mitch had potential, though. He was an assistant district attorney in Kansas City. Because he was dedicated and also worked long hours, he understood her commitment to work. Thankfully, she'd received a promotion a few months ago, which meant not as much travel. She did have to be in Dallas early next week for some meetings, however. Because of that, she would take tomorrow and Friday off and head to her hometown of Hawthorne, Texas, which was only about ninety minutes from Dallas. Her aunt and uncle lived there, along with her brother Sawyer and two of her three cousins. She was ready to get in some family time and see them over the long Labor Day weekend before attending her business meetings. Mitch was in the middle of a murder trial, working insane hours, so she didn't feel bad about being gone this weekend.

Drinks only. Maybe some apps? Swamped with this trial. Luciano's? 7?

He'd named an Italian restaurant in downtown, close to both his office and the courthouse. Darby texted a thumbs up, knowing that's all she needed to do to confirm. As intense as he was in the courtroom, Mitch was easygoing outside it. That's one of the reasons she liked spending time with him.

Her driver pulled up at the Cheer USA national offices, and she brought her luggage into the lobby. Avoiding the elevators, she took a flight of stairs down to the parking garage and left her things inside her trunk. Going upstairs, she went to her office, where her assistant greeted her.

"Messages are on your desk. I prioritized them, so start at the top. I've got a dental appointment and need to leave now."

"Are you getting your permanent crown in?"

"Yes. Finally. See you tomorrow, Darby."

She settled behind her desk, going through all her messages first. Then her cell rang. She saw it was her cousin.

Answering, she said, "Hey, Autumn. How are things in Hawthorne? Better yet, how are you and Eli doing? I can't wait to see you and meet him."

"We're getting married!"

"Whoa! That's terrific news. Congratulations. When is the wedding? I'll put it on my calendar now so I can work around it."

"This weekend," Autumn said surprising Darby. "It's crazy last minute, but we only want close family there anyway. With Summer coming in from New York and you arriving too, Eli and I thought it would be the perfect time to say our I do's."

A small wave of envy rippled through her. Darby wished she could find someone to share her life with. She quickly tamped it down, truly excited for her cousin.

"I'm really happy for you, Autumn. I can't wait to meet Eli in person."

"It'll be Saturday afternoon in Mom and Dad's backyard. You should see the flowers this year, Darby. A kaleidoscope of color. The perfect backdrop."

"What should I wear?"

"It's casual. Not shorts and T-shirt casual, but maybe a sundress. It's still hot as blazes in Texas." Autumn laughed. "We might even invite everyone over to swim after the ceremony."

"Okay. I know what to pack. I land at DFW tomorrow afternoon. No need to get me. I plan to rent a car. I'll stay with your parents or Sawyer this weekend and then drive back to Dallas for a couple of days of meetings."

"Sounds good. Just wanted to let you know before you got here."

"I'm glad you did. And I can hear how happy you are, Autumn."

"Eli makes me giddy, Darby. I've never felt this way before. We're madly in love. See you soon. Bye!"

The connection ended. She was thrilled Autumn had found someone who made her feel loved and treasured. Her first husband certainly hadn't. The entire family had disliked Dr. Flint Ferris, but everyone had kept their opinions to themselves, wanting to stand by Autumn and her decision. Flint had been self-centered and cheated on his wife. Autumn had the guts to stand up to him and demand a divorce. She'd left her nursing job in Houston and returned home to Hawthorne, where she'd landed a job as Director of Nursing for a hospital which had been recently built in town. Eli was the medical director for the facility. Sawyer really liked Eli, and her brother was an excellent judge of character.

Darby finished up some correspondence and then wandered down the hall to Peggy Mortimer's office. The CEO's door was open, and Peggy's assistant waved Darby in.

Peggy was on the phone, but she motioned for Darby to have a seat. She finished her call and hung up.

"How was your trip to Chicago?"

"Promising."

She'd been sent to talk to the CEO of another national cheer organization. Peggy had high hopes of merging the two groups.

"I'll write up my report tonight and email it to you, but I think we have a solid chance of uniting our organizations."

"Not tonight," Peggy said. "Take a break. You work long hours, Darby. I don't want you to burn out."

Actually, she was already at that point. After ten years of working for Cheer USA—not counting the summers she and her best friend Kelby had gone around the country teaching cheer camps—she was getting itchy feet. The travel had gotten old. She didn't feel challenged anymore. Now with Kelby recently returning to Hawthorne and marrying and now Autumn doing the same, Darby felt the pull to return to Hawthorne and put roots down, as well. She wanted to find a good man. Even start a family. And possibly put her teaching degree to use.

"All right. I'll work on it tomorrow first thing. No detail will be left out."

Peggy laughed. "You're a perfectionist, Darby. That's what I love about you."

"I'll see you tomorrow."

She returned to her office, seeing it was time to leave to meet Mitch. She stopped by the restroom and freshened her makeup, spritzing some perfume on her wrists and rubbing them together. Though she was tired, she felt she owed it to Mitch to see him before she left town again. He was a nice guy. Funny. Sweet. But the spark she had hoped would develop hadn't so far. Maybe it was time to cut bait—and think about shaking things up in her life.

It was quicker to walk the three blocks to Luciano's than drive, plus it saved her from having to find a parking spot. She entered the dark restaurant and checked in with the hostess. Mitch wasn't there yet, so she went to the bar and took a seat in a booth for two. As she did, she got a text from Mitch saying he was on his way.

Darby ordered a glass of Chardonnay for herself and a beer for Mitch. She also asked for the sampler appetizer to be brought. It had a variety of items, such as fried mozzarella sticks, calamari, and toasted ravioli.

"I'll bring you some bread and olive oil, too," the server told her.

Mitch arrived just as their drinks and the bread did, looking a little rumpled. He sat, immediately reaching for his beer and downing half of it.

"Are you just thirsty, or do you really need that?" Darby asked, sipping her white wine.

"Both," he replied.

"How is the case going?"

"We rested the state's case today. Just before noon. The judge had some appointment this afternoon, so she said court would resume tomorrow with the defense needing to be ready to put on their portion of the trial."

"Have you got a good read on the jury?"

"Yes and no," he said, taking another swig of beer and then reaching for a roll, breaking off a piece and dipping it into the olive oil. "Eight of them I've got a handle on. The other four? Not so much. Usually by this time, I do know which way most are leaning, by watching their body language and facial expressions. These four baffle me."

As Mitch went into detail, explaining why, their appetizer platter arrived.

"Thanks for ordering this. If I'm inhaling things too fast, slap my hand."

She laughed. "Will do."

They talked about the jury some more and the points the prosecution had driven home. By now, the platter was empty. Mitch had eaten without thinking, something she knew he did when he was heavily involved in a case or when he had something on his mind.

"Darby?" He looked her square in the eyes. "We need to talk."

Instinct told her to prepare herself because a breakup was coming. "What's up, Mitch?"

"You know I've enjoyed spending time with you. You're so easy to talk to. You get my jokes. You're committed to work, and you get that I work long hours. You've never been demanding."

"But?"

He shrugged. "We went into this saying we wanted to keep it casual. I almost thought I might push things to see if you wanted to be a little more serious, but ..." His voice trailed off. "Something happened. With Jessica."

She knew Jessica was his former girlfriend. They'd gone to college together and dated for three years. When Mitch had opted to attend law school, Jessica had enrolled in med school. From that point on, they had been off and on over the next five years, trying to make things work while living in different cities, both deeply immersed in their studies. They'd finally decided to call things off between them. Mitch hadn't dated anyone seriously since he'd ended his relationship with Jessica.

"Are you back together?" she asked. "I get it if you are. She's been a big part of your life."

Mitch nodded. "You're the last obstacle to that. Jess has finished up her residency and some kind of post-training. She knows I'm wedded to staying in Kansas City. I've worked too hard to walk away now." He hesitated. "She's willing to come here. To try again."

Darby placed her hand over Mitch's. "I think that's a great idea, Mitch. You've never really gotten over her. Do you still love her?"

"I think so." He paused, shaking his head. "No, I know so. And it's not fair to you."

"The heart wants what the heart wants," she said,

squeezing his fingers and then removing her hand. "You both had some busy years, training in your separate professions and then diving into demanding jobs. I think you owe it to each other to give your relationship another chance."

"You aren't mad?" he asked.

She smiled. "I could never be mad at you, Mitch. We've had some good times. Enjoyed one another's company. Whether it could have developed into something more serious is beside the point. Jessica's free and willing to come to Kansas City. I think that speaks volumes. Besides, I've been contemplating a career change myself. It would most likely mean a move back to Texas for me. So let's part friends, okay?"

Mitch smiled. "You are the best, Darby." He leaned over and kissed her cheek. "I hope you find whatever—and whoever—you're looking for."

"I do, too," she said softly, glad that they were ending things on a positive note.

The server appeared. "Can I get you another drink? Dessert?"

"No, just the check," Mitch said, looking at Darby. "I've got to get back to the office. The first witness the defense will call is full of technical testimony. I want to be on my toes for whatever unfolds."

"And I've got a report to write," she told him. "It looks as if the chance for Cheer USA to merge with another national organization is a strong possibility."

He paid the bill and walked outside with her. Taking her hand, Mitch said, "I'm sorry this didn't work between us."

She had always been like one of the guys. Comfortable with men. Able to talk sports with them. No one guy had ever grabbed her attention and made her sit up, thinking *he's* the one. Darby knew she could have married Mitch and even been happy with him. But it wouldn't have been a grand, passionate love.

Leaning up on tiptoes, she brushed her lips against his cheek. "I hope you and Jessica make it, Mitch. I'll be rooting for you."

She walked away, feeling a little sad. A little lonely. But she knew it was for the best. At thirty-two, it was time to turn her eyes to her future. To seriously consider if it were time to walk away from Cheer USA and put her teaching certificate to good use. She would talk with both Kelby and Sawyer about it this weekend. Attend her meetings in Dallas.

And maybe by then, she would have a clear idea of exactly what she wanted out of her future.

CHAPTER
Two

HAWTHORNE

"I think it's perfect," Darby told Autumn, looking at the wedding dress her cousin now modeled.

"With it being my second wedding, I didn't want to go all-out bride," Autumn said.

"This hits the mark," Summer told her twin. "You can wear it for tomorrow's wedding, but you can also wear it for other occasions. Personally, I'm all about versatility in clothing these days. My place in New York is so tiny, every piece of clothing needs to double or triple its value in order for it to be a part of my wardrobe." She sighed. "Oh, for the days of living in Texas and having a walk-in closet."

Autumn smoothed the skirt of the tea-length dress. "It seems so odd to be wearing civilian clothes all the time now. For years, I lived in scrubs, both at work and at home. On my days off, it was just easier to toss on a pair of scrubs and do housework or run errands. I've actually had to go out and buy a lot of clothes so I'm dressed appropriately for my job."

"I'm glad you are settling in nicely to your new role at

Triple H," Darby said, using the nickname for Hogan Health Hawthorne. "Overseeing the entire nursing staff is a big career step up for you."

"It has been," Autumn agreed. "I'm glad that Eli had faith in me professionally—and now personally. Oh, I'm so happy, I could burst!" She twirled in a circle, her joy obvious.

Summer leaped to her feet and hugged her sister, and Darby joined in, making it a group hug.

"I need to get going," she told the twins. "I'm going over to Kelby's to see her new house. She said she has a Hawks shirt for me to wear to the game tonight."

"You'll meet us at the tailgate?" Summer asked.

"Yes. And I assume we'll all sit together at the game."

"Right along with Mom and Dad on the fifty-yard line," Autumn said, laughing. "Dad staked out their seats years ago, same as he did his pew at church on Sunday mornings. Now that he's the superintendent of Hawthorne's schools, no one would dare sit in Joe Sutherland's place."

"See you soon," Darby said, fetching the keys to the rental car and her purse.

She drove to Kelby and West's new house, which had only been finished last month. The couple had bought five acres located just outside of Hawthorne so they would have plenty of room to raise their family. For a moment, a pang of jealousy sparked within her at that thought. Kelby had been her best friend since kindergarten, and she was happy that Kelby and West had found one another after so many years apart.

As she pulled up to the sprawling ranch house, she admired the color of the brick and outside design, as well as its landscaping. Kelby answered the door, pulling Darby in for a long hug.

"I'm so glad to see you," her friend said. "Come on. Let me give you a quick tour of the place."

They moved through the house, with Kelby pointing out features she liked about it, including the large outdoor kitchen and firepit in the backyard.

"You have plenty of room here," she said. "It looks as if you'll be hosting family gatherings in the future."

"We're happy to do that." Kelby took Darby's hands in hers. "Oh, I can't tell you how happy I am to be married to West and back in Hawthorne. Remember when we thought this place was boring and couldn't wait to leave?"

"Going to college in Austin together was exciting," she agreed. "And cheering for the Longhorns with you made my college years a dream come true."

She turned away, but her friend pressed, "What is it? You seem off."

"I had lunch with Sawyer today and talked to him a little bit about this. I'm in a quandary, Kelby. I feel as if I'm at a crossroads in my life."

"Is it work? Mitch? Both?"

"Mitch and I are done. He got back together with his former girlfriend. They were a case of being at the right place at the wrong time. I'm happy for him. I think we'll even stay friends." She hesitated. "This is more of a work and life dilemma. If I were older, I'd call it my midlife crisis."

"I thought you enjoyed what you do at Cheer USA," Kelby protested. "You've never led me to believe otherwise. You also got that promotion not too long ago, so that means you won't be traveling as much in the future."

"I don't feel challenged anymore. I feel like I'm simply going through the motions at work," she admitted.

Kelby squeezed Darby's hands. "I know exactly what you

mean. It's been eye-opening to start my own business, but I've never been happier taking the risk. Maybe you'd like to come to work with me at Social Synergy Creations."

"No, that's your thing. Not mine."

"Then what are you thinking about doing? Teach?"

She nodded. "I'm toying with that idea. Of course, school just started a few weeks ago in Texas. It's not as if I could find a full-time position at this point. I've thought about how much I've loved working with cheer campers all these years, and I'd like to put my teaching degree to good use."

"I know you're certified here in Texas. Would you consider moving back to Hawthorne?"

"I think this is where I'm supposed to be," Darby said quietly. "Sawyer's come back. As much as he enjoyed working and living in Dallas, he said he really likes the slower pace and the friendliness of the people here in Hawthorne. I'm thinking about talking to Uncle Joe about it. Going on and putting my application in so that it's on file. That way, when next spring comes and hopefully a few openings pop up, I could already be in line."

"You know you have my support in whatever you decide to do," Kelby assured her. "Even if you want to quit Cheer USA now. You could move in with West and me. You see how big the house is. You could sub. Get your feet wet that way. See if teaching is really what you want to do."

"That's a kind offer, but I don't know if I could give up a full-time salary in order to sub."

"Well, the offer is out there if you want to take us up on it. Rent-free, to sweeten the pot."

"Shouldn't you run that by West first?"

"West adores you. You're his cousin and friend. Family to both of us. He'd be happy to have you here."

"Thank you."

"Now, let's go find something for you to wear. As the new football coach's wife, I already have an extensive wardrobe of Hawthorne Hawks game wear. T-shirts. Hats. Necklaces and earrings. We'll get you decked out."

After Darby changed into a Hawks T-shirt and donned a button and pair of earrings, Kelby said it was time to leave for the tailgate. They arrived and found Uncle Joe and Aunt Meg.

"Hamburger or hot dog?" her uncle asked, turning a hamburger patty.

"Whichever is ready to come off the grill first," Darby said, Kelby echoing the same.

They each took hot dogs and dressed them with mustard and pickle relish. A huge pot of queso caught her attention and she placed tortilla chips on her plate, ladling the queso on top of the pile.

Eli came up to them, introducing himself. "It's nice to meet you in person, Darby," the handsome doctor said. "We're really glad you're in town this weekend for our wedding."

"If I hadn't already been here, I would've flown down in a heartbeat," she assured him. "Autumn has always been more like a sister than a cousin to me. I wouldn't miss your wedding for the world."

Autumn waved them over, holding up bottled waters. They joined her. Conversation turned to Triple H and its impact on the community.

"I drove by it when I came into Hawthorne. It's really large and a beautiful building."

"Come see it inside," Eli said. "We'll give you a tour."

"I'd like that," Darby told him.

"How long will you be town?" Summer asked her.

Darby explained that she had meetings Tuesday and

Wednesday at the downtown Dallas facility which would be hosting Cheer USA's national competition in early February.

"It's never been held in Dallas before, but part of my job has been scouting locations for future competitions. I believe this arena will be the perfect place to hold next year's competition. I also hope Hawthorne's cheerleaders will enter it."

"I'll introduce you to Kay Timmons," Kelby said. "She's the cheer coach at HHS."

Eli told them he needed to report to the field since he was the physician on duty for the game and that he'd see them later. Darby finished her food and when Kelby had done the same, they said they'd meet the others in the stands.

As they approached the stadium, memories flooded Darby. She had grown up going to games here at Hawks Field, and then she and Kelby had cheered for the Hawks during their high school years. This was her first time attending a game since she herself had been a cheerleader as a teen. She could hear the band warming up and knew the cheerleaders were doing the same, stretching their muscles and turning flips and cartwheels.

"I briefly met Kay at a cheer camp this summer held at SMU," Darby said, as they moved down the concrete stairs to the track which surrounded the field.

Just as she suspected, the cheerleaders were already on the track, their megaphones and pompoms placed at equal distance from one another as the girls went through their warmup routines. She spied Kay in conversation with a man Darby didn't recognize.

Touching Kelby's arm, she said, "Let's wait a minute. Looks like they're having a serious conversation."

"That's Kay's husband. Todd. I wonder what's going on. Kay looks upset."

"Maybe this isn't a good time to chat with her," Darby said, hesitant to approach the cheer sponsor.

Todd Timmons kissed his wife's cheek and walked away. By now, a couple of the girls had seen Kelby and Darby and greeted them. They talked to the cheerleaders for a few minutes and then excused themselves, moving in Kay's direction.

"Is everything all right, Kay?" Kelby asked. "This is my best friend and former Hawks cheerleader, Darby Montgomery."

Kay mustered a smile. "I remember meeting you at the Cheer USA camp. My girls really enjoy performing the dances you choreographed which they learned at camp. The squad was a big hit at the pep rally yesterday."

"Glad to hear that," she said, still concerned.

Kay's eyes filled with tears. "I'm sorry," she apologized. "Can we step away from the girls a minute?"

Kay walked away. Darby and Kelby exchanged a glance, following the cheer coach around the end of the stands, which placed them out of sight.

"I didn't mean to get so emotional. Todd just told me that his promotion has come through." Kay looked at Kelby. "Remember, I mentioned that to you last spring? Well, it's finally happened. And it couldn't come at a worse time. Todd will be going up to Chicago, while I stay here and finish out my contract and the school year."

Kelby nudged Darby and then asked, "What if your principal was able to find someone to take your place?"

Kay brushed away tears from her cheeks. "At this time of year? That's almost impossible. First of all, very few people want to get involved in cheer coaching. It's very demanding on a teacher's time. All the after-school practices. Games both during the week and on weekends, year-round. Then all the prep work that goes in for competitions. Not to mention I also am the journalism teacher at HHS. That means I sponsor both the newspaper and yearbook. Finding someone certified to teach those classes, plus agree to take on the cheerleaders, would be difficult."

Darby felt Kelby staring at her and turned to meet her gaze. Her friend nodded encouragingly.

"I have a Texas teaching certificate," Darby shared with Kay. "My teaching fields are English and journalism."

The cheer sponsor seemed baffled. "But you already have a job with Cheer USA. Why would you leave that?"

"I've been with the organization over a decade now," Darby explained. "I'm ready for a change in my life. I was thinking about moving back to Hawthorne."

Kay's jaw dropped. "Are you serious? Would you be willing to take my place at the high school? Then Todd and I wouldn't have to be separated for the entire school year."

An excitement began building within her, but Darby said, "Can you give me the weekend to consider it? This would be a huge change for me. I want to make certain that it's the right one."

"I won't tell a soul," Kay promised. "Not even Todd. Though that'll probably kill me. My cheerleaders are a terrific group this year, Darby—if that helps you with your decision. Sometimes, I've seen little cliques form within the squads, but both JV and Varsity really get along well with one another this year. I know you haven't taught in a high school before, but newspaper and yearbook practically run themselves. I've been doing both for five years now, and I always make certain that there is enough returning staff to keep things running smoothly as we initiate a group of newbies into the fold."

"Do you teach any other classes?" she asked.

"Only Journalism I. It's for kids to get their feet wet and see if they're interested in journalism. I have all my plans. Notes. Handouts. I'd be willing to pass along copies of everything to you if you took the job. A majority of my intro students move on to working on the newspaper or yearbook. Sometimes, even both. I have a class period for each publication, along with Journalism I. Then a period with JV cheer and another with varsity cheer. And my planning period, of course."

"I see," Darby said, recalling her own days working on the *Hawthorne Herald*, her thoughts swirling. "Give me your number so I can text you if I have any more questions."

They exchanged cell phones and typed in their contact information, and Kay said, "I hope you'll really consider this, Darby. Selfishly, I want to go to Chicago with Todd and not have to live apart until next May. We've been thinking about starting a family and have just begun trying for a baby. I hate to put that on hold."

"You've given me a lot to digest, Kay. I promise I'll be in touch soon."

Kay hugged her spontaneously. "Even if you don't take my place, Darby, I think you should try teaching at some point. Especially cheer coaching. You're so effervescent and creative. You would be such a great role model for the girls you work with."

They said goodbye, with Kelby slipping her arm through Darby's, leading her back under the stands and into a far corner so they could talk privately.

"If you ever wanted a sign, Darby Montgomery, you just got banged over the head," Kelby said enthusiastically. "It sounds like an ideal situation. You already have the cheer squads and publication staffs in place. You have a place to live with West and me until you find something of your own.

It just means talking to Cheer USA and telling them it's time for you to move on."

"Talking about moving on—and actually moving on—are two radically different things," Darby said, still feeling slightly overwhelmed at the prospect of changing her life so radically. "Yes, this opportunity has fallen into my lap. I don't want to waste it, but at the same time, I don't want to rush in. I need to think about it for a couple of days. You know I like to mull things over."

"I won't mention this to anyone else. Not even West," Kelby promised. "Will you talk it over with Sawyer?"

"Definitely. My big brother has always been my sounding board." She grinned. "But seeing how happy Sawyer is back in Hawthorne—not to mention you and Autumn—is definitely going to influence my decision."

Kelby hugged her. "We can talk it over whenever you like. Make a list of advantages and disadvantages. I can even ride down to Dallas with you on Tuesday if you haven't made a decision by then. I was already going to drive down there to meet with a client. Just let me know."

"Will do. We better head upstairs now. The game will be starting soon. My aunt and uncle will be wondering where we are, and the head coach needs his wife in the stands cheering him and his players on."

"West does like to know where I am during a game. Even if the first one played was only last week. That was an away game. I'm so ready to see him down on the field, whistle around his neck, where it all began for him."

They joined her family in the stands, along with Kelby's brother, who was best friends with West. Darby tried to watch the game but found her attention straying to the cheerleaders on the track. Kay had done a great job with them. Their motions were sharp and crisp. Each girl knew the dances and cheers well, and the cheerleaders really involved the fans in the game.

Suddenly, Darby knew she didn't have to think about anything. Taking Kay Timmons' place would allow her to come back to Hawthorne.

And start a new life.

CHAPTER
Three

Jace pulled up to the Hawthorne Inn and cut the engine to his Porsche. He sat for a moment, wondering if he were doing the right thing by coming to Hawthorne.

After being disappointed in barely missing out on meeting Eli in Houston, he had decided to bide his time. Since Eli was starting a new job, Jace didn't want to barge into his brother's new life and upset the proverbial applecart. Instead, he forced all thoughts of Eli to the back of his mind, doubling down at work and focusing on his current clients, as well as trying to sign new ones.

Still, he contacted Crawford and told the investigator to keep an eye on Eli for six months. He wanted his brother settled before making contact with him.

Crawford had met with Jace two weeks ago, his report thorough, as always. Eli was thriving in his job as the medical director for Hogan Health Hawthorne. He was well thought of in the community and by his superiors at Hogan's corporate headquarters in Austin. He had begun a relationship with an employee at the hospital, Autumn Sutherland, and it looked to be serious. Crawford had even done a background check on Autumn, learning she was a nurse in Houston for years, though not at the same hospital Eli had worked. She'd been hired to be the Director of Nursing at the new hospital. Autumn had roots in Hawthorne, with her father being the superintendent of schools and her mother the head librarian at the city's public library.

Jace actually knew who Autumn was—because her brother was a client of his. West Sutherland had recently retired from the NFL and had taken a job as an assistant coach at the high school he'd graduated from. When its head coach suffered a heart attack and decided to retire, West had been tapped to take the reins of Hawthorne High School's football program. West was still a client of Jace's, having promotional deals in place for the next few years, but they hadn't spoken in several months. It truly was a small world, with West's little sister now dating Jace's older brother.

He got out of his sports car and retrieved a weekender bag before entering the inn. Thankfully, there had been a cancelation, which had allowed him to book a room for this Labor Day weekend. He didn't know if he'd stay the entire time.

It would depend upon how his meeting with Eli went. Whenever that occurred.

Jace still didn't know how to approach his brother. Whether Eli would even remember him or not. He tried not to pin his hopes on their meeting turning out to be successful. At worst, Eli would want to have nothing to do with him, and Jace could walk away, knowing he'd at least tried to rekindle a relationship with his older brother. At best, Eli would welcome him, with the possibility of them having a future relationship.

He checked in and received his room key, an actual key

that fit into the lock of a door. The inn was over one hundred years old and had originally been the family residence of an oil baron. The family had died out after a few generations, with the house falling into disrepair. It was only within the last five years that it had been purchased and turned into a successful B&B.

"We do have a Sunday brunch, Mr. Tanner," the desk clerk informed him. "It is included in the price of your room. If you'd like to take advantage of it, just let me know. I can reserve a table for you."

"Thank you. I'll think about it."

Going upstairs, he quickly unpacked and changed into jeans and a polo shirt. He'd made sure to bring one in green since the Hawks had a home game tonight. Eli was the physician on call at the stadium and would be on the sidelines. Jace planned to attend the game and study his brother, trying to learn more about him than what Crawford's report had revealed or what Jace had read about Eli on the internet.

He returned to the desk, asking the clerk how far the stadium was from the inn.

"I'd walk to Hawks Field if I were you, Mr. Tanner. Usually, it's about a five-minute drive, but with it being the first home game tonight, the place'll be packed. You could bypass the traffic on the road and get there in about fifteen minutes on foot."

The clerk gave him directions, and Jace set out, seeing the game started in just under an hour. He'd already driven around the town when he'd arrived, even passing by Eli's house, which was a perk provided to him by Hogan Health. It was a beautiful Colonial, with a well-manicured lawn and large oak tree in the front yard, a far cry from the ratty apartments they'd lived in growing up.

He quickly found the masses headed toward the football

stadium, which was located next to Hawthorne High School. The desk clerk's advice had been on target, and Jace was able to reach the stadium without trouble. He saw several groups of people standing by, chatting. Some even tailgated in the parking lot. He kept an eye out for Eli but never saw him. West would have been in the stadium for hours, seeing his team through warmups and then giving them a final pep talk in the locker room before they took to the field.

Not wanting to stick out, he stopped at the concession stand and bought a Dr Pepper and bag of popcorn before finding a spot near the top of the bleachers. From here, he had a great view of the field.

He also spotted Eli talking with West Sutherland.

The two men conversed congenially. Jace assumed since West's sister was dating Eli, they had met on more than one occasion. West was, hands down, Jace's favorite client. It made him feel good to see West so comfortable in Eli's presence.

He continued to watch Eli after West took to the field to supervise drills. His brother was also taking in everything, talking with others, walking around. Eli even ventured over to the other team's bench and introduced himself to the coach. The more he saw of Eli, the more eager Jace became to approach him.

Searching the crowd, he spotted Autumn Sutherland's auburn hair. She was standing with a woman who had to be her twin. Jace recalled West mentioning his younger sisters were twins. While they favored one another in the face, Autumn was several inches shorter and curvier than Summer, who had honey blond hair and a willowy frame. They took a seat and then a few minutes later, waved to two other women, who mounted the stairs and joined them. He heard someone call out to the tall one with raven hair and realized she was Kelby, West's new wife.

But it was the woman with her that really drew his attention.

The sunlight hit her caramel hair, causing it to gleam with an array of colors. She was compact, with a small frame to go along with her small breasts and waist. But even from several rows up, he saw her radiant smile and lively eyes. She was pretty, but it was more the vivacious spirit that seemed to fill her that made her even more attractive.

This would be a woman worth getting to know.

And Jace rarely bothered learning much about any woman.

He had dated only casually over the years. Though his good looks drew women to him easily, he had never wanted to be tied down to one woman. Work was his focus, and he believed females were a mere distraction. When he did go out for social engagements, it was always with a different beautiful woman on his arm. Most had little to no personality and only wanted to be seen with him because of who he was, hoping they might have access to his impressive stable of clients.

He watched the woman as she took a seat with West's wife and two sisters. It was odd, being so intrigued with a stranger. Perhaps when he met Eli, he would also be introduced to Autumn.

And this woman.

Turning his attention again to his brother, Jace suddenly felt a chill race along his spine. Eli must have sensed his presence somehow, because he turned and began searching the stands in earnest. Immediately, Jace lifted the Dr Pepper, placing it so that it blocked most of his face. He took a long drag on the straw, drinking until the entire soft drink was gone, a loud sucking noise alerting him his cup was empty. Lowering the paper cup, he saw Eli had turned away.

Still, it spooked him—so much that he changed seats, moving from the center of the field down to the five-yard line. He kept near the top of the stands, though. People quickly filled in the seats around him, the game ready to begin.

Jace had wanted to play football, but his parents were against it. They thought the sport too violent, fussing over him. He convinced them to let him go out for basketball, and he'd played guard both in middle school and high school. His parents had no interest in sports and had never attended a single game he'd played in. Sometimes, he marveled at the fact that they had wanted another child when they spent a vast majority of their time ignoring him.

During the fourth quarter, the Hawthorne quarterback went down with an injury. Eli raced onto the field, immediately rendering aid to the player. After several minutes, the teen was carted off the field, with Eli accompanying him to the locker room. The back-up went in and didn't seem to have any jitters. Eli appeared again, and the Hawks won the game handily.

Jace blended into the crowd, leaving the stadium. Ironically, he wound up only a few feet behind his mystery woman and Summer Sutherland, who accompanied an older couple. He heard Summer call the woman *Darby*.

It suited her.

He bypassed the traffic, returning to the Hawthorne Inn on foot. He went up to his room and stripped off the clothes he'd worn to the game. Feeling sticky after hours in the humidity, he jumped into the shower. It might be September, but Texas was still hot as hell.

He dried off and checked his email, a habit he couldn't seem to break. He responded to a few and then sent a text to

Crawford, who preferred receiving those to an email. Jace asked if Crawford had learned anything new about Eli that was worth sharing and told Crawford he would approach his brother tomorrow. Tonight had helped Jace make up his mind. He would talk to Eli and see if there was anything between them. He would try not to be disappointed if nothing came of their conversation.

As he turned back the covers, his cell dinged and he picked it up, seeing Crawford had replied.

Source just informed me that Eli applied for a marriage license today with Autumn Sutherland. Will find out when ceremony is and let you know.

It surprised him that his brother was marrying so quickly. Eli hadn't known Autumn long. Then again, Jace knew next to nothing about his brother's personal life. Eli hadn't seemed to have much of one before he left his job managing the ER in Houston. Maybe his new job and living in a small town had changed his brother's way of thinking.

Jace fell asleep, clinging to hope that Eli might want his brother in his life.

Four

G ood as his word, another text from Crawford awaited Jace when he awoke. He silenced his cell from midnight until six each morning, trying to escape from work for a few hours of blessed sleep. During that time, Crawford had sent additional information, including the time the hastily-arranged ceremony was to be held and the address of the bride's parents, where the marriage would take place.

Jace acknowledged the text, again thanking Crawford for the investigator's work on his behalf. Still, he didn't have a clue how to approach Eli. Yes, he had his brother's address, but to go to Eli's home, uninvited, on his wedding day? Jace was uncomfortable with that idea. He waffled the entire day, wondering if he should contact Eli since Crawford had also provided his brother's cell phone number, as well as that of Autumn Sutherland.

At one point, Jace almost called West, assuming he would be attending the wedding, and checking with his client to see if West thought it was a good idea to get in touch with Eli. Or even run interference with him.

He had never been paralyzed with such inaction. All his life, Jace had been decisive. Confident. In charge of every situation. But he didn't want to screw this up. Finally, the time for the ceremony drew near. It was now or never. The urge to speak to Eli before he married Autumn Sutherland became overpowering. Quickly, he dressed in a suit and tie, feeling as if he donned armor to go into battle. His clothing came from the best tailors available, hugging his large frame. In a suit, he believed in himself.

Going to his car, he put in the directions to the Sutherlands' house and drove straight to it, parking across the street from the two-story. He saw West and Kelby approaching the porch and watched as they were admitted. At least he knew he was in the right place.

Ten minutes later, Eli pulled up. Crawford had shared pictures of Eli's car and license plate, and Jace now watched his brother climb from his car. A sick feeling washed over him, knowing he might be outright rejected. Still, Jace sucked it up and exited his vehicle before he lost his courage, crossing the street to where Eli now stood.

He took off his sunglasses, not wanting to hide behind them, and swallowed, his mouth suddenly dry as a desert.

Before he could speak, Eli said, "I can't place you, but I feel as if we've met before."

Jace looked into the eyes of this man, and for the first time, a memory struck him. He could see the little boy his brother had once been. It was as if all the years washed away in that moment, and he was three years old again, needing his big brother.

"Buddy?" Eli asked hoarsely, the question in both his voice and eyes.

Eli recognized him.

Jace beamed, relief sweeping through him. "I'd forgotten that. That you used to call me Buddy."

His brother looked shell-shocked. "I can't believe … it's you."

Suddenly, they were locked in a hug, their arms tightly holding one another. A sense of calm flooded Jace, as if the final, missing piece in his life had now slid into place.

Eli was the first to pull away. Staring deeply into Jace's eyes, he asked, "How did you find me, Buddy?"

Just hearing that nickname brought joy to him. "It's a long story, Eli. Or should I say E-wi? That's what I remember calling you."

Eli studied him in wonder. "What's your name? Your real name. I'm ashamed to admit that I don't remember it. Mom always just told me to look after my little buddy, so I called you Buddy."

It surprised him when his eyes welled with tears. "I … don't know what my name was. My adopted name is Jason Tanner. I've always gone by Jace. My birth certificate reflects that name and that of the couple who adopted me."

He paused, adrenaline surging through him, making it difficult to think, much less speak.

"I don't know who I was before, Eli. Only who I've become. But I've missed you over the years. I always loved you. I knew you were out there somewhere, and I was determined to find you."

Jace wanted to explain more. How he tried to respect the Tanners and not hurt them needlessly once he had learned upon his high school graduation that he was adopted. How he waited to search for Eli after they had been killed. Those words didn't come. Maybe they would sometime in the future. For now, just being here and seeing Eli was enough.

His brother embraced him again and said, "Jace. It suits

you." He studied Jace a moment and then asked, "Were you at the football stadium last night?"

A chill ran through him. "I was."

"I sensed you."

He searched his brother's face. "I saw you gazing into the crowd. You looked as if you were searching for someone. I was afraid to approach you. I left the game, not sure if I'd try and contact you."

His throat swelled with emotion. "But I couldn't stay away. I had to make contact with you."

He cleared his throat, trying to get his out-of-control feelings under control. Jace had always prided himself on being stoic. Seeing Eli now had turned him into a marshmallow, though.

"You've done well for yourself. A doctor. Running a hospital."

Pride filled his brother's features. Despite knowing that Eli had not been fortunate enough to be adopted, he had made a good life for himself, accomplishing far more than most men did. Jace wanted to hear about his brother's early years, as well as what his life was like now. That would have to wait, though. Eli had a wedding to get to.

"What about you?"

Not wanting to take up any more time, Jace said, "I'll tell you about me sometime. I know you're about to get married. I just stopped by to wish you good luck. Give you my number." He looked hopefully into Eli's eyes and added, "Maybe we can get together sometime."

Resolve filled his brother's face. "You're not going anywhere. You're coming to my wedding."

"No," Jace said quickly. "I can't. I don't really even know you."

Eli wasn't taking no for an answer, however. "You're my

flesh and blood, and I've been looking for you, as well. I even registered and sent in my DNA to a few sites, hoping to connect with you that way. You need to meet Autumn and her family. And you'll be *my* family at this wedding."

A thrill shot through him. Eli *wanted* him at his wedding. He wasn't shoving Jace aside, making excuses. It was obvious his brother planned to have a relationship with him, starting immediately. Pure relief poured through Jace, knowing he'd made the right decision to speak face-to-face with Eli.

Eli introduced him to Meg Sutherland, who answered the door. Jace heard the pride in his brother's voice when he did so. Meg, an attractive woman with a kind smile, welcomed Jace with open arms. She brought him inside the house into the den, where she introduced him.

West grinned at him. "I already know Jace. He's been my sports agent for years."

That threw his brother for a loop, but Eli quickly recovered, introducing Jace to Autumn's cousins. Sawyer was an attorney in Hawthorne, but it was Darby Montgomery who drew his attention. She was the woman who had interested him last night. Now, he had a name to go with the face. The very pretty face. Darby was more than pretty, though. She had a vitality about her that drew a person to her. He definitely wanted to spend some time with her.

For now, though, he turned his attention to his brother. Meg took Jace upstairs in order to introduce him to Autumn. He decided the pictures he'd viewed didn't do Autumn justice. She had a warmth about her that made a person feel good about himself. His gut told him that Autumn was a perfect match for his brother.

After she hugged him, Autumn said, "I didn't think this day could get any better, but it has. Your presence really adds the icing onto the cake, Jace. Eli has been so eager to find you. He loves you a great deal. I'm so glad you could be here and share in our wedding." Autumn grinned. "And I have a thousand and one questions for you, but we'll hold off on that, for now. Just having you here means the world to Eli and me."

"Thank you, Autumn. For allowing a stranger to crash your wedding."

She smiled gently at him. "You aren't going to be a stranger for long. I can't wait to get to know you better."

"You can do that after you're married. I'm Summer Sutherland, Autumn's twin. We're glad to have you with us, Jace." She looked to her sister. "I'll take Jace downstairs. You and Dad give it two minutes and then head on down."

"Will do," Autumn replied. She leaned up and kissed his cheek, causing sudden tears to mist his eyes.

Summer led him downstairs, saying, "I thought an unexpected wedding was enough of a surprise, but you turning up has really made this a special occasion, Jace."

"I'm grateful your parents opened your home to me," he replied. "And that Eli even wanted me here."

"You're family," Summer said firmly. "His and ours."

He liked how the Sutherlands had opened their hearts to him and said, "Eli is a lucky guy to be marrying into your family."

Summer chuckled. "And you're also lucky since we'll adopt Eli *and* you into the fold."

They went outside, and he saw the back yard was awash in colorful flowers.

"Someone has a green thumb," he said.

"It's Mom. She always has had a way with flowers and plants. I'm glad Autumn decided to take advantage of how beautiful the yard looks this time of year. Let me let Eli know that Autumn is on her way."

Summer went to Eli and spoke a moment. It surprised him when Eli motioned him over, as well.

"Would you do me the honor of serving as my best man?" his brother asked, emotion flooding Eli's voice.

Jace stood a moment, overwhelmed by the request. Summer nodded encouragingly at him, and Jace beamed at Eli. "I'd be happy to, Big Brother."

Taking the boutonniere Eli handed to him, Jace fastened it to his lapel. Then his brother also gave him a small ring box, which Jace placed into his pocket.

The judge officiating the ceremony had them take their places, and Autumn and her father appeared. The ceremony was brief, the judge's comments full of good humor. Jace studied Autumn's face as she looked up at Eli and spoke her vows. Without a doubt, the bride loved her groom very much. It was obvious Eli also was over the moon about Autumn. He said his vows with love on his face and in his tone. Jace felt privileged to witness their union.

And could only hope that someday he might also live this kind of love story.

After the ceremony ended, Meg Sutherland asked Jace to stay for dinner.

"We've got plenty of barbeque and even a small wedding cake, along with Blue Bell ice cream."

He laughed. "You are talking my love language, Meg. My knees go weak at the mention of Blue Bell."

"Well, I was able to find Bride's Cake. It's Autumn's favorite flavor, and they only produce it for a few months each summer. Fortunately, I have a large freezer in the garage, and Joe picks up a new half-gallon of Blue Bell anytime it goes on sale. I'm not embarrassed to admit that I have no less than six different flavors in my freezer right now."

"It's too bad you're already married, Meg," he teased. "Else I would try to sweep you off your feet."

Darby joined them. "I overheard you mentioning Blue Bell. I couldn't help but hope we're having some after dinner, Aunt Meg."

"We are. In fact, why don't you and Jace go bring two or three flavors in from the garage and put them in the kitchen freezer?"

"Will do," Darby said, eyeing him. "Come on, Jace. I'll pick the flavors. You can be the muscle and cart them in."

He playfully flexed his biceps. "I knew all those gym workouts would come in handy."

She led him into the house and out a door leading to the garage. Opening the large freezer, she said, "You can always count on Uncle Joe and Aunt Meg to have ice cream on hand. I think that's why they bought this freezer years ago."

"Your aunt said Autumn's favorite is Bride's Cake."

Spying it, Darby reached in and handed it to him. "Done. Ooh, Blackberry Cobbler. Definitely this one." She stacked it on top of the carton he already held. "One more. I wish I knew what Eli liked."

A sudden ache of sadness filled him. They'd barely had enough to eat when he and Eli were children. Having access to ice cream was out of the question. Jace could still recall the first time he'd been given the frozen treat on the day the Tanners brought him home. His new mother had asked if he liked vanilla ice cream. Jace hadn't known what she referred to. Still, he was always hungry and figured it must be something to eat, so he'd told her he loved it. One bite—and his love affair with Blue Bell ice cream had begun. That day he'd been given Vanilla Bean. As a treat, his mother had squeezed chocolate syrup atop it.

In his entire life, Jace had never eaten anything as good as that first bowl of Blue Bell ice cream when he was three years old.

"Go with vanilla," he suggested. "Everyone likes that."

"Aunt Meg has a carton of that, but it's too boring. Let's go with Mint Chocolate Chip instead. This is a household of chocoholics."

Darby removed the half-gallon container and closed the freezer. Jace led them back into the house, opening the door to the kitchen freezer and placing his two flavors inside. Darby set hers inside, as well, and closed the door.

"I'm glad you showed up today, Jace. Autumn has shared how Eli really has been trying to find you. You showing up is the best gift imaginable."

"I almost didn't come," he admitted. "Something compelled me to drive here. I didn't have a clue how Eli would receive me. I merely wanted to wish him good luck with his wedding and hoped that he might want to get together sometime in the near future."

"Where do you live?" she asked. "Dallas? I know West said you were his agent, so I assume your offices are there since he played for the Cowboys."

"They are. I live and work in downtown. I started Touchdown Talent Management five years ago. I was lucky to land West as a client my very first week in business. He'd been with another agent and was unhappy with the representation he'd received. I was one of several agencies which pitched to him, and he said TTM checked all his boxes." He paused. "What do you do for a living?"

He saw an odd look cross her face. It was so brief, for a moment he thought he was mistaken about seeing it because she smiled brightly.

"I've been with Cheer USA for over ten years now. Kelby and I cheered together at UT. During our summers in college, we started working for Cheer USA, traveling the country and teaching cheers and dances at clinics. The summer job became my full-time employment after I graduated."

"You continued to teach?"

"I did. I became a choreographer, creating dances at first, and then also moving into coming up with cheers and chants and their motions. I would teach what I'd created to everyone on staff in Kansas City, and then I'd travel the country, leading the choreography. Recently, I've moved more into the corporate end of work. In fact, next week I'll be in Dallas, finalizing plans at the arena Cheer USA will use to hold its national competitions in early February next year."

"How long will you be in town?" he asked, his heart suddenly beating fast.

"My meetings are Tuesday and Wednesday. Depends upon how fast I can finish up as to whether or not I fly back to Kansas City on Wednesday night or Thursday morning."

"Have dinner with me," he urged.

She looked startled at the idea. "Why?"

Jace gave her a smile, one which usually melted any woman's heart. "Because I asked?"

Darby just snorted. "I need more than that."

No woman ever challenged him. No woman ever said no.

It was actually refreshing to hear it.

"Because I think you're interesting. Beautiful." Flashing another smile, he added, "And because we're family now, with the wedding and all. I need to get to know my cousin-in-law? Is that what you are?"

She laughed, a musical sound which he could quickly become addicted to. "I really don't think there's a name for our new relationship."

"Then let's strike up a friendship," he ventured.

And see where it leads.

"Sure. We can have dinner together on Tuesday. It'll give me an excuse not to continue with business after hours. After being with the same people all day, I hate when business spills over into drinks. Dinner. Or both. I like to get away from business, don't you?"

Jace laughed. "I rarely get away from it. I own the company, and there's always something to be done. Then again, I have a superb assistant. Everyone should have an Elena Arturo in their lives. She makes running TTM easy with her help."

"She sounds like my kind of person," Darby said, a teasing look entering her eyes. "Maybe I should have dinner with Elena instead of you."

"Have dinner with me Tuesday," he pressed. "Then if you're still here Wednesday, I can see if Elena is available."

Darby laughed again. "You're on. Let's go grab some barbeque now. While Kansas City is known for their barbeque, I can't help but be partial to the version Texas has."

"I've never been to Kansas City," Jace said as they returned to the backyard.

But if things went well with Darby at dinner Tuesday night, he could picture himself flying up to see her. Jace felt the pull toward her, and from the look in Darby's eyes, she also could sense something between them.

They flirted lightly as dinner went on, and by the time the ice cream was brought out, Jace knew that he wanted to spend time alone with Darby Montgomery.

Today had been a revelation. He'd discovered the brother he'd longed to be reunited with.

And maybe he'd finally found the woman who could hold his attention.

For good.

"I hope the talk with my dad goes well," Summer told Darby. "I know you're making the right decisions. My heart and gut tell me so."

Darby hugged her cousin. "Thanks for listening to me and helping me iron out my life. Now, I'll see if I can make things happen."

She went downstairs, hoping to catch her uncle before he left on his morning walk. She entered the kitchen and found him downing a glass of water.

"Want some company on your walk?" she asked brightly.

"I can't pass up spending time with my favorite niece," Joe Sutherland said.

They headed out the back door and walked for about ten minutes without talking.

Working up her courage, Darby said, "Are you familiar with Kay Timmons?"

"I'm proud to say I know every teacher in the Hawthorne schools by name," her uncle said. "I interview each new hire after the principal sends them to me, and I also go and watch them teach a lesson once they've been placed in a Hawthorne classroom. Why?" he asked, frowning slightly.

"Kay's husband has been transferred to Chicago," she revealed.

"Darn it! Blanche Biggerstaff told me that was a possibility back in the spring. Since no one brought it up again, I thought we were safe for this school year." He frowned. "Normally, I wouldn't hold a teacher to a contract if his or her spouse is asked to move for their job. I'd simply let Kay go with Todd and wish her the best. She will be too hard to replace, though, especially now that the school year is underway. Very few teachers want to take on being a cheer coach, much less adding to it by sponsoring the newspaper and yearbook staffs. That's a lot to put on a person's plate, but Kay's done a fabulous job at the high school."

"What if I told you there's a replacement standing by, ready to take on both the cheerleaders and both publications' staffs?"

"Then I'd give you a big hug since I don't have any kind of bonus money to pay." He stopped in his tracks. "Darby, are *you* interested in the Kay's job?"

She nodded. "For a while now, I've felt I'm at a crossroads, Uncle Joe. I've loved my time at Cheer USA, but I'm ready to try something different. I've kept my Texas teaching certificate current all these years, just in case, and now might be the time to make the change. I realize I need to interview with Blanche Biggerstaff. And you. I don't want anyone to talk about nepotism. I want to earn this job, fair and square."

"Legally, I will have to post the position. You would be ideal for the position, Darby. Not only coaching the cheer squads, but I recall you were the editor-in-chief for the *Hawthorne Herald*."

"My teaching fields are English and journalism," she

confirmed. "Kay said that she teaches an intro to journalism class and promised to pass along all her notes and lesson plans to make for a smooth transition. She also has returning staff members to both the newspaper and yearbook, so those publications are in decent shape now."

"What about Cheer USA? Have you talked to them?"

She shook her head. "I've only been toying with this idea, thinking I'd put in my application here in Hawthorne for any openings next year. Then I talked with Kay at the game Friday night. She was upset. She loves her kids here in Hawthorne but was dreading being separated from Todd for the entire school year, especially because they're trying for a baby now."

"You know I can't guarantee you the job." He smiled. "We have to look at qualifications. And right now, I can't think of a better candidate to take over for Kay. You're certified in the right teaching field. You have experience galore with cheerleading. And you know the newspaper side of journalism. I don't see how we can find a better teacher to step into Kay's shoes than you. It'll just be a matter of crossing our T's and dotting those I's."

Darby flung her arms around him. "Thank you, Uncle Joe. I'll need to put in my notice with my boss. This is actually a good time of year to resign. We're busier in the winter, spring, and summer than we are in fall."

"Let's head back to the house," Uncle Joe suggested. "We can let you apply to HISD online. I'll see that Kay's job is posted right away in order to get the clock ticking, and I'll talk to Blanche about interviewing you while you're in town. We can aim for that tomorrow and do the interview together."

"That's Labor Day," Darby protested. "I can't take away her holiday."

"Teachers and administrators don't really have holidays.

That'll be one of the first things you learn about this business. Most people get to enjoy weekends. Teachers grade papers. Act as a sponsor and chaperone for events. Come on. Meg can feed us some French toast when we get home."

Once they were home and had eaten breakfast, Darby downloaded the application to teach in Hawthorne ISD. It was lengthy, but she felt confident that she was doing the right thing as she filled it out. She couldn't see anyone applying who would have more experience than she did in such specific areas.

She went downstairs and found Uncle Joe in his study, informing him that she'd emailed the application to HR.

"I've already talked with Blanche. I also called our webmaster and had the job listed on our website. Blanche said she was happy to come over to the house in an hour, and we can do the interview here."

"Then I better jump in the shower and look presentable for her," Darby teased.

An hour later, Blanche Biggerstaff arrived. They went into Uncle Joe's office, taking seats.

"I know this is unusual to do an interview on a Sunday," he began, "but it will be important to fill this position as soon as possible." Turning to the high school principal, he said, "You can run with it now, Blanche."

"Thank you, Dr. Sutherland." She glanced to Darby. "Tell me a little bit about your background, Ms. Montgomery."

Seeing that Blanche was keeping things formal, Darby responded, "I'd be happy do so, Mrs. Biggerstaff. First of all, I'm a product of Hawthorne schools, where I received an excellent education. It allowed me to attend the University of Texas at Austin, where I had no trouble with my classes because I was so well prepared academically. I majored in secondary education, earning certifications in English and journalism. While at UT, I worked on the staff of the university's newspaper, *The Daily Texan*. I had previously been on the staff of the *Hawthorne Herald*, serving as editor-in-chief my senior year."

Darby paused a moment before continuing. "I was a cheerleader throughout my school days and cheered for the Longhorns in college. Because of my outstanding performance on the field and in competitions, I was tapped to work for Cheer USA during the summers between college semesters, traveling the country and teaching at clinics for girls ranging from twelve to eighteen years of age. After graduating with honors, I went to work full-time for Cheer USA. I was an assistant choreographer, creating dances, as well as the words and movements to cheers. I eventually became the head choreographer for the organization. I've traveled the country, teaching and running workshops in forty-eight of the fifty states. Right now, part of my role is scouting facilities to hold our national cheer competition. I'm familiar with budgets and traveling expenses, and I know I could sponsor the groups in question."

"That is quite impressive, Ms. Sutherland," Blanche praised.

"I know I'm unproven in the classroom, but I have taught for years at these cheer camps. Although I don't have any experience in putting together a yearbook, I have been assured by the current sponsor, Kay Timmons, that the staff in place is experienced. I believe one of my best qualities is my flexibility and the ability to adapt quickly to new situations."

Blanche asked a few more questions about Darby's teaching experiences within Cheer USA and finished with, "Why now? You're employed by a well-known, national organization. You've risen through the ranks. Are you unhappy at your present job?"

"I wouldn't say unhappy," she began. "It's more that I don't feel as challenged as I once was. After working at Cheer USA for over a decade, I'm looking for new professional experiences. I've enjoyed the teaching portion of my job, and I would love to transition into a teaching job full-time in the public schools. I'm a product of public schools, and I think the best and brightest should go into teaching, to serve as role models for our students."

She took time for a breath and then added, "I'm in my early thirties, Mrs. Biggerstaff. I've traveled the country for ten years, and now I feel the need to put down roots. To come home to Hawthorne. I'm close to my family, and both my brother and two of my cousins have returned to Hawthorne in the past year. Family is very important to me. I feel Hawthorne is a special place, and I would like to be a part of the experience students who live here have."

Blanche nodded, seeming satisfied with Darby's answers. The principal looked to her uncle. "Dr. Sutherland, do you have anything you'd like to add?"

He asked Darby a couple of questions regarding her philosophy of teaching.

"I believe hands-on learning sticks with students better. Yes, there's definitely a time and place for lecture and memorization, but especially with the types of students I would be working with—if I am offered this position—learning by doing is critical. I want to think of myself as more of a guide and mentor to students. I'll teach the journalism students how to get to the heart of a story, using the 5 W's and H. I'll emphasize the importance of integrity and objectivity in their reporting. I want to work with them on how to nail headlines and create a page layout. While I don't have experience in producing a yearbook, much of what is done with a newspaper carries over to a yearbook. I'm a fast learner and will work hard to make certain the yearbook students aren't slighted.

"As far as cheerleading goes, I expect to be very active, working out with the girls and helping them to build strength and durability, as well as teaching them new dances and cheers. I'll critique their performances regularly and offer constructive feedback. I guess I'd sum up my philosophy of education as learning by doing," she concluded.

Uncle Joe nodded sagely. "If you would excuse us, Darby, Principal Biggerstaff and I need to discuss a few matters."

She rose. "Of course." Offering her hand to the principal, she said, "Thank you for your time, especially on a holiday weekend, Mrs. Biggerstaff."

As they shook, the older woman smiled. "Call me Blanche."

Darby returning the smile. "Blanche, it is."

She left Uncle Joe's study and went to the kitchen, finding her aunt and cousin at the table sipping a cup of tea.

"Would you like a cup?" Aunt Meg asked. "It's an orange spice blend of tea."

"Sounds wonderful," she said, finally relaxing.

Summer retrieved a large mug and poured Darby a cup from the teapot. Taking a sip, Darby savored it.

"How did your interview go?" her aunt asked.

"It's probably the best interview I've ever done," she replied. "They're talking things over now."

Aunt Meg snickered. "What they're talking over is the football game played Friday night and the upcoming one this next Friday. You don't have anything to worry about, Darby. This job is yours."

"Have you heard from Autumn today?" she asked.

"No," both Summer and Aunt Meg replied, with Summer adding, "I'm sure Autumn's having hot sex right about now," causing everyone to laugh. "Or maybe they took a time out so they could spend an hour getting to know Jace a little better."

While Darby had talked over the idea of switching careers with her brother, Kelby, and Summer, she had not mentioned to anyone how taken she was with Jace Tanner. Jace resembled Eli slightly. But where Eli appeared handsome and friendly, his younger brother looked dangerous. He oozed a masculinity which was very appealing. She had found herself flirting with Jace without even thinking about it.

Something told Darby that he was a player, though. That he'd never had a serious relationship in his life, continually bouncing from one woman to the next. It wouldn't do to act on the attraction she felt for him. Even if she had agreed to have dinner with him this coming Tuesday. She would treat the meal as a friendly get-together and nothing more.

Uncle Joe and Blanche appeared in the doorway, with her uncle saying, "We have to leave the job posted for ten days, Darby, to comply with state law. If anyone else applies for the position during that time, Blanche will interview him or her. We feel we already have spoken to the best candidate, however. If I were you, I'd turn in my two-week notice to Cheer USA and pack your things."

She sprang to her feet. "Thank you for giving me this opportunity. I am so grateful. While I'm not a green girl straight out of college, I realize I haven't taught in the public schools. That all my teaching experience has been with extracurricular activities in a setting away from a formal classroom. Still, I promise I won't let you down."

"Other than your immediate family, we ask that you don't

share that you've received a job offer from us," Blanche told Darby. "We need to keep this very quiet."

"I understand," she said, wanting to do a happy dance across the kitchen floor. "And again, I'm sorry we pulled you away from your family on a Sunday, Blanche."

"It's not a problem. I was policing visitors to Fred all morning. I think half the football team came to visit him."

"I'm sorry. I neglected to ask about him. How is he feeling?"

"Dr. Carson said the concussion he suffered in the game was mild. I think Fred is tickled he's gotten so much attention. I shooed everyone out and left him to take a nap while I was over here. I guess I'll go home now and start herding cats again. I'll be in touch with you, Darby, regarding your start date. I'm sure it'll take a couple of weeks for you to finish up things in Kansas City and return to Hawthorne. It'll also give Kay time to clean up things on her end and prepare her students for her replacement."

"That's fine. Am I allowed to communicate with Kay?"

"You absolutely can contact her," Blanche assured. "Joe and I have already called Kay and told her the good news. She's thrilled that you'll take over for her."

"Then I guess I have a resignation letter to write."

Darby excused herself and returned to the guest bedroom. She pulled out her tablet and quickly composed her resignation letter, attaching it in an email to Peggy Mortimer. Not wanting her boss to open it without any forewarning, Darby texted Peggy.

> I've just sent you an email. It contains my resignation. I hope a two-week notice will suffice. Enjoy the rest of your holiday weekend. I'll be back in the office on Thursday. We already have a meeting scheduled for 1:30 that afternoon. I'll go over everything about the Dallas site with you then.

Darby read through the text again, correcting a typo. Taking a deep breath, she pressed send.

It was done. Her time at Cheer USA would be over soon.

And a new chapter in life awaited her in Hawthorne.

CHAPTER

Six

Jace dialed DeMarcus Green's number the moment he arrived in the office. Elena said the running back had called and left messages three times over the long weekend, each time saying there was no urgent need to call him back.

Three times was a red flag to Jace.

He paced his office as the phone rang, seeing Elena set a Starbucks cup on his desk. He gave her a quick nod of acknowledgement, knowing it would be doctored just as he liked it. Somehow, she was always in tune with what he needed. Coffee when a hit of caffeine was in order. Cashews when he got the munchies.

DeMarcus' voicemail came on, causing frustration to build within him. Jace waited until the beep and said, "DeMarcus, it's Jace. You have my cell number. I've told you to reach out to me, day or night. No more calling the office when it's a holiday. Call me directly, okay? Anytime you need to talk. And call me when you get this."

He touched his earbud, ending the call, and wandered

back to his desk. Picking up the cup, he took a long drag. As it went down his throat and hit his belly, he could already feel the caffeine trickling through him. He sat, keying in his login and password, and the screen before him came to life.

But Jace couldn't concentrate on it. He sat back in his chair, twirling a ballpoint pen, letting his thoughts drift.

The past few days had been mind-blowing. Being reunited with Eli had been better than Jace ever could have anticipated. It made him mad at himself for not having earlier pursued the leads Crawford had delivered. Then again, right after Eli left Houston, TTM's business had picked up considerably last spring. He'd found himself swamped with work. Of course, that had been an excuse so that he could put off talking with Eli. At least he'd finally put work on the back burner for once and gone to Hawthorne. Attending Eli's wedding—and serving as his best man—would be something Jace held close to his heart forever.

Even though Eli and Autumn had just gotten married, they insisted on spending a large chunk of Sunday and Monday with him. They had taken him to a nearby lake on Sunday afternoon for a picnic, just the three of them, sitting by the water and eating and talking. Some of the memories they'd spoken of had actually been good ones. One of them would recall something, and the other would start to add on to the memory, as they talked about their childhood before they'd been separated by CPS. A few of the things that had come to mind had been painful. Autumn being there helped temper those feelings. She was quiet. Supportive. Understanding.

It was Autumn who began drawing things out of Jace. The more he shared, the more she encouraged Eli to do the same. While he knew much of what Eli talked about, thanks to Crawford's deep dive into Eli Carson, just listening to his brother talk kept Jace mesmerized. Eli was very smart. Quick with his wit. It was also obvious that he was madly in love with his new wife.

Thanks to Autumn, Jace opened up about being adopted by the Tanners, explaining they had lost a son named Jason, and how they'd been unable to have more children. They had wanted him to be Jason 2.0, something Jace had rebelled against from the moment they brought him home. Eli told Jace how stubborn he'd been as a two-year-old, and that hadn't changed by the time he turned three and they were separated forever.

Eli had told Jace he forgave him for being adopted. Somehow, his brother understood that Jace had felt guilty about that all these years. While Eli had moved around to different group homes over the years, Jace had a steady, permanent home. The Tanners may not have been affectionate, loving parents, but at least he didn't have to go without, as Eli had. His brother had said the past was in the past. That they would look ahead to building a relationship now, one which would be strong and carry them into the future.

Monday, Eli and Autumn had her family over to swim and grill. Jace enjoyed getting to know West's wife. Kelby was a spitfire, but she really balanced West. Mid-afternoon, West had disappeared, and Kelby had told Jace that it was part of being a football widow. Even though it was a holiday, he and his coaching staff had gathered at the high school to watch film and prepare a game plan for the Hawks' upcoming game on Friday night. With the team not practicing on Monday, they would be playing catch-up the rest of the week.

Besides spending time with Kelby, Jace had also hung out with Darby. Her brother also came to the cookout, and Jace envied the easy relationship she and Sawyer had. Even though they weren't around one another often, with Darby living out of state, it was obvious that she and her older brother fell into a back-and-forth with ease. He saw true affection between the brother and sister.

And his hands were itching to be on Darby.

They flirted a bit, nothing too overt, but he could sense the sizzle beneath their words. She also filled out her swimsuit nicely. He liked that she wasn't one of those girls who merely lay out by the pool and didn't want to get their body wet, much less their hair. Darby's caramel hair had been pulled back in a high ponytail, and she had dived into the pool, not caring about getting soaked. They had teamed together to play some pool volleyball against Sawyer and Summer and commiserated when they lost at the very end.

He'd enjoyed sitting around, snacking, talking, learning more about his brother and this family Eli had married into. As for Eli, Jace couldn't imagine a happier guy. Every time Eli looked at Autumn, love was clearly written across his face. Jace had actually found himself a bit jealous, having never been in love.

He was back to reality today, however. His schedule was packed. Then he recalled he'd asked Darby to go to dinner. Immediately, he buzzed Elena.

"What's up?"

"What's on my schedule today from five o'clock on?" he asked.

Without having to consult his calendar, the assistant said, "You've got a four-thirty meeting with Penny. I scheduled you through five-thirty. Then at six, you're having drinks with the—"

"No, that doesn't work for me. Reschedule. Both."

"O-kay," Elena said, eyeing him with interest. "Should I also bump your dinner after? You were taking that jewelry designer you met at a party last week to a charity dinner for cystic fibrosis."

He cursed softly. "Yes. Send a healthy contribution to the CF fund."

"When should I put her on your calendar?" By now, Elena had opened the tablet she carried, consulting it for a future time to dine with Penelope Rossi. "Even if you don't want to attend the charity function, it would be the gentlemanly thing to at least take her to dinner."

"Not Wednesday," he said quickly, hoping that Darby's business would keep her in Dallas a second night.

Because he planned to take her to dinner again tomorrow night.

"Wednesday you have a fundraiser for a political candidate."

"Nope. Cut him a check and send it, along with my regrets."

Elena studied him a moment. "What's her name?"

"What do you mean?" Jace asked defensively.

"You never ask to change things around or reserve a night. You keep to the schedule I set up for you, even if you do add to it yourself sometimes. I figure it has to be some woman who's turned your head to have you canceling things left and right."

"I met my brother this weekend," he blurted out.

"Your brother?" she asked, clearly puzzled. "You've never mentioned a brother. To me. Or anyone at TTM that I know of. And believe me, that news would've gotten around. Fast."

"Have a seat," he ordered.

Over the next ten minutes, Jace told Elena about being a foster kid and having been separated from his brother for over twenty-nine years.

"That's incredible, Jace," she said, awe written on her

face. "I can understand you wanting to spend time with him. And his new bride." She frowned. "But you don't want to go overboard. Three really is a crowd. You have the rest of your life to get to know your brother."

"I'm not seeing Eli and Autumn tonight. Or tomorrow night. Autumn's cousin is in Dallas for business the next two days. We decided to have dinner together tonight. I'd like to be free in case we enjoy our time together this evening and want a repeat tomorrow."

"Shall I make dinner reservations for the two of you then?" Elena asked.

Jace winced. "I have no idea what kind of food Darby likes," he admitted.

Elena studied him. "You must really like this woman because you've never given a thought to whether or not your date likes a certain cuisine or not. I'm going to go and start working on making your excuses and sending those checks. You need to see when Penelope is available for a make-up dinner."

She consulted the tablet she carried. "You're actually free on Thursday, if that helps."

"Send her two dozen roses." He thought a moment. "No, just a dozen. I don't want to make too much fuss about having to cancel and have her read more into it than I want her to. I merely asked her to go to the charity event tonight because I needed a plus one."

Elena asked, "To Penelope's home or office?"

"Definitely office. She's the kind of woman who wants others to know she's received flowers and is seen in all the right places. In fact, book a table for seven at The Mansion for Thursday night."

"Before you know she's free?" Elena asked innocently.

"She'll want to go. Because it's The Mansion."

"All right. You do your thing. I'll do mine. We can check in after you've spoken to Darby so I can know where to make reservations for tonight and tomorrow night."

She left his office, closing the door behind her, and Jace picked up his phone, texting Penelope.

> Work crisis has come up. Can't make charity event tonight. How about Thursday instead? The Mansion. 7PM.

Jace waited a moment before seeing the three dots flashing on his screen. He knew Penelope's response would appear soon.

> Sorry we can't attend the charity event this evening. Would love to have dinner with just you at The Mansion. Pick me up at six-thirty.

Before he could respond, a new text came in. Penelope had sent her address to him. He would have preferred meeting her there, but Jace felt he owed it to her and would pick her up. He texted a thumbs up, hoping that would be the end of their conversation. Already, he was regretting asking her to dinner, but Elena was right. It was the right thing to do after canceling on her on the day of the event.

He rarely spoke to any woman on the phone, but he was eager to hear Darby's voice. Still, he knew she was in a meeting all day today. He sent her a text, asking when she might be done with business and where she would like to have dinner tonight. He told her he would make the reservation.

Jace paced his office, knowing she might not be able to reply right away. Suddenly, his phone rang. Darby's name flashed on the screen, making him feel ridiculously happy.

Answering, he said, "Didn't mean to pull you away from your meeting. A text would've been fine."

"I had a few free minutes. We're about to do a walking tour throughout the entire facility, so I will be tied up for several hours. I wanted to touch base with you about dinner."

"I wasn't sure what food you enjoyed eating. I'm happy to book—"

"No reservation is required where I'd like to eat," she told him, naming a restaurant. "It's down on Lower Greenville in a strip shopping center. My favorite Mexican food restaurant in Dallas. Kansas City has a woeful selection of Mexican restaurants, so I have to eat at Adelina's while I can."

Jace had never heard of the spot. Then again, he didn't eat at hole in the wall places. He patronized fine dining establishments, liking to be seen at them.

"Where are you staying in Dallas?" he asked. "I can pick you up."

"I won't be done here until probably five-thirty. Six at the latest. Then I need to go and check in. I'm staying at the Forum. I'd also like to get out of my work clothes and into something more casual. Why don't you pick me up at seven? I'll meet you in the lobby."

His heart sped up at the thought of seeing her again in person. "Sounds like a plan," he said carefully, not wanting to betray how he was really feeling. "Seven works for my schedule."

Jace said goodbye and hung up, trying to keep the foolish grin off his face as he went out to speak with Elena. He waited while she finished her conversation and hung up.

"The CF chair is sorry you won't be able to attend tonight, but she's thrilled at the donation you've made in advance. Flowers have been ordered for Miss Rossi. The reservation on Thursday at the Mansion has been made. You normally don't eat that early," she observed. "Any reason why you wanted dinner then?"

"I want to make certain that it's an early night. I won't be seeing Penelope Rossi again. As far as tonight goes, we're eating at a place I've never heard of. Somewhere Darby likes. Adelina's."

Elena's face lit up. "I love eating at Adelina's. I grew up going there. It's one of the hidden gems of Dallas." She looked at him appraisingly. "If this Darby knows about Adelina's, then I'm all in favor of you seeing her."

He shrugged nonchalantly. "I enjoy her company. That's all. She's only in town a couple of days. Then she'll head back to Kansas City. I may never see her again."

Elena's brows arched again, as if she'd caught him in a lie.

Defensively, he said, "You can get back to work. And if DeMarcus calls, put him through immediately."

Jace returned to his office and took a seat behind his large, cherrywood desk. He was worried he would enjoy Darby's company more tonight than he had this past weekend. That he would want to see more of her. He had never been in a relationship, much less a long-distance one. He told himself that would be a recipe for disaster. No, he'd simply enjoy her company and move on when she left town.

Suddenly, all those empty nights ahead weighed upon him. Jace was a workaholic, often in the office until nine or ten on the nights he had no after-hours social obligations. He thought back to how happy Eli and Autumn were. West and Kelby, too. A feeling of loneliness washed over him.

He shook his head, trying to rid himself of these feelings he'd never experienced before. He had a satisfying, full life. He owned a top sports management agency. A nice car and beautiful condo. Just because his long-lost brother was in love and happily married didn't mean that was also in the cards for Jace. He had built his business from the ground up, and his reputation as a ruthless bargainer proceeded him into any negotiations. He couldn't afford to turn sappy over some woman he might only see sporadically over the years.

His phone rang, and Jace saw DeMarcus Green's name light up the screen. Leaning back in his chair, he tapped his earbud.

"DeMarcus. Thanks for calling me back. What can I do to help you?"

As his client explained something he was unhappy about, Jace relaxed. He was back in the world he knew.

The world he planned to stay in.

CHAPTER
Seven

Darby thanked the event center general manager for his time. The contracts had already been signed well over a year ago when she had previously toured the venue and recommend Dallas be the city where Cheer USA's national competition would unfold. This visit was merely to firm up all the details and agree upon the timeline for the event.

"If you have any more questions, Darby, I'm happy to answer them," Dean Baker said.

"I need to let you know that this is my last official outing on Cheer USA's behalf," she shared. "I'm leaving the organization soon."

"I'm sorry to hear that. You're a real asset to them."

Though Uncle Joe and Blanche had told Darby not to share with anyone about landing the job at Hawthorne High School, she said, "You may see me in February at the competition. I might just be bringing a squad of cheerleaders to compete."

"You're kidding!"

"That's all I can say right now, Dean. Thanks for your

time. I'll copy you on the email I send my boss regarding everything we've discussed. Peggy Mortimer is a perfectionist, but she has a good heart. I'll be passing along all my notes and our previous emails to Peggy and whoever takes my place. Thanks again for your time."

Darby left the arena and returned to her rental car, driving to her hotel a few miles away. A bellman removed her luggage from the trunk as she left her key with the valet, telling him that she was checking in.

Fortunately, she only had to wait in line briefly before speaking to a reservations clerk. Within ten minutes, she was in her room, which had a beautiful view of downtown Dallas. She peeled off her work clothes and took a quick shower, wanting to freshen up before seeing Jace Tanner. The shower revived her after a long day on her feet, and Darby decided to dress in the sundress she'd worn to Autumn's wedding. Jace had already seen it, but that shouldn't matter. This wasn't a date.

Looking into the mirror, she voiced that sentiment aloud. "This isn't a date."

As she applied a fresh coat of lipstick, she told herself this was merely two new friends meeting up for dinner. It didn't' seem to make any difference, though. Her heart still beat more quickly than usual. She had thought about Jace off and on all day, eager to see him again. He was a slick, different version of Eli. A man like Eli was more to her taste. Though Eli had lived in Houston for many years, he had taken to life in a small town with ease.

Darby had a feeling that Autumn and Eli would start a family fairly quickly, and she was happy she would soon be living in Hawthorne and could play auntie to their baby. Kelby had also confided to her that she and West were also in baby making mode, so there would be two little ones to spoil, hopefully, by this time next year. Though Darby had never been someone who thought about having children, the idea of living in Hawthorne and raising a family greatly appealed to her now. She was just happy she would have the chance to move back to her hometown and start a different kind of life. If she found someone to share it with, that would simply be icing on her cake.

She spritzed her usual floral scent on her wrists, rubbing them together. It was getting close to seven, so she slipped into her dress sandals and left the room, heading down to the lobby.

When she emerged from the elevators, she saw Jace sitting in an oversized chair, scrolling through his phone. The man seemed to do nothing but work. Then again, she was also a workaholic, so she understood. She couldn't imagine the pressures he faced in his hectic job and was glad he had been able to take time out of his schedule to have dinner with her while she was in Dallas.

As she moved toward him, he must have sensed her approaching. Jace looked up, a slow smile spreading across his handsome face.

He rose and clasped her elbow, brushing his lips against her cheek. Immediately, Darby was aware of two things. One was the tingles which ran through her. The other was that he smelled divine. A woodsy, masculine scent that made her think of hiking.

Jace pulled away, releasing her elbow, and she fought the urge to step closer to him again.

"You look beautiful," he said huskily. "And smell even better."

She chuckled. "You've seen this dress before, Tanner," she teased. "I wore it to the wedding. As for my perfume, I always wear my signature floral scent. I like something light and airy."

"I like it on you," he said, his gaze intense, causing new tingles to ripple along her spine.

She swallowed, sensing the charged air between them. More than anything, she wanted to take him by the hand and lead him back to the bank of elevators. Back to her room. And have hot sex the rest of the night.

What was she thinking?

"We should get going," she said brightly, pushing the racy thoughts away. "I'm starving. Sour cream enchiladas are calling my name."

"I'm parked right outside," he said, his hand going to the small of her back, guiding her across the lobby and out the front doors of the hotel. All she could think of was the heat emanating from him, especially from the fingers that seemed to scald her back. Even when they reached outside, he kept his hand there.

And she liked it more than she should.

She liked *him* more than she should.

He waited until the valet had closed the driver's door and the car pulled away before greeting the employee.

"Ah, Mr. Tanner. Got you taken care of. You're car's right over here."

Jace finally removed his hand, reaching into his pocket. He handed a bill to the valet and then led Darby to a Porsche.

Opening the door for her, she got in, saying, "You would drive a Porsche Boxter."

He gazed down at her, looking impressed. "You know cars."

"My dad did. It was something he was interested in, and I was a daddy's girl, so I learned all I could about cars."

"Then we'll have a lot to talk about tonight," Jace said,

closing her door and coming around to climb behind the wheel.

He pulled away from the hotel's circular drive, turning onto the street.

"I have to admit that I'd never heard of the restaurant you named, but my assistant lit up when I told her that's where we were having dinner."

"I told you I liked Elena. You should've had her join us. I think she and I would have a lot in common."

He stopped at red light and looked to her. "I'm selfish, Darby. I wanted you all to myself tonight."

His words caused her mouth to go dry. Usually, she had some snappy comeback, but Jace Tanner left her tongue-tied.

"What else did your dad teach you about?" he asked.

"Everything about sports. He was a huge football fan. A diehard Dallas Cowboys fan. And he also worshipped his Texas Aggies."

"Your dad was an Aggie?" he asked eagerly. "Me, too." Jace held up his fisted right hand, where a prominent A&M class ring rested on his ring finger. "I need to meet your dad. I'm surprised he wasn't at the wedding."

"I lost Mom and Dad when I was in college," she said quietly. "They were struck by a drunk driver head on after they were driving home from my college graduation in Austin. They were both killed instantly. The driver walked away with a slight concussion and a broken wrist. He's serving time now in prison."

His fingers found hers, squeezing them. The comforting gesture caused her eyes to mist with tears.

"I know what that's like," he said. "I lost my parents the summer before my senior year in college. They were in a small plane crash."

She looked at him, sensing distress. "I'm so sorry, Jace. Were you close to them?"

His face flushed. "Not really."

He pulled into a parking lot across the street from Adelina's and slid the Porsche into an open spot before turning it off. His gaze met hers.

"Sometimes, I feel guilty. Because I didn't feel anything when I received the news of their deaths. I've never told anyone that. I'm afraid others would judge me pretty harshly if I did."

"Do you think you were simply numb when you heard?" she asked. "Or did you never bond with them after your adoption?"

"It's more that. My adopted parents had a son named Jason. He drowned. Mother couldn't have more children, so she and Father decided to adopt. They looked for a little boy who favored their Jason. Even named me after him. I think they figured out pretty quickly that I wasn't a replacement for their Jason. That I never could be—and that caused them to pull away. They distanced themselves almost from the time they brought me home. They were academics. Professors of archaeology and ancient history. I don't think they knew how to show affection, much less relate to a little boy who'd lost everything he knew."

Darby ached for the little boy Jace had been, stripped of his family, sent to strangers who hadn't known how to care for him, much less love him.

"If they could have given me back to CPS, I think they would have. Then again, that would have looked bad to their friends, and the Tanners were all about appearances. I pretty much raised myself because they were too busy to be bothered with anything. I wound up learning to cook and prepared all my own meals because they were gone or would work through dinner. They went on digs during the summer months, and I wasn't allowed to go. When I got old enough to do so, they asked me once if I wanted to accompany them. I told them I had no interest in anything buried in the ground for thousands of years." He paused. "They never asked again."

She placed her free hand over their joined ones, wanting to lessen his hurt. "That must have been terrible. To have been adopted and yet not feel as if you were a part of a family."

He shook his head. "I don't mean to have a pity party. I had it way better than Eli ever did. I had a nice home. Decent clothes. I was given educational opportunities. I may not have received love, but I had the material things I needed. The Tanners lack of interest in me instilled a drive, one which I still possess today. I push myself, wanting to prove to me and everyone around me that I'm worthy of attention. Notice. That I can produce results. My clients know how devoted I am to them. I always come through for them. I'm merciless when negotiating on their behalf."

"Do you have many friends, Jace?" she asked softly.

He looked away. "Not really. I don't like to ask for help. I don't want anyone thinking I'm weak. I guess I'm what you'd call a lone wolf."

Darby realized Jace Tanner was giving her insight to him that he had never allowed anyone to access before. She didn't know why he had chosen to open up to her. They barely knew one another.

Yet somehow, it felt as if they had always known each other. Forever.

"You didn't have to share any of this with me, Jace. But I'm glad you did."

He finally turned to meet her gaze. "I don't think Eli is

the broken one," he said, his voice raw and hoarse. "I think ... that's me."

Her hand cupped his cheek. His eyes closed a moment, and he leaned into it, seeming to savor the touch as much as she herself did. This smart, confident, sexy man had bared his soul to her. Darby wanted to help him in some small way. Her thumb caressed his cheek for a moment, then she slid her hand to his nape.

And pulled him toward her.

Their lips met.

Jace had kissed his fair share of women and had found kissing to be highly overrated.

Until now.

Darby Montgomery's lips were pillowy soft against his firmer ones, and he had the urge to swallow her whole. He needed her goodness inside him. Her caring spirit. He had shared things with her that he hadn't told another soul, things which he had never really admitted even to himself. He was a push things aside kind of guy. Either he dealt with something head on or he dismissed it, shoving it as far away as he could, hoping no residue was left.

But Darby had drawn confidences from him. It was as if in knowing her, he wanted to reexamine his own life. Make some changes.

Make a life with her.

That thought freaked him out, and he almost pulled away, but the lure of her lips and that intoxicating floral scent drew him back in. Jace told himself to stop thinking and just be in the moment.

He let all thoughts dissipate as he concentrated on the woman next to him. Slowly, he brushed his lips against hers. He didn't rush anything. Instead, he let things unfold naturally. His pulse leaped as her lips pressed harder against his, demanding more from him. Her hand, warm on his nape, held them together. He, too, wanted to hold her.

His hands came up, cradling her face. He kissed her softly, breaking the kiss, then moving in for another one. One kiss became too many to count, each one longer than the one before it. Need coursed through him. He didn't think about whether it was a physical need which cried out to be satisfied or an emotional one. It was time his lips did the talking.

He stroked her smooth cheeks with his thumbs, touching her gently as if she were a precious vessel. Ever so slowly, he teased her mouth open. Her hand tightened on his nape, and his tongue swept inside, ready to explore. Taste. Touch.

Tilting her head back, he deepened the kiss, need pounding him now. Hungrily, he kissed her, taking and giving, amazed at how intimate a kiss could be. She made a noise, one which let him know she liked how he kissed her. How he held her.

It made him want more.

And it was because he wanted to press for more that he stopped. He caressed her tongue a final time and then kissed her rosebud mouth softly. Yet he couldn't seem to pull away entirely. Jace rested his brow against hers, his hands still tenderly touching her face.

What was he supposed to say to her? That this was the most incredible kiss of his life? That he was compelled to learn everything he could about her?

Admitting to these kinds of feelings sent panic surging

through him. His hands fell away, and he lifted his forehead from hers, slowly withdrawing from her, despite the fact his body cried out to stop immediately. Wanting to embrace her so badly made him terrified. Jace had never depended upon anyone. Never needed anyone.

He wasn't about to change his life because of a few kisses.

"Wow," she said softly, wonder in her voice.

"I'm sorry," he apologized brusquely. "I shouldn't have—"

Her hazel eyes, which now shone green with passion, immediately sparked with anger.

"Don't you dare apologize, Jace Tanner," she said threateningly. "I won't let you do that."

Curiosity filled him. He felt if he asked her what she meant, her reasoning would suck the life out of him. Already, he was frightened enough by this woman, which was laughable. She was a foot shorter than he was and probably weighed barely over a hundred pounds. A brisk wind would likely blow her away. Yet Jace saw a strength within her. A resolve which might be as strong as his own.

"Then I won't apologize," he told her.

Her eyes narrowed. Darby studied him. "You have no idea why you started to apologize, much less why I would be angry about you doing so, do you?"

Darby Montgomery didn't pull any of her punches.

"No. And no. It's just that we don't know one another."

"We don't?" she asked, snorting. "Jace, you opened up to me. You shared some pretty deep things. I am honored you would confide in me. Yes, we may not have known one another until a few days ago, but I'm more comfortable with you than I have felt with any man. My gut tells me we are two old souls. Maybe ones who knew one another in a different life."

She paused, assessing him. "Because from the moment

we met, I have been drawn to you. And not just physically, even though there's that. I sense something about you. I feel as if I've known you a lot longer. That I want to know you better. Whether we become friends or lovers is still up in the air for me. But I'm drawn to your essence."

"How do you do that?" he asked. "It's like you're inside my head. Talking to you is a little like talking to myself."

Taking her hands in his, Jace said, "I'll admit that I'm a typical guy. I have surface conversations with everyone. Because of my agency, most of those discussions are about sports. When I talk sports—and combine that with business—I don't have to dig deep. Think too hard on anything. My entire life, I've pushed myself to achieve. I set a goal and reach it. I set another one. Big. Small. In-between. I'm climbing this invisible ladder. Laser-focused. Never looking down. Always moving ahead."

He gazed deeply into her eyes, ones which drew him in. "You make me want to think about things. Especially myself. I'm not really sure I like that, Darby."

"Self-analysis is good for you," she encouraged. "We're always growing. Learning. Changing. Evolving. That's simply a part of life."

Jace shook his head. "I'm afraid I'm more like a shark. I'm cutthroat when it comes to business. I would do anything for my clients. I'm merciless when I'm negotiating on their behalf. They know how devoted I am to them. I'll get them more money. More benefits. More of whatever they want. Whatever they dream of. I'm in the business of making those dreams of theirs come true."

She cocked her head, studying him. "Then what do *you* want, Jace? What do you dream of? And don't say more money. You have plenty of that already. It's easy to see by the way you dress and the car you drive. I'm talking about deep within you, not a business goal you wish to achieve. You can only take on so many clients and negotiate so many contracts and make so many sponsorship deals.

"What I'm asking is what makes Jace Tanner tick? And what makes—or would make—you happy?" Her words were both encouraging and challenging at the same time.

And Jace had absolutely no idea what he truly wanted.

"Can I think on that and get back to you?" he asked lightly, trying to downplay the serious turn of their conversation.

Darby pulled her hands from his. "Joke all you want, but I think until you figure out what you want out of life, you'll simply bull your way through it, trying to get your own way in everything you do."

"That's what being a sports agent is all about."

She rolled her eyes. "There's more to being a sports agent. I think you do an outstanding job, setting goals for yourself and your agency. You should be proud of all you have achieved. I'm impressed by it." She paused. "But I also want to get to know the man you are, Jace. And I think before I can, *you* need to get to know the man you are—and the man you want to be."

Jace felt as if she'd thrown down a gauntlet like a knight of old, challenging him in a way no one had ever done before.

What did he really want out of life?

Darby was right. He had a successful business. An expensively furnished condo. A sports car which drove smoothly and was flashy. He wore custom-made clothing. Dined at the best restaurants. Was seen with the most stunning women on his arm.

But what did he truly want out of life?

His tone serious, he met her gaze. "I really do think I

need to stop and assess things and think about what I want. And when I know? I want to talk to you about it."

Her smile radiated warmth. "That's a much better answer. Not flippant. Thoughtful." She leaned over and kissed his cheek. "I think we've done enough deep diving for tonight, Tanner. Let's go relax and chow down on some great Mexican food."

He saw the pendulum swinging. Darby was once again playful. Confident. Flirtatious. He liked that side of her, but he also liked this deeper side of her. The one which challenged him. Once he dropped her at her hotel this evening, he would have a lot of thinking to do.

He got out of the car and went around to open her door. Jace offered her a hand and helped her from the low-slung passenger seat. He got a nice flash of toned, tanned legs, which caused his pulse to jump.

Possessively taking her hand in his, they crossed the street and entered Adelina's. Even on a Tuesday night, the place was almost full.

Jace held up two fingers, and the hostess led them to the only empty booth available. They passed couples, families, and even those still dressed for work, looking as if they were meeting colleagues for dinner.

Darby slid into one side of the booth, and he took the other, glad he had the table between them because desire still raced through him. He told himself to do all the looking he wanted but that touching was off-limits.

Unless Darby made the first move.

The hostess handed them their menus and promised their server would arrive soon.

"What's good here?"

"Everything," she said, thanking a teenager who set a bowl of tortilla chips and another bowl of salsa on the table.

"I'm partial to their enchiladas, but everything from burritos to tamales to tacos rock."

The server appeared, setting down two glasses of water. "What else can I get you to drink?"

"Dos Equis for me," Darby said.

"Make it two," Jace told the server.

"Any apps?"

He looked to Darby. "You've been here. Order what you want."

"Tableside guac, please," she said.

"Be right back."

He chose a chip and dipped it into the salsa. After one bite, he finished the chip with enthusiasm.

"That's delicious."

"They make their salsa with both sweet and smoky flavors," she explained. "It's actually a peach and mango salsa, with three different kinds of chili peppers. Not too spicy. Just the right kick."

"If the salsa is any indication, I think I'm going to enjoy dinner."

The server returned after Jace perused the menu, delivering their beers. Darby ordered sour cream chicken enchiladas, while he went with spinach and chicken ones. His meal also came with a puffed taco. The server put in their order and then returned pushing a cart. Jace had eaten plenty of guacamole, but he had no idea what went into it.

Fascinated, he watched as a couple of avocados were halved and shred of their skin. The server mashed them in what Darby told him was a molcajete, a mortar and pestle created for this process. Tomatoes and jalapeños were diced and blended in, as were tiny bites of onion. A sprinkling of salt and cilantro completed the process, and the server mixed everything together in a large bowl before dishing it into a smaller one.

"Enjoy," she said, placing it on the table.

"My mouth is watering," he confided, dipping a tortilla chip into the bowl.

Darby did the same and proclaimed, "Heaven," after swallowing.

"You aren't kidding. How have I not heard of this place?"

"Maybe because it doesn't have a Michelin star?" she teased.

"Guilty as charged," he told her. "I've made a habit of dining at the best-known restaurants in the area. I'm in a business where being seen at the right place is the best way to get a foot in the door. No one wants a sports agent who frequents Whataburger."

"Hey, watch your mouth," Darby said, grinning as she downed another bite of dip and chip. "I was thrilled when Patrick Mahomes missed Texas and Whataburger so much that he bought a franchise and had it built in KC. I'm able to get my fix of Texas in a basket once every couple of weeks by stopping there."

"Only every few weeks?"

She nodded. "You wouldn't believe it from being around me this weekend, but I'm a very healthy eater. With the wedding and barbeque and then the cookout, I've overindulged while I've been here. Same tonight. But how can I come to Texas and not eat fabulous Mexican food? When I return home, my regular food habits will reappear."

"What do you like to eat?"

"That's good for me? I'm very fond of fish and eat it at least three times a week. I love vegetables. I have a piece of fruit a couple of times a day. A protein shake. Salad with a protein in it, usually chicken. I've had to live on the road for ten years now, and it's very easy to get into lazy habits and eat poorly. The clinics I've taught at have hundreds of girls focusing on me—and my body—as they learn the choreography. I want to be a good example to young women. Eating right helps them stay healthy and also aids in endurance. I also have taught exercise classes. I'm a big fan of PiYo."

"I know PiYo. I did it for about six months. It nearly killed me," he joked.

"What do you do to stay in shape?" she asked, eyeing him with interest.

"I lift weights twice a week. More than that, and I get too bulky. Besides weightlifting, I hit the gym another three days a week. Use machines, like a lat pulldown or a leg press. Run on the treadmill or use the stationery bike. Anything to break a sweat. I also play in a basketball league. It runs November through early March."

"You look like a basketball player. Not just because of your height but the way you move. I dated a power forward for a few months in college."

Hearing that caused a pang of jealousy to ripple through him. Jace knew that was ridiculous. She referred to a boyfriend from ten years ago. Why would that bother him?

The server returned with their food, and it was every bit as delicious as Darby had promised. He raved over his enchiladas, giving her a bite of them.

Jace had never offered a bite of anything off his plate to anyone.

They talked about college some, with him declaring them mortal enemies after learning she had cheered for the Texas Longhorns.

"As a loyal, Fightin' Texas Aggie, I shouldn't even be seen in public with you," he told her, finishing his last bite of rice mixed with beans.

"My dad said I was his daughter three hundred and sixty-four days a year, but on that one day of the year when the Aggies and Longhorns met, I was nothing but a burnt orange stranger to him."

He smiled. "I think I would've liked your dad."

Looking direct at him, Darby replied, "He definitely would have liked you."

"So, what was your major?" he asked. "Besides majoring in cheerleading and dating."

"Secondary education," she replied. "I'm certified to teach English and journalism. At one point, I thought I would go into journalism. I was the editor-in-chief of the *Hawthorne Herald*, the newspaper at HHS. Then Kelby and I got a chance to lead cheerleading workshops in the summer. It allowed us to travel all around the country and see places we wouldn't have had the opportunity to otherwise. Leading clinics also helped us stay in good shape. And it involved teaching, which I found I really enjoyed, so journalism merely became a teaching field to me as I focused on my education classes. I assume you were a business major."

"Guilty as charged," he told her, sipping on his water since he'd finished his beer. "I was selected as a President's Promise Scholarship student, which meant I had a full ride at A&M. Because of that and the education I received there, I am a generous donor to the school and that fund, in particular."

He paused, deciding to see what she would think about them seeing one another again in the future.

"Maybe we should attend the game between the Aggies and Longhorns this November," he ventured.

She smirked at him. "You mean the Longhorns and the Aggies?"

"Tomato, to-mah-to."

Darby looked at him. "You're serious."

"I am. I suppose since I've seen you do nothing but smile since I've known you, I should get to see when you're teary-eyed and morose after a Longhorn loss."

Darby shook her head. "You talk a big game, Tanner."

He grinned. "You afraid to be seen with me decked out in maroon, Montgomery?"

"Not in the least. You'll be the one crying in your beer." She paused. "I'll need to check my calendar, though." She swallowed, toying with her napkin, slowly shredding it.

"Hey, I'll fly you down from Kansas City. My treat. I usually attend the game. It'll be easy to get another ticket for you." He saw hesitation in her eyes and wondered if he had read things wrong between them. If she had a steady boyfriend back home. If she'd been caught up in the kisses they'd shared but was now feeling guilty about them.

Whatever it was, he deserved an answer. Jace could feel a protective layer of ice encircling his heart. He kicked himself for letting down his guard and being so open with this woman.

Worse, he worried he was already addicted to the taste of her.

"What's going on, Darby?" he asked gruffly. "I think you owe me an explanation."

She shook her head. "It's not what you think. You see, I won't be in KC come that game in November." She hesitated and then caused his world to begin spinning.

"I'm moving to Hawthorne, Jace. I'm going to be the new cheer coach and publications' sponsor at Hawthorne High School."

CHAPTER
Nine

Darby knew what she had revealed surprised Jace, yet no reaction flitted across his face. Once again, her heart went out to the little boy who had been torn from his loving, protective brother and sent to parents who tried to use him as a replacement son, instead of loving him for exactly who he was.

The server came and refilled their water glasses, and Jace handed her his credit card.

"I'll take care of this right away," she promised, leaving them in awkward silence after she departed.

"Everything has gone so well between us tonight," she finally ventured. "I don't want for us to end on a bad note, Jace."

For a moment, she caught a flash of anger in his eyes. "You let me talk your ear off, sharing things I've never told anyone, and yet you held that little bombshell."

She could tell by how tight his voice sounded how truly upset he was, yet the control he displayed was incredible.

"I'm not supposed to tell anyone about the job. I learned

about the job opening at the game Friday night. The current cheer coach's husband is being transferred out of state, and she was upset because she would have to finish out her contract and remain in Hawthorne the remainder of the school year."

Darby leaned back, taking a deep breath before continuing.

"I've been ready for a change in my life, Jace. I've worked for the same company for ten years now. I'd even planned to talk to Uncle Joe this weekend and ask him for some career advice. I had also decided to put my application on file and hopefully be considered for a teaching job next school year."

She tucked a lock of her hair behind her ear. "This simply fell into my lap. Not only have I been a cheerleader my entire life, I'm certified to teach journalism. Kay Timmons coaches the cheerleaders and is also in charge of the newspaper and yearbook staffs. It's as if a genie in a bottle gave me one wish, and I asked for a tailor-made teaching job. I immediately applied online and interviewed with my uncle and the HHS principal over the weekend. Because of my unique background, I'm an ideal candidate for Kay's position. By law, they must post the job for at least ten days. If anyone else does apply, they'll give them the courtesy of an interview, but they told me to put in my notice with Cheer USA."

Jace gazed at her for a long moment, as if he saw deep into her soul. Then he slid from the booth, and Darby thought he was going to walk out. She couldn't blame him. She had held back when he had shared confidences with her. Instead, he slid into her side of the booth and slipped an arm about her.

His voice husky, he said, "This is a huge change for you."

Darby nodded. "It really is. It's exhilarating to think I'll be starting a new career. Working with students on a daily basis. I always thought I would make for a good teacher, but the opportunity to work at Cheer USA came along right before I graduated from college. I decided I could always fall back on teaching at a later point in my life."

She swallowed. "That point has come, Jace. I've been feeling burned out, the same as Sawyer. My brother was a high-profile attorney in the Dallas District Attorney's office. For a long time, he thrived on the pressure of the cases he tried. The adrenaline high that came from a victory. But he missed the slower pace of life that could be found in Hawthorne. That's why Sawyer moved back. Because he was teetering on the edge of burnout. I've seen my brother and now two of my cousins return to our hometown, and a part of my soul was crying out to do the same."

Darby hesitated a moment and then turned to look him directly in the eyes.

"I didn't mean to hide this from you. Legally, I haven't been officially offered the job yet. Uncle Joe and Blanche Biggerstaff knew the family would learn about it, but they asked me not to share my news with anyone else. Other than my boss at Cheer USA, that is." She blew out a breath, shaking her head. "Boy, that is a whole other conversation."

She was aware of his arm about her shoulders, and it felt so good, having it wrapped around her protectively. Their bodies were also pressed closely together, and he radiated that wonderful heat and masculine scent, which she was quickly becoming addicted to. If they hadn't been in a public place, she would have initiated another kiss between them.

But what good would that do?

Jace lived an entirely different lifestyle from the one she wanted to be a part of in Hawthorne. He represented athletes who were millionaires and was seen in all the right places in Dallas, wearing custom suits that cost more than she earned in a month. All she wanted was to be a part of small-town life, a far cry from anything Jace Tanner would ever want.

The server returned with their bill, and Jace scrawled his name across the receipt. She couldn't help but see that he left the server an extremely generous tip, and that made her like him all the more.

"Let's go somewhere we can talk some more," he suggested.

"You aren't angry with me?"

He smiled slowly. "I was. Not anymore."

They returned to his expensive sports car, and he asked, "Would you be comfortable coming back to my condo?"

She appreciated that he would understand her concern, one any woman would have when asked to go back to a guy's residence. Instinct told her she could trust this man, though.

"Yes. I'd like to see where you live."

They didn't speak for the next ten minutes, and Darby wondered what he was thinking about. They arrived at his building, and he parked in the garage, coming around and helping her from the car. Small gestures like that went a long way with her, and she told herself not to fall for this man.

Riding the elevator to the top floor, she figured he would have settled for no less than the penthouse. Once they entered his condo and he flipped on the lights, she glanced around and couldn't help but chuckle.

"What?" he asked.

"It's exactly what I thought it would be. Sleek. Modern. Masculine. It's very you."

Darby walked about the room, running her hand over the back of the dark leather sectional. Everything was chrome and glass and leather. Sterile, in her opinion. No photographs or knickknacks were on display. Nothing personal marking the room. Anyone could live here.

And no one would learn anything about Jace if they saw this place.

Their gazes met, and he said, "I'm looking at my place with a critical eye now. I hired a top interior designer to put it together for me. I'm seeing it through your viewpoint, Darby." He frowned. "And I don't like what I see."

She reached for his hand and slipped hers around it. "Why would you say that? It's a gorgeous room. Why, it should be featured in a magazine."

Jace gave her a rueful smile. "It has been, along with me. This past January, in case you're interested in looking it up online. *Texas Monthly*."

"I might just do that," she said, releasing his hand and turning to move away.

He caught her wrist, his thumb slowly rubbing it sensually. "Can I get you something to drink?"

"No," she said, her pulse jumping.

"Then let's sit on my very expensive, chosen by a super-expensive decorator, sofa."

She couldn't help but laugh at his remark, and it broke some of the sexual tension building between them.

Some. Not all.

Darby slipped off her sandals and sat, tucking her feet underneath her. Jace took a seat, as well, not beside her but still fairly close. He rested his arm along the back of the sectional and faced her.

"So, tell me what you're leaving behind in Kansas City. What you look forward to most by returning to Hawthorne."

"I'm definitely a workaholic. I'm hoping in Hawthorne that I'll be able to have more of a work/life balance, though. I live in the same apartment I've had for a decade. It's close to my office."

For the next few minutes, Darby explained to Jace what her job entailed at Cheer USA and why she was in Dallas.

"Fortunately, the event center manager and I were on the same wavelength. We were able to accomplish everything we wanted to do today."

"That means you're free tomorrow?"

The intensity of his gaze almost had her coming undone. It took everything she had to maintain her poise and answer intelligently.

"I had thought I would still be in meetings all day tomorrow. Then fly back tomorrow night or early Thursday morning. I have an afternoon meeting with my boss on Thursday to talk about the Dallas facility and the upcoming national competition." She paused briefly. "And the resignation which I submitted."

"I guess that's not going over too well with your boss."

"It isn't. Peggy knows I'm a true workhorse. That I have a passion for Cheer USA and what we do there. I'm the ideal representative for the organization. I think she'll try to talk me out of resigning, but I've submitted my two-week notice. That clock is already ticking away, and I intend to follow through and move to Hawthorne."

"Will you leave behind friends? A boyfriend?" he asked casual.

"Because of all the travel I've done over the years, I really haven't had a steady, serious relationship. I had been dating a lawyer these past few months, hoping a spark would ignite between us because he's a really nice guy. Instead, he told me just before I flew to Texas that he's getting back with his longtime girlfriend from college. They were on-and-off all during his law school and her med school years. She's completed her residency now and is willing to move to KC to give them another try. I'm all for it.

Mitch and I are better off as friends. You can't force chemistry."

Their gazes met, and she saw the heat in his eyes. It caused her belly to flutter with butterflies.

Blinking, she turned away. "As far as moving to Hawthorne, I enjoyed growing up there. It's an ideal place to raise a family. My mom and Aunt Meg were sisters. Also close friends. Because of that, our families got together often. Sawyer and I have always been tight with West, Autumn, and Summer. I'm looking forward to being able to seeing more of them in the future."

"What will teaching be like?"

"Busy. Probably just as busy as I have been with Cheer USA, but it'll be a different kind of busy. Working with the cheerleading squads will be time-consuming."

Darby explained her class schedule to him and how she would have periods to meet with both cheerleading squads, the two publication staffs, and a beginning journalism class.

Laughing, she added, "At one point, I thought I was going to light the world on fire as a journalist. Travel to far-flung places around the world and report on the news. Either writing about it or being a part of a broadcast team. That's why I started college as a journalism major."

"What changed your mind?" he asked, and she could see his interest was genuine.

"I just kept thinking about how my teachers had influenced my life. Prepared me for the world. Helped to mold me and my character. I decided there was plenty of adventure in my own back yard of Texas and that I could teach and make a difference in the lives of many students over the years. That's when I switched majors to secondary ed."

"I think the passion you had at Cheer USA will transfer to your new career at Hawthorne High School," Jace declared with confidence. "They'll be lucky to have you on staff."

"To me, it's like one of those circle of life moments, me getting to return to the place I grew up and teach at the school I graduated from. I know a lot of things will be new to me. As a rookie, I'm going to make mistakes and will have to learn how to forgive myself for them. But I'm really thankful and excited to have the opportunity to be back in Hawthorne. It's a special place."

Jace threaded their fingers together. "You would succeed at whatever you chose to do, Darby Montgomery."

"Thank you. That means a lot to me. I know we've only known each other a short time, but I can see you're a good judge of people. You must have to evaluate both clients and situations instantly. Tell me more about what the world of being a sports agent is like."

His gaze pinned hers, the look in his eyes stealing her breath. "We can talk about that later. Right now, all I want to do is kiss you senseless. Will you let me do that, Darby?"

Hesitation filled her. Her attraction to Jace had been obvious from the moment they met. Even now, knowing they were two very different people with careers and lifestyles that didn't mesh, she wanted him.

Wanted him ...

The thought of his mouth on hers, his hands on her body and hers on his, was something she couldn't pass up. Darby had always been the good girl who went for good guys.

Jace Tanner might have good in him, but she sensed he was dangerous to her.

Somehow, she didn't care.

She placed her hand on his, the one which rested along the back of the sofa, close to her.

Boldly, Darby said, "I'm ready for whatever lies ahead tonight, Jace."

103

CHAPTER
Ten

Darby saw his eyes widen slightly, followed by desire flaring in them. His eyes were hazel, the same as hers, but they turned almost the green of a cat's as he slid into place next to her.

Suddenly, his mouth was on hers. Hot. Demanding. Aggressive. Unlike before, there was no warming up to more heated kisses. Jace came out of the gate as if he were on fire, and it lit a fire within Darby, as well.

Without missing a beat, he lifted her into his lap, their mouths fused together. She wrapped her arms about his neck, wanting to be as close to him as she could. Her breasts pressed against his chest, which seemed harder than granite. Already, her nipples were tightening, as was her core.

He eased her mouth open, and she gave way, admitting him. Their tongues began mating immediately, both fighting for control of the kiss. But there were no losers tonight. Every stroke of his tongue against hers brought satisfaction pouring through her. She pushed her fingers into his thick, brown hair, marveling at the softness of it. They tightened as he deepened the kiss, and she held on for what was the wildest ride of kisses ever. They were all-consuming. Drugging. Invading her very soul.

She wasn't shy, either. She gave as good as she got, taking from him as he did her. He broke the kiss, giving them a moment for a quick breath, and then he dived into it again. His hands now roamed her back. One fell to her thigh, rubbing up and down it, only the thin material of her sundress between them. His hand went lower, capturing her calf, massaging it, causing her to moan.

"You like that?" he asked against her mouth, his hand moving higher, slipping under the hem of her dress. It rode higher, reaching her thigh, kneading it.

Sparks began igniting within her, and she felt as if she were out of control, running for the edge of a cliff, ready to dive into the abyss without thought.

His hand skimmed up her thigh and down it, then moved between her legs. She let out a whimper as he dragged a finger along the seam of her sex. It tightened, and she wanted his finger inside her. The thought shocked her. Surprised her. She didn't take the idea of sex with any man lightly.

But she wanted Jace Tanner in her. Now.

His mouth was on hers again, devouring her, keeping her from asking him for that very thing. His finger continued to tease her, sliding up and down her slit, causing her to whimper. Then he moved it to the edge of her panties and seemed to hesitate.

Breaking the kiss, she panted, "Do it," frantic for the feel of him.

He did as she asked, sliding his finger beneath the silk material.

And into her.

She gasped at the intrusion, tightening about it.

"You're wet for me. Dripping," he said, his voice low and raw. "I want to touch you. Taste you."

"Do it," she echoed, need coursing through her.

Instead of continuing what he'd started, Jace came to his feet, bringing her with him. He was a good foot taller than she was and lifted her easily. He left the living room and went down a hallway, entering his bedroom, which was in the dark. Gently, he placed her on the bed and turned on a light sitting on the nightstand beside the bed.

His eyes were dark now, a dark gray-green, glowing like liquid heat. As she lay there, he peeled off his jacket. Unknotted his tie and slid it from his neck. Slowly unbuttoned the starched dress shirt, all while she watched, her breathing shallow.

He was bare to the waist now and the most beautiful man she had ever seen, his chest sculpted with muscle, his belly flat, ridged into an eight-pack. He reached out, pulling her to her feet, pressing his body against hers. She could feel his stiff cock pushing against her.

"I want to give you the best orgasm of your life," he said. "May I do so?"

Again, he asked. He wanted her consent. That was about as sexy a thing as she had ever heard.

"Yes," she said breathlessly.

"Good."

He took a small step back, his hands going around her to unzip her sundress. He peeled it away from her pulsing body. It pooled at her feet. He lifted her from it, placing her on the bed again. She hadn't worn a bra with the dress and only wore the scrap of silk panties. Leaning down, he slipped his fingers into the top and worked them over her hips and down her legs, tossing them over his shoulder. She watched each move he made.

Wetting her lips, she swallowed, her heart racing madly. Jace lay down beside her, propping his elbow up and bracing his head in the palm of his hand.

"I want to watch you," he said.

"All right."

He moved his free hand, placing it flat on her belly. The heat was immense. Slowly he dragged it downward, his fingers finding and parting her. One finger slowly entered her, causing her to gasp.

And him to smile.

"You're so beautiful," he said.

"I'm pretty. Not beautiful."

Giving her a wolfish smile, he said, "Beauty is in the eye of the beholder. And I think you are stunning."

As he spoke, his finger moved within her. Stroking her. Stretching her. Another one joined it, and she began to writhe from his touch. Then whimper. She begged him to hurry. He only smiled.

Then he stroked her deeply, causing her hips to rise. His finger pressed against the perfect spot, and she sighed.

"You like that."

"I do," she said, trying to sound playful, but what he was doing to her was slowly driving her out of her mind.

He pressed hard, then began circling the place. Her breath quickened. Little mewls came from her. All the time, he watched her, satisfaction on his face.

Then the pressure mounted, building inside of her, pushing her over the edge. His fingers continued to move as she cried out his name, her body no longer hers. The orgasm slammed through her, flooding her, making her dizzy and then causing her to float on a cloud of pure bliss. She finally came back to earth, her gaze meeting his.

"How was that?" he asked.

"Better than anything I can ever recall," she said truthfully.

"I think we can do better."

With that, he got off the bed. His fingers wrapped around her ankles and tugged, pulling her across the bed until her feet dangled from it. Her bottom was at the very edge.

Grabbing a pillow, he placed it on the floor and knelt on top of it. His lips brushed against her inner thigh, traveling slowly upward. She held her breath for a moment and then forced herself to take a breath, afraid if she didn't, she would pass out and miss all the fun.

His fingers kneaded her thighs, their heat scalding her bare skin. Then he moved closer to her. Rationally, she knew what oral sex was, but no man had ever performed it on her before. Excitement raced through her.

His tongue licked her inner thigh, moving closer to where the pounding was at her core, the beat sharp and fast and demanding. Then his tongue stroked her seam, and she cried out. Her fingers plunged into his hair, tightening in the thick locks. He pushed his tongue inside her, causing her to jump.

The next few minutes passed in a blur. He used his tongue. His teeth. His fingers. The combination of all three turned her into a pleading mess. She begged him, holding him close, feeling his smile against her body. Then the wild sensations tore through her again, and she rocked her hips, crying out, taking the ride of her life.

When the orgasm ended, she was completely limp. She couldn't have lifted a finger and didn't try to do so. Jace removed his shoes and socks and stripped off his suit pants, leaving him in boxer-briefs. Again, she marveled at his sculpted frame. His legs were incredible, thick, muscular thighs and beautifully shaped calves that made her want to sink her teeth into them.

He climbed into bed with her, dragging her up to where the pillows were. Then he wrapped his arms about her. She was being held tenderly, yet possessively, and it made her eyes sting with tears.

"Sleep," he urged, kissing her hair.

"I ... want ... but I can't move."

"Close your eyes, Darby," Jace ordered.

So, she did.

* * *

JACE WAS IN DEEP TROUBLE. He'd played with fire, thinking he was invincible.

Darby Montgomery had brought him to his knees.

All his life, he hadn't needed anyone. Hadn't wanted to need anyone. He was strong. Independent. Unemotional. Focused. While he had always wanted to reunite with his older brother, he hadn't made room for anyone else in his life. The closest thing he had to family, beyond Eli, was his office staff.

Darby had waltzed into his life and changed everything.

Suddenly, nothing seemed important. Not the business he'd built from scratch or the fat bank account he had. The condo. His investment portfolio. He could kiss everything goodbye and never miss it—if he had Darby.

That frightened him to his core.

He lay in bed now, holding her in his arms, listening to her even breathing as her light, floral scent danced up to tease him. He wanted to make love to her. Possess her. Never let her go.

How could that be?

They'd only met days ago. If you considered tonight a date, then they'd been on a grand total of one. Hell, he hadn't even had sex with her yet. Oral, yes, because he'd wanted so bad to get her off. To hear his name come from her lips. And oh, it had. She had been like lighting a candle. Watching it begin to flame and then burn, higher and higher. And she had.

He'd kissed her. Brought her to orgasm twice. And he was already thinking about making things permanent.

He'd gone bat-shit crazy.

Yes, she was attractive. Yes, they had sexual chemistry. And yes, she had a brain. A good one. She was quick-witted and could easily carry on a conversation about all kinds of topics, unlike the vapid beauties he usually hooked up with. Jace didn't want something quick and easy with her. A brief, torrid affair. No, he wanted more.

But that wasn't going to happen.

They were cut from very different cloths. She had made the choice to return to her hometown, a place that seemed as All-American as the mythical Mayberry of TV. Hawthorne was a good place. A small town with nice, decent people. Darby would easily weave herself into its fabric. Teaching kids. Making a difference. Finding someone to love and marry. Having kids and her happily ever after.

That was not the kind of life he wanted. He was all about glitz and glam. Fast cars and Michelin star meals. Custom-made suits and first-class air travel. Going for the jugular and scoring a victory. Making millions for his clients and himself. The idea of giving all that up to rot away in a small town was not his style. He'd come from less than nothing and had made it big in the world. His name meant something. He could buy whatever he wanted. Whoever he wanted. He didn't want slobbery babies or dropping kids at soccer practice or attending piano recitals. He wanted to push himself to the fullest. Live life on the dangerous side.

He and Darby Montgomery simply did not mix.

Jace told himself she was simply the new, shiny thing he'd seen. Something he thought he wanted. But he couldn't have her and give up who he was. He must be true to himself. Even as he told himself this, he glanced down, seeing Darby slumbering in his arms. Wanting to wake her. Kiss her. Make love to her.

Whoa. He was not a making love kind of guy. He was a have hot sex and stay uncommitted man. The more time he spent with Darby, the more he would crave her. He needed to cut ties with her now. Before it was too late. Because Jace knew they would both be burned if he didn't.

Still, he let her sleep for another hour. Was content to keep her in his arms because it gave him the most satisfying feeling he'd ever experienced.

When he did wake her, he did so gently. He turned her, kissing her softly, pushing aside the thought that it would be incredible to wake up to this woman every day.

She kissed him back, causing a deep yearning to fill him. He tamped it down and broke the kiss.

"I should get you back to your hotel."

He ignored the flicker of disappointment in her eyes.

"Yes. Good idea. Let me freshen up a moment."

She gathered her clothes and headed into his bathroom. Jace quickly dressed, combing his fingers through his hair, thinking how she had held onto it tightly.

When she came back into the bedroom, he opened his mouth to tell her that he'd enjoyed this evening but that he didn't want to see her again.

Instead, he heard himself saying, "Since you're in Dallas for another day, how would you like to spend it with me?"

CHAPTER
Eleven

Darby finished getting dressed, putting on the freshly-laundered Hawks T-shirt Kelby had gifted her with only a few days ago. Who knew when she had donned this shirt that she would once again become a Hawthorne Hawk?

She looked intently into the mirror at herself, wondering if she could see a change in her.

Because of Jace Tanner.

The handsome sports agent had certainly rocked her world last night. Not only had she thoroughly enjoyed getting to know more about him over a leisurely dinner, but she blushed now at the intimacies which had occurred between them. Her orgasms had been earth-shattering. She had been completely depleted by them, along with being overwhelmed by Jace himself. Though she still felt he had the capacity to upend her world, Darby wanted more of him.

After awakening in his arms, a feeling of safety she had never experienced with another man had washed over her. Then he had told her he was taking her back to her hotel, and disappointment flooded her, knowing that she was obviously lacking in whatever he was looking for and hadn't been able to hold his interest.

Then he caught her off-guard, asking if he could spend today with her. Darby was grateful that she had finished up her business with Dean Baker and decided not to fly back early. Spending all day with Jace today seemed like a bit of heaven on earth to her.

Her phone chimed, and she picked it up, reading the incoming text from Jace.

In the lobby with breakfast. Do you want to come down—or should I come up?

For a moment, she hesitated, not certain how she wanted to respond. Then Darby decided simply to go for it.

I'm in Room 317.

Darby left the text at that, nervously pacing until she heard the light tap on her door. Opening the door, she could only stare. While she had thought Jace incredibly handsome in his suit and tie, he appealed to her even more in a dark brown, fitted T-shirt and light brown cargo shorts which showed off his muscular calves spectacularly.

"Come on in," she invited, surprised her voice sounded so normal because her heart was racing in double time. "Thanks for picking up breakfast for us."

He went to the table near the window and set the bag and two, tall drinks on it.

As he began removing items from the bag, he said, "I didn't know what you usually ate for breakfast. I got a couple of bagels. Two donuts. A yogurt and a fruit bowl."

She took a seat at the table, and he sat in the other.

"I didn't know if you were a coffee or tea drinker either,

so I went with coffee. One regular and one decaf. Hope that's okay."

"I probably drink an equal amount of coffee and hot tea," she told him. "I always go decaf on the coffee and herbal on the tea, though."

"This is the decaf," he said, pushing one of the cups her way.

Opening the lid, she stirred in some sweetener he'd brought.

"They're both vanilla lattes," he added, seeming nervous to her.

"I love a good latte. As for breakfast, I'll claim the fruit and yogurt. It's time to start eating healthier again."

She opened the container of Greek yogurt and spooned a bite from it, savoring its tartness. Meanwhile, Jace spread cream cheese on half a toasted bagel and took a large bite from it.

"What will you do now that you'll be back living here?" he asked, a teasing glint in his eyes. "With the temptation of cheeseburgers and enchiladas and Blue Bell?"

"I'll keep to my healthy habits, and then I'll splurge a couple of times a week. Hawthorne has an amazing pizza place. Pizza Palace. The owners are from New York, and they really know how to produce an incredible pizza with a perfect crust. How about you?" she asked, turning the focus back to him. "What are your eating habits like?"

"As far as eating goes?" He shrugged. "I like stuff that's good for you, but I also like stuff that's not so good for you. Because I work out so often, I can pretty much eat whatever I want and maintain a steady weight."

"Besides doing PiYo, I also meditate," she told him. "It really has helped me to keep focused over the years."

"Hmm. I've never tried meditation. Then again, I'm a

pretty focused guy already." He grinned. "Focused on *you* today," he flirted.

She felt the blush stain her cheeks. "Are you sure you're able to take an entire day away from work? I don't want to keep you from anything important."

"I'm the boss. I can do whatever I choose. Today, I choose you."

His words caused her stomach to erupt with a mass of fluttering butterflies. It surprised her because no man's words had ever affected her.

But Jace Tanner's certainly did.

They finished their breakfast and coffees, talking about everything from things in the news to a new movie they'd both seen and enjoyed. The more time she spent talking with Jace, the more she enjoyed being around him.

She knew that she couldn't let her heart become involved, though. This was a man who lived a vastly different lifestyle from her own, especially now that she would be living in a small town. She would simply enjoy this one day with him— because it wouldn't be repeated in the future. It was a day for them to both play hooky and revel in doing so. The fact that her partner in crime was so devastatingly handsome only added to the fun.

"What are we going to do today?" she asked. "You said dress casually, preferably in shorts, and I've complied."

"First, I'd like to take you by my office. I want you to see it."

Darby frowned. "Then I better change."

"No, you don't need to do that. There's no reason to dress up with everything we're doing today being super casual."

"I guess I still have enough of that small-town girl in me, and I want to make a good impression on people."

He frowned. "You want to impress my office staff?"

"You've built your business from scratch, Jace. You've surrounded yourself with people who are not only terrific at their jobs, but they're ones you enjoy being around. I don't want to embarrass you by waltzing in, looking like a slob."

He reached and took her hand. "You are the least slob-like person I've ever seen. You look terrific today."

"If you say so."

"I do," he said firmly, their gazes meeting. "And I don't give out compliments lightly."

They left her hotel room and went down to his Porsche. Again, she thought she probably could buy four or five practical, economical cars for what he had paid for this one sports car. Darby told herself to stop thinking about all the differences between them and just enjoy this day.

It only took about ten minutes to reach his office and park. Naturally, he had his own parking space with his name prominently displayed on it. They rode the elevator to one of the top floors in the glass office building and stepped from it.

"I'm eager for your opinion about my office and my staff."

She wondered why he would care what she thought of either but kept quiet, telling herself not to rock the boat today. Keep everything at face value. Don't read anything into what he said or didn't say.

They entered the Touchdown Talent Management offices and were greeted by the receptionist. Jace took Darby through the place, introducing her to Penny Hiller, who handled all the company's marketing, and Steve Butler, who was in charge of social media and graphics for the agency.

In the breakroom, they came across a tall, wiry man with dark hair and sparkling blue eyes.

"Darby Montgomery, I'd like you to meet my partner in TTM. This is Mark Walton. He's an attorney and handles contracts and anything else legal for us."

Mark gave her a warm smile and offered his hand. "It's a pleasure to meet you, Darby. If you want to know any dirt on this guy, I'm your man and will spill all I know for a Butterfinger."

She laughed. "I may do that, Mark. I like cheap info."

Jace said, "I won't be in the office today. Anything I need to know about?"

"If I could steal you for five or ten minutes, that would be helpful," Mark said.

"Let me go and introduce Darby to Elena." He looked at her. "You can wait for me in my office if you don't mind."

"Take as long as you need," she told him.

They left the breakroom and approached the desk of a pretty woman in her mid-thirties, with long, dark hair and brown eyes.

"Elena Arturo, meet Darby Montgomery."

The assistant came from behind her desk, and the two woman shook hands.

Darby said, "He may not tell you this, but Jace has bragged on you. And from everything he said, you're smart, efficient, and keep him in line. In other words, you're my kinda gal."

Elena chuckled. "I'm glad to hear he's full of compliments when I'm out of earshot. Maybe I should use this info to wrangle a raise."

"I'm all for that," she told the assistant.

Jace said, "Excuse me for breaking up this lovefest, but I'm taking today off, Elena. Reschedule whatever needs to be shuffled. Mark needs me for a few minutes, so show Darby my office and have her wait there."

Elena nodded. "Will do, Boss. Come this way, Darby. You're going to see a spectacular view of downtown Dallas."

They entered Jace's office. One entire wall was floor to ceiling windows, and the view was incredible.

She glanced around. "This office is as big as my apartment in Kansas City," she declared.

"A lot of what transpires at TTM happens here. Jace does a lot of work from his desk, but many of our meetings with important clients happen in the sitting area over here. And instead of the conference room, Jace likes to have work meetings with various employees at this table area."

"I know you need to get back to work, Elena. I'll just have a seat here and catch up on a few emails."

The assistant studied her a moment. "I worked with Jace at a different sports agency. When he started TTM, he asked me to come along. The man is a machine, working sixteen-to-eighteen-hour days. He has never come in and announced he was taking a day off. You must be someone very special, Darby, for that to happen."

Hearing this helped her to understand that Jace was feeling some of the same things that she was.

"We met in Hawthorne this past weekend," Darby volunteered. "My cousin was getting married to Jace's brother. We hit it off. I was in Dallas on business for a few days, and we decided to get together."

"Jace never told anyone here about Eli," Elena confided. "I only learned that he had a brother yesterday. Jace keeps a lot to himself. His personal life and his emotions. The fact that he shared that he found Eli with me is huge. It's even bigger that he's taking the entire day off to spend with you. I know you had dinner last night at Adelina's. It's my family's favorite restaurant. I've eaten there from the time I was in a highchair."

Elena touched Darby's arm. "I think you're exactly what

Jace needs, Darby. I hope things go well between the two of you. Today—and beyond."

Darby didn't see the point of explaining to Elena how she and Jace came from incredibly different worlds. How he would remain here in Dallas while she began a new life, teaching in Hawthorne. She had never been a woman who'd had a casual fling, but that was exactly what this was. Something short term. Heady. Intense. But nothing permanent.

"Can I bring you something to drink?" Elena asked.

"No, thank you. I'll just check my emails now."

She went and sat on one of the two sofas in a corner of the room. It was plush and comfortable, exactly what she had anticipated.

Darby didn't let the view distract her. She answered a couple of emails and then read over her notes from yesterday's tour. She would write up her report for Peggy tonight if she had time or on the plane tomorrow morning.

Jace appeared a quarter of an hour later. "I think we're ready to head out."

"Are you sure we shouldn't just put things off and let you work today? We could have dinner tonight," she suggested as an alternative.

He scowled. "I told you that I wanted to spend the entire day with you. That's what I meant." His features softened. "And tonight, as well."

She didn't know if that meant he wanted to have dinner—or spend the night with her.

If it were the latter, she was all in.

They returned to the parking garage and left downtown, heading east.

"What did you think of the TTM offices?" he asked.

The question might have sounded casual, but she knew her answer was important to him.

"They convey exactly what you want your clients to feel. It's got clean, modern lines. It's tastefully decorated. The layout is excellent. I know you've only hired people who are tops in their field. Overall, if I were thinking about signing with you, I would have a very favorable impression of TTM."

"Good. Would you change anything?" he pressed.

"I'd have to think on that," she responded. "Let me get back to you."

They drove in silence for a few minutes, and Darby was surprised how comfortable things seemed between them after such a short acquaintance. She had been on dates where awkward pauses drew out into long, even more awkward silences. With Jace, she didn't feel as if she had to keep the conversation going the entire time. It was a relief to find things were so easy between them.

"You wonder where we're going? We got sidetracked on that topic."

"You're the guy from Dallas. You should be able to take me wherever you'd like today."

"I hope we'll start out at a place you haven't been to before. If you have, I can switch gears. I'm taking you to the Dallas Arboretum."

"I went there when I was maybe eight or nine years old," she told him. "It was Christmastime, and they had this beautiful display at night of the Twelve Days of Christmas. It was so dark, though, that I really didn't get to see the grounds, but each of those twelve days was like glimpsing into a winter wonderland. I'm eager to see what the arboretum looks like in daylight during a different time of year."

He nodded, a satisfied smile on his face. "Today's weather is going to be really nice. Low seventies, with a slight breeze. Sunny."

Jace glanced to her, their gazes meeting. "I think we're going to have a good time together, Darby."

She thought the exact same thing.

CHAPTER

Twelve

After Jace had left Mark, he spoke with Elena, telling her how he wanted a fun day outdoors with Darby and thought to take her to the Dallas Arboretum. He had attended a client's wedding held there last spring, and the grounds were breathtaking. Elena had told him she would handle everything there. Parking. Tickets. Seeing that a picnic lunch was provided. She also recommended after leaving the arboretum that they visit White Rock Lake, telling him they could walk around it or choose to rent bikes. She even gave him the option of renting kayaks, and he had instructed her to set up reservations for both kayaks and bikes, not knowing which Darby might prefer.

Elena had given him a look. Actually, she had several of them. The Angry Look. The Get Out of My Face Look. The Don't You Know I've Already Done That Look. Each of her distinctive looks told Jace to back off.

This new one, however, was different. Subtle. Intrigued. Analytical. He didn't have time to ask her about it. He just wanted things done. She promised she would handle the arboretum and the lake—and that she would have a special surprise after those activities, which he figured would take most of the day. Jace supposed she would make dinner reservations for them, hoping she would give them enough time to get cleaned up after a day spent outdoors.

He pulled the Porsche into the arboretum and pulled up to where a security guard waited. Quickly searching his phone, he found an email from Elena, with parking and tickets attached. He showed the guard and was waved through, easily finding a parking place. With the arboretum just now opening and kids in school, he figured the crowd would be small for a weekday. Probably moms with young children in strollers or retired couples strolling the grounds.

"Let me read the rest of Elena's email," he told Darby, not wanting to miss anything his assistant had sent.

Sixty seconds later, a pleased smile crossed his face.

"Good news?" asked Darby.

"Elena has everything handled. She truly is the best."

"Then I hope she gets that raise which was mentioned," Darby added.

He liked the fact that she spoke up in support of another woman. All too frequently, he had seen women in competition with one another, tearing down instead of building one another up.

Going around to her side of the car, he opened her door and pulled her from her seat.

"Let's go enjoy the day," he told her.

Once their tickets were scanned, he turned his phone's ringer off, leaving it on vibration in case Elena sent him more info. For now, he wanted to devote his sole attention to Darby.

As they entered the grounds, she said, "Oh, this is lovely. I know besides Christmas, they also dress up the park for fall and Halloween. It's considered one of the top botanical gardens in the world. I've been to the one in Phoenix, where desert plants were prevalent across the landscape. This will be a much different experience."

He took the map they were handed and said, "Let's get familiar with the property."

Leading her to a bench, they reviewed the map. He was specifically looking for the DeGolyer House and easily found it and the gardens surrounding the house, which was over twenty thousand square feet.

"We should go to the DeGolyer House first," he told Darby.

She rose from the bench. "Lead the way."

They reached the gardens in front of the house, which featured a gorgeous fountain and an abundance of flowers. Darby knew gardening and told him the difference between the seasonal and perennial blooms which surrounded them.

"I've never had a house of my own," she explained. "I've lived in the same apartment in KC since taking the job with Cheer USA. I used to love helping my mom, though. We'd weed the flowerbeds. Plant some seasonal flowers. Lantana in the spring. Black-eyed Susan and Star Hibiscus for the summer. Fall asters and goldenrod for autumn. Pansies and snapdragons for winter."

She bent and sniffed a bunch of flowers. "For perennials, Mom planted gorgeous purple Mexican bush sage and purple fountain grass. And salvia." Darby rose, a smile on her face. "You've brought me to the perfect place, Jace."

Happiness washed over him. Suddenly, he realized he was more interested in making Darby happy than himself. He'd been a loner for so long. Selfish. Taking care of only himself. It was as if a light had been switched on inside him, and he could now see what was important.

This woman made him happy. And he wanted to keep her awash in happiness.

"Let's go inside the house."

"Oh, I don't think you can. That one time we came, the house was off-limits. Dad said they gave tours once a month, but we weren't here at the right time."

"We can get in. I promise."

She studied him a moment. "You're pretty darn cocky, Tanner."

"I like to call it confident." He threaded his fingers through hers. "Come on."

Leading her to the front of the house, he opened the door, hoping that what was in Elena's email was correct.

"Mr. Tanner?" a woman in her mid-forties asked. She had dark hair and very blue eyes.

"Yes. Are you Rebecca?"

She smiled. "Rebecca Wimsey. I'm here to show you the DeGolyer House. Or as some say, the DeGolyer Mansion. If you'll follow me."

Darby flashed Jace a perplexed look as they moved from the foyer.

"The DeGolyer House sits on part of the sixty-six acres which make up the Dallas Arboretum," their guide explained. "The home is listed on both the National and Texas Registers of Historic Places. It is built in the Spanish Colonial Revival style and was designed by two architects from Los Angeles, Burton Schutt and Derman Scott."

They entered the first room, and Rebecca continued.

"Originally, the house was called Rancho Encinal by its owner, Everrette DeGolyer, who commissioned it in 1939. Its formal gardens were designed by Arthur Berger, a prominent landscape architect. Mr. DeGolyer made his money in the oil industry, first as a petroleum geophysicist and then an oil company executive. He was quite well known for his phil-anthropy, and the library he built at this house, full of early editions and rare books, became one of the most famous private libraries in the nation."

He and Darby gazed about the room, and she said, "It's incredible."

Rebecca smiled. "Mr. DeGolyer was born in a sod house in Kansas, so you can see he really came up in the world. The library now is very small compared to what it was in its heyday. He donated parts of his collection to SMU, the University of Texas at Austin, and the University of Okla-homa. Everything from law books to the history of Mexico to seminal works of science. Mr. DeGolyer also helped found St. Mark's School of Texas here in Dallas, and he served on the board as President of the Dallas Public Library."

They followed Rebecca throughout the large house for an hour as she told them stories of various pieces of furniture and portraits which hung in the house.

By the end of their tour, Jace was fascinated and could see Darby had also enjoyed their time with Rebecca.

"Thank you for your time today, Rebecca," he said. "I know this was last-minute."

"Oh, I didn't mind at all, Mr. Tanner. And your generous donation will go far to help with programs here at the Dallas Arboretum."

They left the one-story house, and Darby said, "That was incredible. I'm sorry it cost you a hefty donation, but I thor-oughly enjoyed hearing all the history of the house and its occupants. It was like stepping back in time. Everything is so well preserved. I would love to come again at Christmas since Rebecca said they decorate it as the DeGolyers did."

"We'll have to do that."

He saw her frown slightly but didn't press her. Glancing

at his Patek Philippe watch, he said, "We have time to visit one garden, and then we need to make a stop."

"Another surprise?"

"You'll see."

They ventured to the Lay Family Garden, filled with beautiful flowers and plants. It contained two water features. One, the Lay Grotto, had a waterfall and koi pond. The other had a cascading water element beneath a trellis of greenery. No one was in the garden, and Darby snapped a few pictures of it.

He pulled out his own cell phone and slipped an arm about her waist, pulling her close.

"Smile, pretty lady," he said, snapping a selfie.

He appreciated when she didn't ask to see it. Too many times, he'd been around women who deleted picture after picture, waiting to capture a perfect snapshot. Darby seemed happy to pose and move on.

Another thing to like about her.

"Time to go to Guest Services," he announced, where he retrieved a picnic hamper and a blanket.

"What's this?" she asked, clearly curious.

"Lots of people picnic on the grounds. I thought we could do the same. Elena recommended we go to the Jonsson Color Garden." He consulted the map. "Here it is." Handing her the map, he said, "You lead the way."

When they arrived, he saw many flower beds of what he thought were seasonal flowers, with reds, golds, and oranges dominating. The large lawn of lush, green grass in front of these flowerbeds had a few scattered picnickers on it. He guided them toward a place to the side, where they had an excellent view of all the garden and a bit of privacy.

Handing Darby the hamper, Jace opened the blanket and spread it out. They sat, Darby opening the basket and pulling out a variety of food. Cheeses and crackers. Fruit, including red grapes and slices of apple. Chicken salad sandwiches. There was also bottled water to wash it down, as well as a bottle of a crisp Chardonnay with a corkscrew and two plastic glasses.

"Remind me that Elena deserves a *really* big raise," Jace said.

"I told you so," Darby replied, placing a slice of cheese on a cracker and feeding it to him.

Damn. He could get used to this.

They took their time eating and then packed up the basket and folded the blanket. He returned it to Guest Services, telling the clerk that she was welcome to keep everything.

After that, they strolled the rest of the grounds. Darby fell in love with the Woman's Garden, with its scenic view of White Rock Lake behind the large infinity pool. They also visited A Tasteful Place, an ornamental garden which also had a nearby kitchen and pavilion and had been inspired by the movement to eat fresh, sustainable, locally-grown food. They even enjoyed a free tasting.

When they reached the secluded McCasland Sunken Garden, they saw a bride was having her portrait made. They started to leave, but the bride called out for them to stay.

"I don't want to monopolize a public place," she told them. "My fiancé and I are actually getting married in this exact spot next month. I'll walk down that staircase. We'll have the wedding over in the courtyard. My grandparents will sit on that bench." The bride-to-be smiled. "This is the place my parents met thirty years ago. They got married at the arboretum, and we wanted to do the same."

They took a seat on the bench, watching the photographer as he made suggestions for poses.

"She radiates happiness," Darby observed. "I hope I'll be that happy when I fall in love someday."

Jace found his throat tightening with emotion.

Because he was in love with Darby Montgomery.

Yes, it sounded totally insane. He'd known her less than a week, but she was already as necessary to him as the air he breathed. He couldn't say anything, though. Besides sounding as if he should be committed, Jace didn't want to scare Darby away. She was the best thing that had ever happened to him, and that even included finding Eli. He supposed he wanted what Eli and Autumn had. No, he *knew* he wanted what the couple had.

And he wanted to spend the rest of his life with Darby.

Instead, he simply smiled at the woman wearing the bridal gown, thinking how much he wanted to see Darby in something similar.

They wished the bride well and continued walking the grounds before setting out for his car.

As they walked, he asked, "What was your favorite place we saw?"

She grew thoughtful. "Maybe the Red Maple Rill. Those Japanese maples growing along that stream was a beautiful contrast. How about you?"

"I think I liked Crape Myrtle Alley. The way the trees arched in a natural tunnel was pretty cool. And I liked the fountain at the end of Toad Corner."

They reached his car, and Darby sighed. "This was wonderful, Jace. I think I'll want to visit the arboretum every year in the future. Maybe during different seasons, so I can see the different varieties of flowers. Oh, especially spring. Tulips are my favorite flower. I'll bet they have plenty of those come April."

He wanted to tell her he would bring her to visit as many

times as she wanted, but he was afraid to voice that. Except for their fiery lovemaking and the fierce attraction between them, everything between them had been casual. Friendly. He didn't want to put any pressure on her. And he certainly didn't want to declare that he loved her. It was hard for him to understand these new, fragile feelings he'd never felt before, much less voice them to Darby.

"More to do," he told her, pushing aside thoughts he wasn't ready to deal with just yet.

"I don't think you could top this."

He gave her a cocky smile. "Challenge accepted, Montgomery." Opening the car door, he helped her into the vehicle. "Let's see what you think an hour from now."

Darby was having the time of her life. Not just because of what they were doing.

Because she was doing it with Jace.

They drove to nearby White Rock Lake, which they had been able to see from the DeGolyer House. Jace parked, and they went to the trail which encircled the lake. Though it was afternoon and mid-week, there were several people out enjoying the fine weather, with joggers, walkers, and moms pushing strollers. Even a few rollerbladers passed them.

Jace threaded his fingers through hers, and Darby felt a blanket of calm envelop her. She wanted to keep things light between them, but these small gestures of his continued to steal pieces of her heart.

As they strolled along the path, he said, "We can walk part of this if you'd like, but I know we've already done our fair share of walking at the arboretum."

"I never mind walking," she said. "I enjoy it, especially walking outdoors. Besides, we're both in great shape." She deliberately pushed away thoughts of just how great his shape was.

"We do have two other options available to us," he explained. "We can rent bikes and ride them around the lake if you'd like that."

"Ooh, I haven't been on a bike in ages. That sounds like a lot of fun."

"Duly noted. Or we could rent kayaks and take them out on the water."

She beamed at him. "Now, you're talking, Tanner. I love to kayak. I haven't been in over a year. Are you up for that?"

"I want to do whatever makes you happy, Darby," Jace said quietly, causing a tingle to dance along her spine.

He consulted his phone and told her they had a few minutes' walk to get to the kayak rental stand.

"I suppose I have Elena to thank as much as you for today," she said.

"She did help arrange a few things. Making the reservations for the kayak and bikes. Helping to arrange the private tour at the DeGolyer House."

"And don't forget the heavenly basket of food and wine for our picnic," she reminded. "You have a real gem in Elena."

"I saw tremendous potential in her when we worked together at a different sports agency. Put my time in a few places, learning the ropes. I thought she was being underused and undervalued, so when I started TTM, I asked her to come along for the ride. She understood it would be a drop in pay at the beginning, until I signed enough clients. With her help, though, we got off to a quick start. Elena has a very warm, welcoming presence which puts the clients at ease. She's probably the smartest person I know, and I'm including myself when I say that. Frankly, I don't know how much longer she'll want to work for me. I can see her branching out on her own, and I would support her one hundred percent if she did."

Darby liked hearing that. Many men were jealous of the success of women or held them down, preventing them from progressing up the ladder. The fact that Jace was so supportive of Elena spokes volumes about his character. The more she got to know him, the more she liked him.

And liking him too much wasn't an option.

She reminded herself that she was taking things a day at a time. That the goal was to enjoy this one, perfect day with him and cherish whatever memories came from it.

At the kayak stand, he gave the clerk his name, and they were led to a group of kayaks. She choice once which was sky blue, while Jace went for a fire engine red one. They were provided with life jackets and slipped into them, buckling them up before taking their oars and kayaks to the water's edge.

Once they had both pushed off and had paddled away from the shore, they floated side by side for a few minutes, with Jace pointing out a few things to her. Darby was itching for more of a workout, though, and began paddling, with Jace following, his strokes long and even.

They were out on the water for two hours, soaking up the sunshine and enjoying being out in nature on a beautiful day. She would have to think about buying a kayak and using it on Lake Hawthorne once she moved to Texas. It would be easy to talk Kelby into going with her since her friend loved the water so much. Maybe even Sawyer would enjoy kayaking with her. As a former college athlete, her brother was adept at every sport he tried.

Jace checked his watch. "We need to head back," he

informed her. "I have something planned after this, and we can't be late for it."

She smiled at him. "I don't see how today could get any better."

"Hold that thought."

They reached the shoreline and stepped from their kayaks. Jace whipped out his phone and took a selfie of them by the water before they dragged the kayaks back to the rental stand. They removed their life jackets and handed them over, thanking the worker for the use of the kayaks.

"Anytime," he said cheerfully. "We're here seven days a week."

Darby walked with Jace back to his car, saying, "I'm tired but in a good way. That was a good workout. I'm sure my shoulders and arms will be a little sore tomorrow."

"The next thing we'll do will relax you," he promised. "And help with the soreness."

Though she was curious about that activity, she decided to go with the flow and be surprised.

Twenty minutes later, they pulled up to a building surrounded by lush landscaping. No signs adorned it, so Darby had no idea what the place was.

Once inside, she quickly figured out that it was a spa from the décor and the Zen vibe. Jace was warmly greeted by the receptionist.

"Good afternoon, Mr. Tanner. We have everything waiting for your couples massage."

Darby now knew she was definitely in a world much different from her own. She had only had one massage in her life, using a gift certificate she had received years ago. While she had thoroughly enjoyed the experience, splurges such as massages and facials were beyond her modest salary.

They were escorted to an area and into a private room, where they were given fluffy robes and asked to disrobe. Darby suddenly felt shy around Jace. She appreciated when he turned his back to her and pulled his T-shirt over his head. She turned and did the same, hurriedly removing her clothing, slipping into the plush robe which felt luxurious against her bare skin.

The room had two chairs and a small table between them. Soft instrumental music was being piped in. Jace took a seat, and Darby followed suit, supposing they would be called soon by the massage therapist.

Instead, the door opened, and a woman rolled in a cart which held a platter of strawberries dipped in chocolate. It also contained a bucket filled with ice. In the bucket stood a bottle of champagne. Jace thanked the woman. She left, and he skillfully opened the champagne without spilling any. He poured the liquid into the two accompanying flutes and returned the bottle to its bucket, scooping up the flutes and handing one to her.

His gaze warm, he clinked his glass against hers. "Here's to us—and the perfect day."

She merely nodded, sipping from the flute, the bubbles tickling her nose as she did so.

"I hope you like strawberries and chocolate," he said.

"Chocolate—especially dark chocolate—is my biggest vice," she admitted. "Actually, dark chocolate is very heart healthy. I usually keep a bag in the freezer and indulge in a piece after dinner when I'm home."

They finished the strawberries, with Jace pouring her a second glass of champagne. Darby felt a little lightheaded after drinking it. She didn't know if it was simply the champagne or the euphoria of being in Jace's company.

The same woman who had brought the champagne

opened the door and asked, "Are you ready for your massage now?"

"We are," Jace replied for them both.

"I'll let your masseuses know. They'll be here shortly." She looked to Darby. "We see Mr. Tanner on a regular basis, Ms. Montgomery, but you'll need to let your therapist know the type of massage you wish to have today, as well as discussing any specific points which are bothering you."

"Thank you," she said, not having a clue as to what she should ask for.

Jace must have picked up on her distress because he said, "There are different kinds of massages you can have."

He walked her through the difference between several, explaining Swedish, deep tissue, sports, and hot stone massages.

"I think I'll go Swedish," she said.

Two women arrived, and Darby spoke with her masseuse, asking for a Swedish massage and telling the woman that she sometimes carried a little tension in her lower back.

"We'll get that taken care of, Ms. Montgomery. Please follow me."

Jace linked their fingers together again as they moved along a long corridor and entered a room. Two long tables sat side by side. The room was dim, lit by scented candles, with soft music playing in the background.

"We'll return in a couple of minutes," her therapist told them. "Please disrobe and slide beneath the sheet, lying face down. We'll start from there."

Again, Jace turned away from her, shedding his robe, allowing Darby to remove her robe and slip under the sheet unseen by him. She had gotten a glimpse of his muscular back, and her fingers longed to stroke the sleek muscles.

"Oh, it's heated," she said, feeling warmth rising from the

table. "Even though it's hot outside, this feels wonderful." She turned her head so that she faced him. "This was really thoughtful of you, Jace."

"I get a massage once a week. My job is pretty stressful. Working out and having a massage are ways that I alleviate that stress."

She smiled and rested her head so that her face was lying against the opening in the table. Once more, she thought about how this was considered a luxury to someone like her. To Jace, however, being pampered in this manner was a necessity. Just a part of his weekly routine.

A light tap sounded at the door, and she sensed the two massage therapists entering the room. For the next hour, Darby luxuriated in the long, deep strokes which penetrated her muscles. Although it would have been easy to drift into sleep, she made certain to stay awake so she could enjoy every moment of the session.

When the hour was up, they were led back to the room where their clothes were and dressed.

"I feel as if I'm floating," she said. "That was one of the best experiences of my life."

An odd look crossed Jace's face, and she decided he must be figuring out how limited her world really was compared to his.

They sipped on the cucumber water provided to them, and then Jace picked up two bottles of water, saying, "Let's drink these in the car. It's important to hydrate after a massage."

He drove back to her hotel, and Darby supposed their magical day had come to an end.

Pulling into the loop in front of the hotel, Jace turned to her. "We still need to have dinner. Are you up for that?"

Happiness spread through her, hearing they would still have time together.

"I'll definitely need a shower."

"Same. Can I pick you up at seven?"

"Yes. Seven is good. What should I wear?"

"What were you going to wear today during your business meetings?" he asked.

"A suit. Heels."

"Wear that." He leaned over and brushed his lips against her cheek. "I'll see you at seven."

"I'll come down and wait in the lobby for you," she said wanting to streamline things.

Darby went upstairs to her room and got into the shower, letting the warm spray strike her body. She washed away the last traces of the massage oil and then shampooed and conditioned her hair since the masseuse had massaged her scalp with some kind of scented oil. She put on a light bit of makeup and dressed, blow-drying her hair. It struck her that she hadn't made a reservation to fly home to Kansas City, so she did that. Her flight would leave at eight-thirty tomorrow morning, giving her plenty of time to reach the office for her meeting with Peggy.

Gazing into the mirror, she thought Cinderella would be leaving the ball without her prince and returning to her hovel of an apartment in KC. Darby realized today had been a fantasy, like a planned date on *The Bachelor*. Jace had lavished her with attention, and they had participated in a picture-perfect day. But reality was sinking in fast. She would wrap up her life in KC and drive herself and her belongings to Hawthorne soon. She would need to talk with Sawyer to see if she could move in with him temporarily because she didn't feel right staying with Kelby and West. Sawyer's place was small, though, so she might ask Aunt Meg and Uncle Joe if she could use their guest bedroom while she found a place of her own.

Her new chapter in life would then start, one which Jace Tanner would not be a part of. Darby wondered if it was even a good idea to have dinner with him this evening. It was too late to call it off, though.

She left her hotel room and took the elevator to the lobby. A few minutes later, Jace texted, saying he was a couple of blocks away. She replied, telling him she would leave the lobby and wait outside for him.

When he pulled up, he immediately jumped out, coming around to open her door. Jace wore one of his tailored suits which fit him well, showing off his broad shoulders to perfection. Darby caught a whiff of the same woodsy cologne, thinking she wanted to bury her nose against his neck.

In the car, he asked if she were hungry.

"Well, strawberries and champagne only go so far," she teased.

"I think you'll like the menu where we're going." Jace named the chef and the restaurant. Darby had never heard of either, but then again, she didn't live in Dallas, much less frequent fine dining establishments.

They pulled up to a large building. Jace gave his key to a valet and then escorted Darby inside. The interior of the restaurant looked as if it were a part of the Palace of Versailles. Everything was gold and shiny, ostentatious and over the top. Already, she felt out of place, and her discomfort only grew as they were escorted to their table. She saw what other women wore and felt woefully underdressed, especially when she saw a few of them looking at her surreptitiously, their noses crinkling in judgment.

They were seated at a table and handed menus bound in smooth leather. She opened hers and saw no prices listed, which only added to her distress. Discreetly, she pulled out her phone and googled the name of the restaurant, bringing up its menu. Online, she could see the prices. One appetizer was the price of what she would normally pay for an app, entrée, and dessert when she went out to eat.

Hesitantly, she turned the page, skimming the menu as she slipped her phone back into her purse. She closed the menu and placed it on the table.

"You've already decided?" Jace asked. "Or are you waiting to hear tonight's specials? Usually, that's what I get because they're both unique and delicious."

Darby glanced around the room and felt small and insignificant.

"What's wrong?" he asked.

Reluctantly, she met his gaze. "I don't think I can eat here," she said quietly.

Frowning, he asked, "They don't have anything that appeals to you?"

"I don't mean to ruin anything, Jace, but could we leave? Please?"

"Of course."

He stood and pulled out her chair, helping her to her feet.

The maître d' hurried over to them. "Is something wrong, Mr. Tanner?"

Darby watched Jace pass some bills to him. "A work emergency, Maurice. I'm sorry that we have to leave before being served."

"I understand, Mr. Tanner. I hope we will see you again soon."

They didn't speak as they waited for the valet to bring

their car. Once they got inside, Jace drove a couple of blocks and then pulled over on a side street. He cut the engine and looked at her.

"What's really going on, Darby?"

J ace had been excited to take Darby to Le Ciel Étoilié . It was one of the top restaurants in the city and a special favorite of his. Its chef had trained in France but had come home to draw on his Texas roots, and the creative dishes that came from Le Ciel Étoilié 's kitchen were the talk of Dallas.

From the moment they had entered the restaurant, though, Darby had seemed uncomfortable. He'd watched her face and seen the dismay as she looked at the menu. Disappointment had filled him because he'd wanted to share a place he loved to eat with her. Then she'd discreetly gotten on her phone, and the next thing he knew, she wanted to leave.

Confusion filled him. Also, a little jealousy. He wanted to know who had texted her or sent her an email which had upset her enough that they'd had to leave dinner before they had even ordered.

He looked intently at her now, seeing her tremble slightly. It caused him to soften. His question had come out a bit harsh, and he didn't want to upset her even more or worse, have her frightened of him.

"If I told you, I doubt you'd understand," she finally said, blinking several times.

He hated when women turned on the tears to get what they wanted. He hadn't thought Darby was that kind of woman, but then again, they'd only known each other for a short while. He told himself all those crazy feelings of falling in love with her were just that. Crazy. He didn't love her because he didn't know her well enough to do so. He did like her. At least, until she'd pulled this stunt.

"Try me," he said, pinning her gaze.

She wet her lips nervously, which was the wrong thing to do, because it caused desire to flare within him. He had hoped after dinner that he could take her home with him and make love to her. See if they were truly compatible.

"Focus," he said under his breath, causing her to frown. Then more loudly, he said, "I really want to know. What's got you so upset?"

Now, she bit her lip, causing a flood of desire to pour through him. *He* wanted to be the one who did that to her luscious, bottom lip. Jace told himself to focus. Ignore everything except her words.

"I didn't fit in," she said.

It was the last thing he would have expected to come out of her mouth.

"What?" he asked, confused.

She took a deep breath and slowly let it out. He saw determination fill her eyes, and he couldn't help but be attracted to her because of it.

"I live a completely different kind of life from the one you do, Jace," she began, seeming to choose her words carefully. "I don't want to insult you. In fact, I am very impressed by all that you have accomplished. You own a thriving business. You have a gorgeous condo and drive a car worth more than I'll make in a year. You run with a crowd who drips money. To you, eating at a restaurant like the one we just left is simply ordinary, something you do when you're hungry and go out to dinner. You wear designer suits. For goodness' sake, you get a massage every week! I could only dream about a luxury such as that."

Braver now, she continued. "I like you, Jace. I really do. I've enjoyed spending time with you. You're bright. Quick-witted. Kind. Generous. But when you compare our jobs and lifestyles, you are a world apart from me. I was so out of place in that room just now. It's the kind of thing men miss, but I was being judged by the women present and found lacking. My clothes. My hair. My jewelry, or lack of it. They didn't even list the price of the dishes, Jace! I called up the menu on my phone and when I saw what a single appetizer costs, I was sick to my stomach."

Darby paused, tears brimming in her eyes. "I don't belong in a place like that, much less in the company of a guy like you." She swallowed. "Would you please take me back to the hotel now?"

Everything she said had knocked him for a loop. He took her hand, and she tried to tug away, but he held fast to it.

"You are a beautiful woman, Darby."

"No, I'm not. I'm pretty. Not beautiful."

"Then you need to take another look in your mirror, because you take my breath away."

She sucked in a quick breath, staring at him.

"You know I'm blunt. Decisive. I wouldn't flatter you. I tell the truth, in business and beyond. You are beautiful. You graduated from a top-tier university. You've had a steady, successful career. You're vivacious and charming and you look good in whatever you wear. Hell, you look good *not* wearing anything."

His words caused her to blush.

"We're not so different. I grew up middle class. Well, upper middle class," he amended. "I told you that my parents were university professors. I didn't want for anything but at the same time, I didn't get everything I did want. Yes, I've made something of myself. I'm successful. I negotiate multi-million dollar deals for the athletes I represent, and I get a healthy percentage of the contracts they sign. Even with the salaries I pay and the business expenses I have, I'm doing better than good. Do I celebrate that success with material things? You bet. I'm in an industry where you are judged by the watch you wear and how expensive your shoes and haircut are. I have to present a certain image in public because of the high-profile clients I represent.

"But do I need all that? Hell, no. I'm still me. Middle class Jace Tanner, just dressed up a bit to play the part of the sports agent I am. Don't let that turn you off from me."

He brought her hand to his lips, kissing it tenderly. "I really like you, Darby. In the short time we've known one another, I've let you in more than anyone my entire thirty-two years. Maybe that's because of being adopted and feeling abandoned and lost and lonely. I know I've kept people at arm's length in the past, but I don't want to do that with you. I want to know more of you. I'm begging you. Don't judge me by the car I drive or what I wear. Me in a t-shirt and shorts today *is* the real me."

She bit her lip again, and he leaned closer, brushing his lips softly against hers. Jace wanted more, but he couldn't afford to push her away. She was already a scared rabbit, running for her life. He needed to lure her back into the fold. Calm her. Assure her that all was well.

"I don't mean to judge you, Jace. I understand how a lot of this is a façade. Still, it's your life. You do what you do, and you're not going to change your lifestyle anytime soon. I would never ask you to do so. I'm just not comfortable being around all that. It's foreign to me."

"I'm sorry I didn't ask you where you wanted to eat dinner tonight. I should've known after going to Adelina's with you that it was the kind of place you enjoyed."

He reached out, brushing the back of his fingers against her cheek. "Are you still hungry? I'll take you wherever you want to go."

"I don't really feel like going anywhere," she said, her voice small.

"But you're still hungry, right? Why don't we get some takeout and head back to my place? Or even your hotel."

He knew his eyes pleaded with her. Jace wasn't ready for this day to be over. Everything had gone so well. Until now. He knew Darby had to go back to Kansas City and wrap up her life there before she returned to Texas. They wouldn't see each other during that time, and already, he was dying inside, wondering how he could get through a day without her sunny smile.

"My hotel," she decided. "And I need comfort food."

"Like a cheeseburger?" he asked, drawing a smile from her.

"Cheeseburgers qualify. But only if you take off the lettuce."

He grinned at her. "I thought you were a healthy girl. A salad-eating girl. The last time I checked, salads were chock-full of lettuce."

She sniffed. "Lettuce is wasted on a burger. If you're going to be bad and go the cheeseburger route, then it should have grilled onions and maybe mushrooms on it."

"I can arrange that."

She frowned slightly, and he knew that although she had enjoyed everything they had done today, all the arrangements Elena had made had been overwhelming to Darby.

"Let's find a Sonic and drive through. I bet you wouldn't turn down tots."

Darby tried to keep from smiling and lost that battle. "Tots are good," she told him. "With ketchup."

"There's no other way to eat them," he agreed.

Jace searched for the nearest Sonic on his phone and found one two miles away. He pulled in and ordered for them, turning to ask her what she wanted to drink.

"A diet cherry limeade," she said primly, causing him to laugh.

"You're eating two thousand calories with a diet drink?" he teased.

Darby nodded. "You have to save calories when you can."

As they waited for the carhop to bring their order, he took her hand. She let him do so, and he held it, trying to memorize the feel of her skin against his, slowly rubbing his thumb in circles in the palm of her hand. Jace closed his eyes, wondering what life was going to be like with Darby gone for a couple of weeks.

The food came, and Jace tipped the carhop a ten. He would have given her a twenty, but he didn't want Darby to think he was showing off and distance her from him anymore than he already had. He placed the drinks in the cupholders and handed the bag to her.

"Keep it sealed," he warned sternly. "No sneaking a tot."

She giggled, and it was the sweetest sound Jace could remember hearing.

He drove a few blocks and pulled into a park.

"Why are we here?" she asked.

"Tots deserve to be eaten when they're hot," he declared. "By the time we got back to your hotel room, we'd have a lot of cold grease on our hands. Let's eat while it's hot."

"I see a picnic table." She opened her door and climbed out with the bag of food, and he followed suit.

Jace sat on the same side as Darby did, their legs brushing against one another as they ate. Again, their conversation flowed naturally, never stilted. He thought he could sit under this tree for a thousand years and never run out of things to talk to her about.

When she finished her burger and wadded up the wrapping, she turned to him.

"Thank you. For understanding. For letting us walk out of a fancy place and choose a cheeseburger for dinner instead."

He slipped his hand around her nape. "I want to please you, Darby. If you're uncomfortable somewhere, I don't want to stay."

"I appreciate how open you are," she said, sincerity shining in her eyes. "Not every guy would have understood, much less offered to leave."

"I'm not every guy. And the guys who wouldn't have left are jerks."

That brought another smile to her rosebud of a mouth. Jace leaned in for a slow kiss, his hand steady on her nape. Her palm flattened against his chest, and he felt his heart rate speed up.

Breaking the kiss, he asked, "Where to now, Montgomery?"

Without hesitation, she said, "My hotel room. It's been a perfect day with you, Jace. Now, I want a perfect night."

"Are you asking me to stay?" he asked, his throat thick with emotion.

"As long as you want."

Coming to his feet, he brought her to hers before gathering their trash and dumping it in a nearby trash can. They walked to his car, and he felt like a schoolboy. Nervous. Excited. Anxious. But ready.

Very, very ready.

He drove to her hotel, leaving the car with a valet. They rode the elevator up in silence. When they reached her room, she removed her keycard. He took it from her and unlocked the door, opening it and holding it open for her to enter the room.

Stepping in behind her, he closed the door and snagged her waist, bringing her back against him. One arm went around her waist, holding her to him. The other began fondling her breasts. As his fingers brushed against her skin, he felt the beat of her heart, pounding in her chest. His lips went to her neck, kissing it, then grazing it with his teeth, getting a rise from her. Her hands clasped his arm, her nails digging into it as he continued to kiss her neck. He moved to her earlobe, tugging on it with his teeth, bringing a loud gasp.

Needing his mouth on hers, he turned her, and their mouths fused together in a long kiss. Her arms came about his waist, holding him to her. Her breasts brushed against his chest, and all he wanted to do was suck on them. Their kisses became more frantic as they both began tearing at their own clothes and each other's. Once they were bare to the waist, he tugged on her hair, tilting her head back, deepening the kiss, demanding more of her.

They stopped for a moment, both gasping for breath, and took the time to remove the rest of their clothes. He kept his head enough to fish a condom from his pocket before discarding his trousers and placed it on the nightstand. Then he took Darby in his arms again, seizing her mouth and ravishing it. He couldn't seem to get enough of her taste. She was like a drug, and he was now addicted.

For life.

That thought caused him to pause a moment. He broke the kiss, searching her face, understanding that whether she knew it or not, he had made a commitment to her. Her alone. One which would carry them through the rest of their lives.

Together.

He took her mouth again, and they fell onto the bed. Touching. Kissing. Wanting. Greed consumed him, and he kissed her ravenously, as if he had been starving until she came along. Now, she satisfied him in every way. He was changed. Because of her.

His hands roamed her curves, and he hovered over her, kneading her breasts. He took one into his mouth, teasing the nipple with his tongue and teeth before sucking hard, causing her to writhe beneath him. He lavished attention on her other breast, heat filling him. He kissed his way down her body, finding her core. He brought her legs over his shoulders and dived in, greedily tonguing her, drinking in her sweet juices. He brought her to orgasm, her cries lusty. He smiled as she shattered, calling his name.

Kissing his way back up her body, he reached her mouth, kissing her deeply. When he broke the kiss, he reached for the condom and tore it open, sheathing himself before collapsing beside her.

"Tired?" she purred, turning toward him, her fingers dancing along his chest and down to his abs. Her nails lightly stroked them, and the muscles bunched beneath her touch.

"Never," he said, clasping her waist and lifting her with ease so that she now hovered above him. Slowly, he brought her down, and she took him inside her. She was tight and warm, her hazel eyes now a brilliant green.

"Set the pace," he encouraged. "I'll follow your lead."

She framed his face with her hands and bent, giving him a sweet kiss. "Thank you," she whispered against his lips.

Then she began to move, and everything up until that moment had been in black and white. Suddenly, his world changed into full, living color as she danced above him. He molded his hands to her breasts, the pads of his thumbs caressing her nipples. She moved with ease, the dancer in her establishing a sweet rhythm they both began rocking to. The speed increased. So did the intensity. And then his hips were moving, jerking, pumping into her. She clung to his shoulders, their dancing playing out, both reaching their climax and calling out hoarsely.

She fell against his chest, exhausted, and he cradled her to him, his hand stroking her hair.

Darby pulled up so their gazes met. "That was incredible."

"It was the tots," he said, keeping his face serious. "They'll put you over the top every time."

She laughed, a sound so musical that he thought it a song. He tucked her hair behind her ears and pulled her back down to him, kissing her. Holding her. Never wanting to let her go. She remained sprawled atop him, stroking his arm lightly. More than anything, Jace wanted to tell her that he loved her. That he wanted to be with her. That whatever differences they had, he would see them worked out.

He remained silent, though. It was too soon to make a declaration of love. Hell, he didn't even know if he might *be* in love. He never had been before. Maybe this was merely lust.

If so, he had a bad case of the lusts for Darby Montgomery.

They fell asleep and awoke, making love again. Not as

frantic this time. It was slower. Sweeter. And just as satisfying.

She said, "If you want to leave now, I understand. I have to be at the airport by six-thirty tomorrow morning. I've still got to pack."

"I'll take you," he told her, wanting to spend every second he could with her. Reaching for his cell, he said, "We should leave here no later than six. What time do you want me to set the alarm?"

"I'll need fifteen minutes to pack. Another thirty to shower and get ready."

"Okay. Four-thirty," he said, setting the alarm and placing his phone on the nightstand again.

"Uh, Mr. Genius, that would be five-fifteen. Unless you're getting up to shower before me."

He grinned at her. "I was building in time to make love to you a final time."

Her eyes widened, and then she burst out laughing.

"Should I be offended that you're laughing because I'm scheduling sex?" he asked mockingly.

Darby kissed him. "Not at all. In fact, make it four. We might need to make love in the shower, too, Tanner, and I need to give you time to recover."

"I like the way you think, Montgomery."

And I like everything about you.

CHAPTER
Fifteen

Darby told herself not to cry. To live in the moment. These last moments with Jace.

The alarm had gone off. At four. Though they had barely gotten any sleep, she seemed not to need much. As for Jace, he was on fire, working her into a frenzy and then slowing down. Teasing her to the brink and pulling back. Finally, she had begged him to enter her, and he had.

It was the best sex of her life.

Not that she had all that much experience. She hoped it didn't show. Jace seemed to be satisfied, and that's all that mattered to her.

He was a generous, considerate lover, taking care of her needs before fulfilling his own. She had come to crave his touch. His scent. His confidence.

How was she going to go back to Kansas City? And it would only get worse. At least in KC, she was far away. When she moved to Hawthorne, though, he would only be ninety minutes down the road. Close—but not nearly close enough.

Besides, this was probably it. Despite his reassurances, she couldn't see a world with them winding up together. He had his life. She had her new one to go to.

Nothing could change that.

So, Jace would be close once she moved to Texas, but in a way, they would still be worlds apart.

He drove through the tollbooth, which meant that her terminal was coming up. How could she thank him for such a magical time together? They'd made love twice this morning, once in bed and once in the shower. While she was getting ready, he'd gone out and picked up breakfast for her to eat in the car. She glanced at him, seeing his strong profile. The set jaw. A man full of determination, ready to rule the world.

Darby turned away, feeling tears sting the back of her eyes. She told herself again not to cry.

"This is it," he said, pulling to the curb. "I checked on your gate just before we left."

"Okay."

They both got out of the car. He popped his trunk and removed her backpack, turning her to place it on her shoulders, and then spinning her around again. He leaned in for a kiss. It was lingering. Sweet.

And just about broke her heart.

Jace lifted her carry-on and extended the handle. "Here you go."

She swallowed down the huge lump so she might have a chance to speak.

"I guess this is goodbye. Thank you for yesterday. I think it was the best day of my life."

He moved closer, his forehead resting against hers. "Mine, too." He kissed her quickly again and stepped back. "Text me when you land."

"All right. Bye."

Darby turned, wheeling her suitcase up the ramp to the sidewalk and entering the terminal. She glanced around to see where the TSA Precheck was since she didn't need to check a bag and could bypass that line. As she rolled her luggage along, her heart grew heavy.

Joining the TSA line, she removed her wallet from her purse and pulled out her driver's license to present as her ID.

Suddenly, she was whirled in the opposite direction. Jerked hard. A hot mouth came down on hers.

Jace ...

She kissed him with everything she had, ignoring that they were in a public place. She tasted the bittersweetness in their goodbye but was grateful for one last kiss.

He broke it. "Sorry. I just needed one more." He gave her a lopsided grin.

"You better go outside before your car gets ticketed. Or towed."

His hand came up, cupping her cheek. "Maybe I could fly up to see you this weekend," he ventured.

Knowing that he'd already played hooky today, she shook her head. "You're behind at work as it is. And I bet if you pulled up your calendar, you'd have to cancel a ton of things."

Looking glum, he said, "You're probably right."

"I've got a lot to do as it is," she said, making small talk. "Turn in my notice. Get boxes. Start packing. Notify the electric company. The cable company. The newspaper."

"Newspaper?" he asked. "You take an actual newspaper? I didn't know anyone under sixty did that." He gave her a teasing smile.

"My dad always subscribed to one. Remember, I wanted to be a journalist at one point. Yes, I get most of my news from the internet or TV, but I like the in-depth articles of a print newspaper. And they have the best cartoons."

He smoothed her hair. "I guess I'll have to check it out."

"Goodbye, Jace."

He studied her a long moment. "Goodbye, Darby. I'm glad I sought out Eli—because it led me to meeting you."

Before she could reply, he turned and strode away. She watched him until he was out of sight and then sighed, taking the handle of her suitcase again and moving back into line.

The rest of her trip went without a glitch. She boarded on time. Wrote her report for Peggy since she needed to present it in a few hours to her boss. Darby was thankful she had something to work on because it kept her from dwelling on Jace.

At the airport, she disembarked and used her rideshare app to arrange transportation to her office. On the way, she texted Jace to let him know she was back in KC. His reply was a thumbs up. She tried not to read too much into that or be hurt by such a curt reply. He was a busy man who had a lot on his plate. The fact that he even texted her back right away was enough.

Once she arrived at the Cheer USA offices, she placed her things in the corner of her office and closed her door. No one knew she was leaving yet, other than Peggy, and she doubted her boss had shared that news, especially since Peggy was going to make a case for Darby staying at Cheer USA.

Going through her emails, she answered several and made notes for what to do on others. With the time left before her meeting, she began composing a list of things her successor would need to do. It was about two-thirds finished when she stopped and ran hard copies of her report to take to the meeting, one for her and one for Peggy. She also emailed the report to her supervisor.

With five minutes until the meeting began, she congratulated herself for having successfully kept her thoughts from straying to Jace.

And that terribly romantic gesture of coming into the airport to kiss her goodbye a final time.

Gathering her report, her notes, and her tablet, Darby left her office. She passed a few co-workers and said hi to them, preparing herself for what lay ahead. Peggy's assistant waved her in, and Darby went into her boss' office, closing the door behind her. While the report regarding the Dallas facility wasn't confidential by any means, whatever they discussed regarding her job would be.

"Have a seat at the table," Peggy said, her fingers dancing across her keyboard. "Just finishing up an email."

She made her way to the table and placed her things on it before sitting, taking three deep breaths and slowly letting them out in order to calm herself.

Peggy stood and went to the mini-fridge, retrieving two sparkling waters. Darby had a weakness for them and nodded. Peggy placed each can in a koozie bearing the TTM logo and brought them to the table.

Taking a chair, she said, "Welcome back. How was your trip to Dallas?"

"I went in a little early so I could attend a family wedding," she shared. "My cousin was getting married. Although I'd FaceTimed with her and the groom, this was the first time I'd met Eli in person."

"And you approve of him?"

"Very much. Eli is smart. Personable. Handsome. And he worships the ground Autumn walks on."

"I wouldn't know what that's like," Peggy joked. "Two husbands have bitten the dust. I think I've sworn off marriage for good."

"Third time might be the charm," she said. "What can I say? I'm a hopeless romantic."

Peggy eyed her. "You never mention much about your personal life, Darby. Are you seeing anyone? I know you travel a great deal. It's hard to maintain a relationship with that kind of schedule."

She felt heat fill her cheeks. "I've met someone recently. I don't think anything will come of it, but we've had some fun together." Wanting to steer the conversation back to work, she passed over her report. "Let's go over the details of how nationals will work in Dallas come February."

For the next hour, Darby walked Peggy through everything, answering questions her boss had. She'd had the foresight to take pictures on her tour, knowing Peggy would want to see them. They scrolled through her phone, discussing everything from concessions to practice rooms to the setup backstage.

Her boss leaned back, a satisfied look in her eyes. "You always have such attention to detail. It's one of the reasons I hired you all those years ago. Yes, you were a fantastic cheerleader. Cute figure. Clear, sharp moves. You could dance like nobody's business. You've done a great job teaching cheers and dances to campers across the nation, and your choreography is inventive and fun. Girls across America are dancing to the moves you created. You have a lot to be proud of."

Peggy took a sip of her drink. "That's why I promoted you a while back, Darby. You have a clear vision. You tend to the details, but you can also see the big picture." Peggy paused. "I had hopes of you succeeding me as the head of Cheer USA someday."

Darby had sensed this was coming. "First, we both know you won't retire anytime soon, Peggy. You're a workaholic and enjoy what you do. While I've enjoyed my new role with the organization, I'm ready to move on."

"What if I set a date for my retirement and named you as my successor to the board? Would that change your mind?"

She shook her head. "Maybe a few years ago it might have, but I'm ready to do something different. What I trained to do in college. I want to teach, Peggy."

"But you've taught for years here at Cheer USA," her boss protested.

"This is different. I want to have my own group of cheerleaders to take through a school year. I want to interact with students in the classroom." She paused. "I have a wonderful opportunity to step into a situation immediately. A teacher's husband has been transferred out of state. I would take over the cheer program, as well as sponsor the newspaper and yearbook staffs. I wanted to be a journalist at one point and then decided I could teach journalism and coach cheerleaders."

Darby paused. "This kind of opportunity is rare, Peggy. If I don't take it, this combination might not ever pop up again. Not to mention that it's in my hometown. I could see my aunt and uncle frequently. My brother also lives there, as do two of my cousins, whom I'm close with."

Peggy sighed. "I can see that your mind is made up, Darby. Offering you more money or more responsibility won't move the needle."

"It won't. I'm eager to return to Hawthorne High School and make a difference in the lives of kids."

And maybe see Jace Tanner on occasion.

Resignation filled her boss' face. "I guess I should be happy that Cheer USA kept you as long as we did." She stood, and Darby did the same. "You've been a wonderful employee, Darby. I know you're ready to get a fresh start."

"I am. I'm working on a document now of all the things my replacement will need to know."

"How long will it take you to finish that?"

"Probably another hour or so."

"You do realize there will be a line of people clamoring to take your position?"

"I know you'll choose the best candidate for the job, Peggy," she said diplomatically, knowing several people who would campaign to land the job. While she had a favorite in mind, it wasn't her place to tell Peggy whom to hire as her replacement

"Email me the list when it's complete."

"I'll do that before the end of the day."

Peggy embraced her. "I wish you the best, Darby. And because I think so much of you, I'm going to let you leave for good at the end of the day. My assistant will walk you through a few things regarding shutting down your email account, turning in your badge and keys, that kind of thing. I know you want to reach Texas as soon as possible. We'll make this our exit interview."

"Thank you, Peggy!" she cried. "Oh, this will really help. The sooner I can get back to Hawthorne, the better." She wiped away her tears. "You'll be seeing me again. I plan to take my squad to nationals."

Her boss smiled. "I can't wait to see you and your cheerleaders, Darby."

She practically floated from the office. Peggy's assistant returned to Darby's office with her, and they went through the protocols for her voluntarily separating from Cheer USA. She finished her list for whoever would take her spot and emailed it to Peggy. Then Darby sent out a general email to the staff in the corporate office, telling everyone that she was leaving for a new job opportunity. That was all the goodbye she needed. No cake. No happy hour. No tears. No fuss.

When she left the Cheer USA office for the last time, she texted Uncle Joe, Blanche, and Kay, telling them she had wrapped up her job in Kansas City and would be back in Hawthorne by Saturday at the latest. She would take tomorrow to close all her accounts and give her landlord notice that she was moving out. Kelby had already said that Darby could have movers bring her stuff to their house since she and West were slowly going to furnish the place, room by room, and had several empty ones Darby could use for as long as she needed.

On her way home, she called Sawyer. "Guess what? Peggy isn't making me finish out the two weeks. As of now, I am officially unemployed until I start work at HHS."

"That's fantastic, Darby," her brother enthused. "Will you head this way soon?"

"I'll contact movers ASAP. Hopefully, they can pick everything up by Saturday. I'll shut everything down here and drive to Hawthorne on Saturday." She paused. "Do you think I could bunk with you until I find a place?"

"Absolutely. As long as it's just you and not all your stuff. You know my place is small."

"The furniture and the bulk of my clothes will be stored at Kelby's," she assured him. "It'll be me and a couple of suitcases."

"Then the extra bedroom is yours for as long as you'd like it."

"Thanks, Big Brother. I really appreciate it."

"Not that I'm rushing you, but if you'd like, I can scout out a few places. See what's available and pull some info together for you."

"Oh, that would be terrific. It's going to be hectic as it is, moving to Hawthorne and starting a new job, and then moving again to my own place. Anything to streamline the process will help."

"Do you have an ETA for Saturday?"

Darby thought a minute. "It takes about seven hours. Maybe a little less. Let's say mid-afternoon."

"Then I'll make a big pot of chili and some cornbread for dinner. I know West and Kelby wouldn't mind hosting. I'll holler at Autumn and Eli, too. We can make a celebration of your return."

"That's so thoughtful, Sawyer. Thank you. It sounds great. I'll talk to you tomorrow or the next day and let you know how things are going."

"It'll be great having you in Hawthorne, Darby. Love you."

"Love you, too."

She hung up—and wondered if she should let Jace know that she'd be in Hawthorne sooner than she'd planned.

CHAPTER
Sixteen

Jace got into his car, angry that he had to pick up Penelope Rossi. He had been in a foul mood all day, snapping at others for no reason. Elena had even pulled him aside, warning him to back off. He'd apologized to her and the others he'd been sharp with.

The day had started so perfectly, waking up with Darby snuggled against him. Making love to her. Then he'd had to take her to the airport, and that's where everything went downhill.

He hadn't wanted her to go.

He hadn't known how to ask her to stay.

It was silly to have developed such incredibly intense feelings for her in such a short span

of time. He'd avoided the love bug, but he hadn't just been bitten. It sank its teeth into him like a bulldog.

And wasn't willing to let go.

Jace had gotten into the car, watching Darby enter the terminal. Logically, he knew she had to fly back to Kansas City. Finish out her two weeks at Cheer USA before coming back to Texas. But he didn't have to like it. He'd done something completely out of character by following her inside and grabbing her, kissing her goodbye a final time. If that wasn't the move of some lovesick sap, he didn't know what was.

He'd driven home and changed clothes, not willing to put his shirt in the dirty clothes hamper because it still smelled like Darby. Work had been excruciating today. To top it off, he had the obligation with Penelope to check off. As he drove to her place, he caught a whiff of Darby's floral perfume lingering in his car. It made him angry, that she had encroached in every area of his life. Immediately, he rolled down the windows and stepped on the gas, his hair flying as the wind tore through the car.

Then he heard the siren and caught a glimpse of the flashing lights in his mirror. Great. A ticket, all because he was trying to eliminate all traces of Darby before he went completely mad.

Jace pulled over and stopped the car. He placed his hands on the wheel, waiting for the policeman who approached him. The cop stopped next to him.

"May I see your license, please?"

"Yes, I'll get it for you. It's in my back pocket."

He unfastened the seatbelt and pulled the wallet from his pocket and license from the wallet. Handing it over, he tried to get his out-of-control feelings under control before he said or did something foolish.

"Do you realize you were speeding, Mr. Tanner?" the policeman asked patiently.

"I do." He sighed. "I deserve the ticket. Write away, Officer."

The cop pulled out a pad but hesitated. "Is everything okay with you, Mr. Tanner?"

"I smelled her," he said, out of the blue. "And I couldn't

get her—or her scent—out of my mind. I rolled the windows down and thought if I went fast enough, the smell would blow away."

The cop looked at him sympathetically. "So, it's woman troubles."

"Yeah."

The officer studied him for a moment. "If you broke up, then you need to let her go, Mr. Tanner. And if you did something dipshit foolish, you need to try and win her back," he advised.

"She doesn't live in Dallas," he said morosely. "She flew back to Kansas City this morning. I took her to the airport."

The policeman shook his head. "I did a long-distance relationship once. It about killed me."

"What happened?" he asked.

The cop grinned. "I wound up marrying her and moving to Texas." He slipped the pad into his back pocket. "I'm letting you off with an unofficial warning, Mr. Tanner. Roll your windows back up. Keep your speed in check. And figure out a way to be in the same place as your girl. Either move where she is or have her move here. The long-distance thing sucks."

He'd been apart from Darby less than twelve hours. "Yeah, it does. Thank you, Officer. I've got it under control now."

"You have a good night."

"You, too."

Jace watched the policeman return to his squad car and then placed his driver's license back into his wallet. He put the wallet in the cupholder and buckled his seatbelt, determined to keep all thoughts of Darby at bay. He'd get through this date. No, not a date. His obligation.

Then he would think about Darby.

He might call her. He'd been swamped by the time she texted him that she'd landed and sent her a thumbs up. Thinking back, he should've waited instead of doing that. Sent her a real text. Or called her.

Cursing under his breath, he couldn't believe how muddled his thinking was. He was utterly confused by Darby. Jace did know one thing, however.

He loved her. He really, really, absolutely loved her.

Ten minutes later, he pulled up at Penelope's building and texted her to come down. Jace was not going to pretend this was anything more than dinner.

It took another ten minutes before Penelope appeared. He was a gentleman and did get out of his car, coming around and opening the door for her. Once inside, he asked how her day had gone. She launched into some complicated story that had something to do with a clasp on a necklace, and it lasted until they pulled up at The Mansion. He valeted the car and led her inside, thinking he would be nothing but bored the next two hours.

"Though I am sorry we missed the charity dinner, I am glad I have time alone with you for dinner tonight, Jace." Penelope's voice was husky.

Not a good sign.

He smiled tightly and nodded at the maître d', who led them to Jace's favorite table.

"Let me know if there is anything I may do for you, Mr. Tanner."

"I will."

The wine list was brought, and Penelope fretted over it. He finally told her what was good and ordered a bottle for them.

"I like when a man takes charge," she purred. "Assertive is sexy, no?"

It was time to set her straight. "Penelope, I know you agreed to accompany me to the charity event because you wanted to be seen with me. Have me introduce you to people who you hadn't met, ones who might help you with your business, by either becoming clients or investors. You don't have an interest in me. I don't have one in you. You were simply a plus-one. Tonight is a make-up call for me having to cancel on you, but I don't want you to get the wrong idea."

She smiled seductively. "Oh, I am full of wrong ideas, Jace. I'd like to show you a few of them."

He frowned. "Any more of that and I'll end dinner before we even order. Understood?"

She pouted prettily. "Of course."

Penelope then proceeded to order the most expensive things on the menu. Tonight would cost him a fortune, but at least he would be rid of her for good.

He ordered a steak and baked potato, thinking Darby would have ordered the salmon. He caught himself smiling at the thought.

"What is so funny?"

"Nothing. Just thinking of something that happened today."

Penelope sniffed. "Well, it wasn't business. A man doesn't get that look on his face when he is thinking of business."

Wanting to distract her, he asked more about her jewelry designing, and she was off to the races. Jace nodded occasionally but didn't hear a word she said. Penelope talked nonstop through the entire dinner. It was exhausting, but at least he wouldn't have to see her again.

"So, I assume many of your clients are interested in bling?" she asked innocently.

He scowled. "If they are, it's up to them to purchase it. I

advise them to see a financial counselor and invest in things beyond jewelry."

Jace nodded subtly to their server, who brought the check. He placed his credit card on the tray just as his cell buzzed. Pulling it from his jacket, he saw Eli's name.

"Penelope, please excuse me. It's a very important call that I must take. Why don't you have another glass of wine?"

"Champagne," she demanded.

He told the server, "Bring Miss Rossi whatever she wants."

Excusing himself, he left the dining room, answering his phone. "Hey, Eli. What's up?"

"I wanted to check in with you and see if you wanted to drive up to Hawthorne this weekend."

As much as Jace wanted to, he didn't want to be a third wheel. Eli and Autumn had just gotten married last weekend, which seemed an eon ago now.

"Thanks, but I've got a lot on my plate."

"Autumn said you would say that," Eli said, chuckling. "She also said that you wouldn't want to come because we just got married. Let me tell you, little brother, that we already act like an old married couple as it is. Seriously, I want to see you. *We* want to see you. You won't be interrupting anything. It's just life in Hawthorne. A slower pace. A friendly crowd. I'm not even tied up with a football game Friday night. The Hawks play away, and the home team has to supply the physician for the game."

Eli paused. "Please come. Autumn and I really enjoyed the time we spent with you after the wedding. Besides, if you say no, I'm going to catch hell from my wife. She doesn't get mad often, but I don't want to join Atticus in the doghouse."

"Atticus has a dog bed in your great room," Jace said, his resolve weakening. "That would mean you sleeping on the couch. While Atticus sleeps with Autumn." He sighed. "Okay. I'll come. But not until Saturday. I've got a commitment Friday night I can't get out of."

He didn't know what was on his calendar, but he was usually busy on Friday nights. This way, Eli and Autumn could unwind a little after their work week and have alone time before he showed up on Saturday.

"Okay, but don't waltz in late in the afternoon. If you aren't here by noon, Autumn and I will get in the car and drive down to Dallas."

"Hey, that's not a bad idea," he said. "You could come stay with me. I've got a guest room at my condo. I could show you a little of Dallas. My office."

"Maybe the next time," Eli said. "Just come, Jace. Don't make me beg. I want to see you."

"All right," he agreed. At least by going to Hawthorne, he wouldn't spend all weekend moping about Darby. "I'll be there no later than noon."

"Thanks. We'll see you in a couple of days."

Jace returned to his table. Penelope pouted and took the last sip of champagne from her glass. He summoned the server, who had prepared a new bill. Jace saw it was not one but three glasses of champagne charged to his account. Penelope must be sloshed, drinking that much in such a short amount of time.

He signed the bill and thanked the server before going to pull out Penelope's chair. She was a bit wobbly on her feet, but he managed to keep her standing while his car was brought around. Getting her settled into the passenger seat, Jace even buckled her in, doubting she could do it herself.

Immediately, she leaned her head against the window and began snoring. Loudly. He drove to her building and decided he better see her inside. Going around to the passenger side, he opened the door and unbuckled the seat-belt. Jace clasped her elbows and brought her to her feet, where Penelope swayed.

"Let's get you inside," he said, retrieving her purse from the floorboard.

Guiding her to the door, the doorman opened it for them, giving Jace a sympathetic glance. He steered Penelope to the concierge, who looked up, concern on his face.

"Miss Rossi indulged in a bit too much champagne," he told the man, not mentioning the three glasses of wine she'd drunk during dinner. "We had a business meeting and frankly, I'm a bit uncomfortable seeing her to her apartment. Would you be willing to do so?"

"Of course, sir," the concierge said, coming out from behind the desk and taking Jace's place.

"Goodnight, Penelope," he told the jewelry designer.

"It was fun," she said blithely, giggling. "Call me."

Jace watched as they got on the elevator and then returned to his car. Once more, he rolled the windows down to air out his car. Penelope had been wearing a heavy musk scent, and it hung in the air. This time, however, he watched his speed.

Once he arrived home, he doffed his clothes and show-ered, wanting to remove every trace of her. He debated on whether or not he should call Darby and decided to give her a little space. Today would have been a difficult one for her. She was to meet with her boss, and she had expressed concern that Peggy would not take her leaving Cheer USA well. He would call her tomorrow. It was Friday and the end of her work week.

He didn't want to seem too eager. Yes, he knew he was in love with her, but he had no idea how she felt about him. Darby had enjoyed their conversations. She had certainly enjoyed the sex. But she seemed to have in her head that the differences between them were too great for anything serious to develop between them.

Jace reflected on what the cop had told him earlier this evening. That he and Darby needed to be in same place for things to work between them. The trouble was, she would soon be starting a new job in Hawthorne, while his agency was in Dallas. Even if she finished out the school year, he doubted she would turn around and resign a job which seemed perfect for her.

He had a lot of thinking to do about her.

And hoped Darby was doing the same about him.

U nfortunately, Darby hadn't been able to schedule the movers until the Saturday morning she was leaving. They arrived at seven-thirty, though, and loaded everything quickly and efficiently. One even took both her suitcases down to her car for her.

She signed the papers presented to her, learning that her things would not be delivered to Kelby's house until sometime Monday afternoon. She thanked them and headed to the manager's office, where she dropped off the keys to her apartment. It was the last thing on her to-do list as she jettisoned her life in KC and turned an eye toward Hawthorne.

She waited until she got out of Kansas City proper and was headed south on I-35 before she called Sawyer.

"Hey, Darby," her brother said cheerfully. "Do you have an ETA?"

"I should be there around four-thirty. Five at the latest. I'll have to stop once for gas and a restroom break. Other than that, it should be a clear shot to Hawthorne with no other stops. How's the chili coming?"

"The chili's coming along fine," her brother assured her. "It's on top of the stove now. Two big Dutch ovens of it. I've got Mom's old Crock-Pot that you didn't want for one batch. I borrowed a second one from Aunt Meg and will put the rest of the chili in it to take to West and Kelby's house."

"Thanks for putting together the welcome home party for me, Sawyer. It means a lot to me."

"I think you're going to be really happy here, Darby. Moving back to Hawthorne was one of the best things I've ever done. I know the dazzling lights of the big city lured me to Dallas, but I'm a much happier, more relaxed person ever since I moved back last spring. I know West would agree with me." He chuckled. "Kelby, too."

"Isn't it cool that they reconnected all these years later? I know they dated those last few months of high school, but with West playing football at A&M and Kelby and me cheering at UT, their lives just went in different directions, in college and after. It's nice to see them come back together. I know from talking with Kelby that she's the happiest she's ever been."

"West, too. And it's not only that they found each other again, but they have rewarding careers. West is happy as a clam coaching high school football, and Kelby is a dynamo, running her own social media business. How are you feeling about shifting careers?"

"Right now, I believe it's the best decision I've ever made. Don't get me wrong. I enjoyed all my years at Cheer USA, but the opportunity to come back to live and work in Hawthorne was too great to resist."

"Do you know when you'll be starting the new job?" he asked.

"I talked with Uncle Joe yesterday. He said not this week but mid-week of the next one. Still, I've been in touch with

Kay Timmons. I'm going to meet with her. She'll hand over lesson plans and talk to me about the JV and varsity cheer squads along with what I need to know regarding the schedules for both publications. Kay is making a reference list of things which need to get done throughout the year for each group, along with tagging some responsible students who will help my transition into the classroom."

"I know we both received an excellent education in the Hawthorne schools," Sawyer said. "It's one of those full circle moments, you coming back to teach after graduating from HHS."

"It's what I wanted a long time ago, but the timing wasn't right. I'm actually glad that I lived away from Hawthorne this past decade. Being on my own taught me a lot about myself. I think I'm a better person now and will certainly be a better teacher because of my experiences away from Texas."

"You've done a lot of traveling these past ten years. You must be happy you can sink some roots here."

"Yes, it's something important to me. So is family, Sawyer. I'm happy to be back near you. Aunt Meg and Uncle Joe. Our cousins. And Kelby, of course. She's like a sister to me. I'll let you go now. I need to touch base with Kelby and let her know not to expect the movers today."

"I'll be at home all day, nursing the chili, in case you need anything done here before you arrive. See you soon, Darby."

She couldn't help but smile. Sawyer had always been not only a protective older brother, but he was a good sounding board for her. It was nice to have a sibling who was also a friend. Though they'd both been busy since they'd left Hawthorne, she looked forward to growing closer to him with them being in the same town.

Darby called Kelby and explained how the movers had two more stops today before they headed south.

"They said it should be mid-afternoon on Monday when they would deliver my stuff," she shared. "If you don't mind, I'll come over and wait for them so that you can keep working."

"That would be appreciated," her friend said. "I have a meeting in Ft. Worth with two clients. I'll be leaving Hawthorne about nine-thirty Monday morning. I've already had a key cut for you and can give it to you tonight when I see you at dinner. And if things get too cramped at Sawyer's, you know you can come and stay with West and me."

"Thanks for the offer, and thanks for hosting dinner tonight."

"I hope you don't mind, but I asked Chance to come tonight."

"I haven't seen your brother in forever. You know he's one of my favorite people. I'll be glad to visit with him and hear how the ranch is going."

Kelby sighed. "We're so happy to have you coming back to Hawthorne, Darby. Do you realize we haven't lived in the same place for over ten years? To think I'll have my best friend back permanently has me walking on air."

Kelby chatted a little bit about a project she was working on, and then said, "I'm getting another call from a client. I'll see you tonight at seven. You will be here by then, right?"

"Easily. Love you."

"Love you, too."

The rest of Darby's drive was uneventful. She did stop for gas and a restroom break, picking up a Dr Pepper and a package of peanut butter crackers to tide her over. Sawyer's chili was legendary in the family, and she wanted to have plenty of room when it came to dinner this evening.

She pulled up to the curb in front of Sawyer's small, two-bedroom frame rental. Her brother had told her that because of Triple H opening this past summer, housing was at a premium. He was biding his time, waiting to see if he wanted to buy an existing home when it came on the market or if he wanted to build from scratch, as West and Kelby had done.

As she got out of her car, her brother came out to lend her a hand. He took her two suitcases from the trunk, while Darby grabbed her backpack.

"Good drive down?" he asked.

"No problems on the road," she confirmed. "I'll need to get gas the next time I go somewhere, though. I'm pretty low now."

"Want me to gas up for you while you unpack?"

"Would you? I appreciate the offer."

Darby fished in her purse for the key fob and handed it over to Sawyer.

"Your room is ready for you. As you know, it's nothing fancy. We'll have to share a bathroom."

She laughed. "We haven't done that in years. I think we'll manage just fine. Did you have any luck with listings for me?"

"Nothing yet. As I told you, things are tight right now. A new apartment complex is being built near the hospital, though. That's a possibility if you want to go the apartment route. I looked to see what houses were available to rent. Not much to choose from. Only two are available. I drove by both. One looked like a shack about to fall down. The other had four bedrooms."

"Nope. Way too much house for me. I'll stay with you for a while then. If you get tired of me and need some space, I can always go to Aunt Meg's or Kelby's."

"We'll be fine together, Little Sister."

He carried her suitcases into the house and deposited them in the spare bedroom. Darby unpacked, hanging clothes in the closet and placing others in the empty dresser. All her cosmetics and toiletries were in a long, folding bag. She went to the only bathroom and found a hook on the back of the door. She hung the bag there. This way, it would leave the entire countertop free for Sawyer's things, as well as the medicine cabinet. She had lived out of this toiletry bag while on the road for years now. A couple more months wouldn't make a difference.

Sawyer returned and gave her the fob, which she dropped into a side pocket of her purse, zipping it closed. They sat and talked for a few minutes, and then he said it was time to dish up the chili into the crockpots.

As they did so, he said, "Kelby said she would have all the trimmings for us. Onions. Cheese. Whatever chili needs. Autumn is bringing the cornbread."

Before Darby could protest, he said, "Don't worry. I provided her with my recipe. She promised to follow it with no deviations."

"Thank goodness. My mouth has been watering for your cornbread all day. I don't know what you do to make it so different from everyone else's, but it's the best I've ever tasted."

He laughed easily. "I could share my cooking secrets, but they would probably be wasted on you. Dare I ask to see if you've learned to cook anything?"

She flushed guilty. Cooking had never been something she was interested in. Sure, she could toss a salad together with ease, but the rest of the time she was home, she either snacked on fruit and raw vegetables or depended upon take-out. On the road, it was easier because she could order fish and sautéed vegetables from her hotel's restaurant.

"Maybe that's something we can do together, now that I'm back in Hawthorne. You could cook even when we were teenagers, Sawyer. I know it was simple stuff. Spaghetti. Tacos. But you knew what to do."

"My skills have improved over the years, as have the dishes I attempt. I suppose my palate became more refined, living in a place like Dallas. Yes, I still have standbys I fall back on. Mom's meatloaf, in particular. But I've become more adventurous, both in my eating and cooking. If you're really interested in me teaching you how to cook, though, I'd be happy to do so."

He grinned at her. "Or *try* to do so."

That earned him a punch in the arm from her.

"I cook pretty much every night for myself once I get home from the office."

As they finished transferring the last of the chili, and Darby said, "I'd like that. How is work going for you, Sawyer?"

He shrugged. "It's different. I can say that. No more high-profile murder trials. No prosecuting drug cartels. I got my fill of those cases, Darby. A lot of days are slow, but family law is something important for citizens of a small town to have access to. People here need wills drawn up. Custody agreements drafted. I'm not limited to family law, though. I've handled traffic tickets. Larceny. Aggravated assault. Overall, I'm happier than I have been in a long time."

"Are you dating anyone?" she asked, curious about his love life, especially since he did seem happy.

I've had a stray date, here and there, since coming back home, but no one has caught my eye yet." He paused. "It's just hard to move on from Elizabeth."

Sawyer had dated Elizabeth Pope his last year in law school and two years after their graduation. They had become engaged, but Elizabeth was struck head on by a drunk driver two months before their wedding. Sawyer had grieved deeply for his fiancée and had never dated anyone seriously since her death. Darby suspected that he had moved back to Hawthorne, in part, to separate himself from memories of Elizabeth and their time together in Dallas.

"I know what you're going to say," he said. "It's been almost eight years since Elizabeth has been gone, but I just haven't felt that spark with anyone else that I felt with her, Darby. Do I hope to marry someday? I do. I want to be a husband and father. Coming back to Hawthorne has given me a clean start. We'll see what the future holds. For you and me."

As they transported the slow cookers to Sawyer's truck, she said, "I met someone. Someone I have pretty deep feelings for."

He looked at her sympathetically. "Here you go, all these years without someone. And now that you're leaving Kansas City, you find him." He shook his head. "Fate can be pretty cruel, Darby. I know it was a big decision to walk away from him to return to Hawthorne for this teaching and coaching opportunity."

As Sawyer backed out of the driveway, she said, "The thing is, he's here in Texas. And no, it didn't influence my decision at all to take the job at HHS."

Darby grew quiet, collecting her thoughts. Fortunately, her brother gave her space to do that very thing.

"I really like this guy, Sawyer. He lives in Dallas. While I was there, I spent most of my time with him. I'm feeling things I've never felt before, but he runs in a completely different world than mine."

He stopped at a stop sign and looked at her. "It's Jace Tanner, isn't it?"

She nodded. "We hit it off at the wedding. Teased.

Flirted some. But as I said, I spent a lot of time with him this past week."

"Do you think he's The One?" her brother asked quietly. "With Elizabeth, I knew from the first time she sat down in Constitutional Law next to me."

Darby bit her lip. "I don't know. He comes from a world of money. His clients are famous. He negotiated multi-million dollar deals for them, and his percentage of those contracts is hefty. He thinks nothing about dropping hundreds of dollars for dinner, while I'm happy with a meal at a Mom-and-Pop place in a strip shopping center."

"Besides the money angle, are you compatible?"

Her eyes misted with tears. "I would say very much so. What can I do, though? He's in Dallas, living a kind of life you only see in the movies. I'm on the cusp of starting a job teaching here in Hawthorne. We all know teachers are one of the most underpaid professions, especially here in Texas. I just don't see our worlds meshing."

"I'm of the opinion that if it's meant to be, it'll happen for you, Darby. Maybe Jace is a stepping stone to the guy you'll eventually wind up with. A way to transition to life here in Texas. You can see each other. Dallas isn't that far away."

She frowned at him. "Dallas is a world away from here, and you know that, Sawyer Montgomery."

He shrugged. "Then keep it casual. See him once, twice a month. If it goes somewhere, you can cross that bridge then. But not now. Don't borrow trouble, Darby. Don't fret over things which you have no control over. Focus on you. Your new job. Jace is simply on the periphery right now. Pull him into your world when you can and see where it goes."

By now, they had reached the Sutherlands' spread. Sawyer pulled his truck in the circular drive, behind another truck, and cut the engine. She figured it was Chance's truck since it looked ancient. Her old high school friend wasn't much for change. She thought it might even be the truck he'd driven in college.

West appeared, Kelby right behind him, and West carried in one of the Crock-Pots of chili, while Sawyer grabbed the other one. Kelby hugged Darby tightly.

"I'm so glad to have you back here. To be in the same zip code is wonderful," her friend declared. "We're going to see a lot of each other, Darby."

Kelby linked her arm through Darby's and led her inside the house. She couldn't help but think how much had happened in her life since she'd last been here to pick up a T-shirt to wear to the Hawks football game.

In the kitchen, the men plugged in the slow cookers and turned them on. Chance grabbed her and twirled her about.

"Good to see you, Montgomery. I hear you're coming back to Hawthorne for good."

"I am. I thought you might've been at the wedding last weekend."

"I had a horse auction to attend." Chance grinned at Eli and Autumn. "These two got hitched so fast, I didn't have time to make other plans." He looked around. "I see the chili. Where's that cornbread you're famous for, Sawyer?"

"Autumn's bringing the cornbread," Kelby told her brother. "I've got all the other fixings. We can start pulling those from the fridge now. Green onions. Sour cream. You name it, I've got it."

As they filled the island with the condiments for the chili, a sense of peace washed over Darby. Though she still hadn't heard from Jace since his thumbs up text, she decided she would make the first move and contact him now that she was back in Hawthorne.

And see not only where things stood between them, but if Jace wanted to explore a deeper relationship with her.

187

CHAPTER
Eighteen

Jace left the TTM offices just after ten on Saturday morning. He'd been up since five, getting in a lengthy workout before showering and heading to the office to meet with a client in town for the weekend. Tevin Wakeland's Detroit Lions had an off-week, and so he had headed to Dallas to see his former high school play last night. He was going to shoot a commercial while in town. Penny and Elena would be overseeing things, but Jace had wanted to drop by and say hello. He liked his clients to know he was hands on.

He did pull Elena aside, telling her to text him once the shoot finished.

"You're not sticking around?" she asked, clearly surprised.

"I'm going up to Hawthorne to see my brother and sister-in-law for the day. I may not come back until tomorrow."

She smiled at him. "Good for you, Jace. It's nice that you're not working the entire weekend. Time with Eli will be nice." She hesitated. "Have you been in contact with Darby?"

"She's back in KC. I may touch base with her this weekend."

His assistant pursed her lips, looking unhappy. "If you screw this up, you know I'm going to take her side. Because she'll be right." Elena paused. "And I'll be hell to work with. Just keep that in mind. Treat her right, Jace. Darby is a keeper."

"Thanks for your advice, Dr. Elena. Let me know when our next therapy session is."

She put fisted hands on her hips. "Therapy wouldn't hurt, you know. You come with a lot of baggage, Jace. A *lot*. I don't know what it is, but I know you well enough to get that you have a lot weighing on you. Connecting with Eli is a start, but you could use some professional guidance."

"You better be glad I like your work so much because you're crossing a line, Elena," he cautioned. "Let's leave my private life private."

She sniffed and walked away, going back to Tevin and checking on him. Jace regretted bringing Darby to the office because he had kept much of his private life quiet. Sure, he had his professional biography on the agency's website and LinkedIn, but no one really knew much about the real Jace.

Except for Darby.

He hoped Eli would, as well. He'd been able to open up to his brother and Autumn some, but he knew after years of being separated, it was going to take time to grow comfortable with his brother and vice versa. Fortunately, Eli seemed to be a patient guy, and Autumn was very encouraging.

Jace went to tell Tevin goodbye and ask if he needed anything.

"Nah. I'm good. You've really come through for me, Jace. I'm happy with my contract and the new endorsements. I may be sending a couple of guys your way soon. One is my favorite wide receiver. The other is a former teammate at LSU. I told them you'd take good care of them."

"Happy to meet with them. I can fly to where they are. Zoom. FaceTime. Whatever they're comfortable doing."

"I'll let 'em know," Tevin said.

"Okay, I'm off. Going to see my brother and his new wife."

"Have fun, man," Tevin said. "Catch you later."

He shook hands with Tevin and left, returning to his car. Traffic was light, and he made good time, reaching the outskirts of Hawthorne by eleven-twenty and Eli's house by eleven-thirty.

The door opened, and Atticus came bounding toward him. He knelt and petted the rescue, telling him what a good boy he was. Eli ambled over, and Jace stood.

"You ever think about getting a dog?" his brother asked. "You sure seem to get along with Atticus."

"No. Too busy."

"That was my reason. I worked in my ER eighteen or more hours a day. Slept and showered at home and that was about it. I didn't think it was fair to leave a dog all alone for so many hours. Now that I've got steady hours, though, Atticus has been really good company. He's a gentle soul."

"I'm sure he'll be good around kids." Jace paused. "I assume you're already trying, even though you're newlyweds."

"We are," Eli confirmed. "I'm thirty-four. Autumn is about to turn thirty. One thing we're sure about is starting a family quickly." He grinned. "And the trying for one is pretty fun. Come on in."

They started toward the house, Atticus following them. Inside, Autumn greeted Jace, giving him a tight hug.

"Thank you for coming up," she said. "We're happy to have you any time."

"Same with me. I've got room for you at my condo. If you want a taste of big city life again, you're welcome to come down. We could have dinner. See a play. Or I could drag you to one of the many charity events I'm invited to."

"That would be fun," she said. "We'll definitely take you up on it. Are you hungry?"

"I rarely eat breakfast. Yes, I'm definitely hungry."

"We're going to grab lunch at the local diner," Eli said. "Then Autumn said you and I have got the entire afternoon together. I'm sure we'll find some trouble to get ourselves in."

They went to the Hawthorne town square and parked in front of Dizzy's Diner. Jace wasn't about to admit that he'd never eaten in a diner. His university professor parents had been snobs, belittling fast food joints and small Mom and Pop places in favor of fine dining experiences. While he'd eaten his fair share of fast food while at A&M, Jace had never set foot inside a diner.

An older man greeted them. Eli even hugged him.

"Dizzy, I'd like you to meet my younger brother, Jace. Jace, this is Dizzy, the first friend I made in Hawthorne. He owns the place."

The diner owner beamed at Jace and offered his hand. "Nice to meet ya, Jace. Your brother wandered in here, looking lost as a lamb. I told him a little about Hawthorne, and he landed the job at Triple H. We're so happy to have him here." Dizzy looked to Autumn. "And always glad to have you stop by, Autumn." To Jace, he added, "Autumn's parents have been eating here for decades."

Dizzy grabbed three menus from a stack near the register. "Let's get you a booth and some good food."

A server brought them three glasses of water, while Eli told Jace that while everything was good, he couldn't go wrong with the chicken fried steak or meatloaf.

"I'll take the meatloaf," Jace said. "With green beans and squash."

"No," Eli said. "Trade one of those for the mashed potatoes. They're out of this world."

Dizzy waved his hand. "You can have those vegetables, plus a bowl of potatoes."

Autumn and Eli ordered, and then Dizzy departed for the kitchen.

"He's quite a character."

"Dizzy's got a heart of gold," Eli said. "He was so friendly when I met him. It's people like Dizzy that make Hawthorne special."

The server returned with the iced teas they'd ordered, and ten minutes later, their food arrived. Jace tried the meatloaf first and sighed after the first bite.

"That's amazing."

"Keep eating," Eli encouraged. "Everything is good."

His brother was right, especially about the mashed potatoes, which were covered in a cream gravy speckled with black pepper. After eating at Adelina's and now Dizzy's Diner, he realized there was something after all to a smaller establishment. He could see Darby in a place like this, and a yearning for her washed over him.

When they finished their meals, Dizzy asked if they wanted dessert.

"I'm pretty full," Jace said.

"Let's split one. The three of us," Autumn suggested. "You can't leave Dizzy's without trying a slice of pie."

They talked it over and decided to go with the coconut

cream pie. Between the three of them, he only had a few bites, but it was the perfect way to top off a meal.

Jace pulled out his credit card, but Eli waved it away, saying, "Dizzy won't charge you for your meal. I'll pay for ours."

"Why wouldn't he charge me?"

"Your first time eating here," Autumn said. "Dizzy always comps a first meal. He just hopes you return for a second, third, and fourth."

They told the diner owner goodbye and returned to the house, where Eli said, "I'd love to take you to Triple H and show you around. Are you up for a tour?"

He knew how proud his brother was of the hospital. "That sounds like a terrific idea, Eli."

His brother kissed his wife. "We'll be back."

"It'll be a while," she warned Jace. "There's a lot to see."

"I'm eager to view everything," he replied. "Even though Eli is involved in the medical field, he may show me something or I may see something that might transfer to my sports agency. I'm always looking for new ideas and different ways to approach things."

"Y'all have fun," Autumn said.

They took Jace's two-seater this time, parking in the spot reserved for Eli.

Chuckling, he said, "Folks are going to wonder if I'm having a mid-life crisis a decade early if they see this fancy sports car parked here."

"Maybe you should try driving one. I think you'd enjoy it. In fact, why don't you drive us home?"

Eli shook his head. "As much as I'd want a baby like this, I want a human baby more. That means car seats—and this Porsche isn't built for that."

Once inside, Eli took Jace floor by floor. The facility was clean and modern and didn't have a trace of that hospital smell which permeated so many other medical buildings. Everywhere they went, his brother greeted workers by name. In turn, they all seemed happy to see him. Usually, no one was glad to cross pass with the big boss, but it was apparent that Eli had made a positive impression on his staff, as well as the folks in Hawthorne.

Their final stop was his office. They sat for a few minutes, with Eli telling him some about the differences in the Hogan Health system verses other healthcare companies. It wasn't anything Jace didn't already know, having received a thorough report from Crawford on Eli and his place of employment. He listened all the same, interested in Eli's take on things, happy to be in his brother's company after decades apart.

"Sorry, didn't mean to talk your ear off. Ready to go home?" Eli asked.

"Sure."

He insisted Eli drive them home, just to give Eli a chance to sit behind the wheel of a Porsche. Yet he recalled how Eli was eager to start a family, and a sports car would be impractical. His brother's enthusiasm for marriage and family life bubbled over, and it got Jace to thinking about what Darby might want. He resolved to call her on his way home from Hawthorne tomorrow. He'd been radio silent long enough with her. If he didn't call soon, she might think he was ghosting her, which was the last thing he wanted her to believe. There was a fine line, however, in giving her space and not keeping the lines of communication between them flowing.

Eli took the long way home, wanting to drive Jace by

everything in Hawthorne. He saw shops on the square. The post office and city hall. A gas station, hair salon, and donut place. Then they drove by Hawthorne High School, where Darby would be teaching soon, and the adjacent football field.

"How are you liking being the team physician for the Hawks?" he asked.

"I enjoy it a lot. It's allowed me to get to know West better. His staff and players. I feel a real part of the town as I watch the game from the sidelines."

They returned to Eli's house and went inside. Autumn was busy in the kitchen, and so they retreated to the media room, tuning in to a football game between Ohio State and Michigan.

"I didn't know squat about football when I came to Hawthorne," Eli admitted. "I'd never seen a game before. Autumn's family is crazy in love with sports, though, especially football. West played for the Dallas Cowboys." He paused. "Oh, you know that. You were his agent. It's hard for me to think that West is the one degree of separation between us."

"West is my best client. Friendly. Easy to work with. Knows what he wants going into any kind of negotiation, but he's also willing to compromise. I still rep him, despite the fact that he retired from the NFL. He still does product endorsements."

"Autumn has taught me a lot about football. We've also been to a Rangers baseball game. She's promising me we'll drive down and see the Mavs and Stars play once their seasons start."

"Let me know. I have clients on both teams. I'd be happy to get tickets for you." He chuckled. "And a parking pass. That's almost worth as much as a ticket to the game."

"Maybe we could all go together," Eli suggested.

He could see Darby rounding out their party once she returned to Hawthorne. The thought of being with her, along with Eli and Autumn, seemed perfect.

Autumn stuck her head in the room. "It's almost time to head over to West and Kelby's." She looked at Jace. "We're having dinner with them. Hope that's okay."

"Sure. I'm the one crashing on your weekend. Whatever you have planned is fine with me," he said.

In the kitchen, Eli pulled two six-packs of beer from the fridge. Autumn also had a pan covered with foil in her hands.

"Cornbread," she said. "First time I've made this, so I hope it turned out right."

"I could always sample it for you," Eli said, waggling his eyebrows at his wife.

"You will stay out of it," she told him. "Because I'm sure it's so good that you wouldn't be able to stop with one square."

Jace laughed, enjoying being around these two. He thought ahead to holidays and other celebrations, and he knew that he wanted Eli and Autumn to be a part of whatever he did.

"West and Kelby built the house," Autumn informed him on the drive over. "They looked around town, but they decided they wanted a little land. The house sits on five acres. They worked with an architect on the design and then had it built to their specifications. They've only moved in recently."

"I look forward to seeing it," Jace said, happy that his client had settled in to life in Hawthorne and his marriage.

They pulled up in the circular drive in front of the house, where two trucks already sat.

"Can I take the cornbread for you?" Jace asked, helping Autumn out of the vehicle.

"I trust you as much as I trust your brother. Which is not much at all when it comes to food," she teased. "Thanks, but no thanks."

"I doubt I could eat that much cornbread between here and the door," he said. "In fact, I can tell you that I've never eaten cornbread."

"What?" she asked. "You're joking, right?"

"Nope, not at all. And today was the first time I've eaten meatloaf."

"Were you raised by wolves?" Eli asked. "Maybe it's a good thing you were the adopted one and not me."

"My parents were what you'd call snobs. They liked upscale things. Country food simply wasn't on their radar."

They reached the door, and Jace rang the doorbell.

"I'm sorry to hear that," Eli said. "I guess we'll have to help you discover all you missed out on."

West opened the door. "Greetings to the Carsons and to my wonderful agent." West shook hands with both men and kissed his sister's cheek. "You've got a birthday coming up, Fall. The big three-oh. We need to figure out what we're going to do for it." He ushered them into the foyer.

Autumn looked to Jace. "My sister was born a few minutes before midnight on the last day of summer. I arrived a few minutes after midnight. Hence our names, Summer and Autumn." She sighed. "I wish Summer could be here to celebrate with us. I'd do anything to get her back to Hawthorne."

"We're in the kitchen," a voice called out.

"That's Kelby, reminding me to be a better host and not keep you standing in the foyer," West said, biting back a smile. "Hope you like chili, Jace, because we've got two big pots of it. Sawyer is our resident chili master."

They followed West through the great room and into the kitchen.

That's when Jace spied Darby, laughing at something a tall, dark-haired man with gray eyes had just said. She put her hand on his arm familiarly.

And Jace saw red.

Nineteen

Darby laughed at what Chance said. Despite the fact that he always looked so serious, he had a dry sense of humor, which she had always appreciated. She, Kelby, West, and Chance had been a tight foursome all through high school, being the same age and in the same grade. Some of her best memories involved the four of them and things they had done together. Being able to be around Chance again was just another reason moving back to Hawthorne would be good for her.

She glanced up at him. "I hope to be seeing a lot more of you now that I'm back in town." He leaned over and kissed her forehead. "Same."

Then she became aware that the room had changed. Glancing over, she caught sight of Autumn and Eli. Then her heart stopped as her gaze fell upon Jace.

He was angry.

Her hackles rose. Well, she was angry at him, too. She had reached out and texted him as he'd requested, and he had barely replied. He hadn't made any effort beyond that to reach out. See how she was. How her meeting with Peggy had gone. A big fat nothing.

Ignoring him, she went to Autumn and hugged her cousin.

"I'm so glad you and Eli could make it."

"We wouldn't miss celebrating have you back in Hawthorne full time," Autumn said. She turned and indicated Jace. "I'm sure you remember Jace from the wedding."

She coolly looked to him. "I certainly do. It's nice to see you," she said politely.

His face was unreadable now. The brief emotion he had shown was now gone. In its place was the stoic sports agent who never let anyone know what he was thinking.

And never let anyone in.

Darby turned her attention back to Autumn. "I hear you've baked the cornbread today using Sawyer's recipe."

"I did. I'm only hoping it tastes half as good as his does."

Sawyer, who leaned against the kitchen counter opposite Darby, said, "If you followed the recipe I gave you, it should be fine. Then again, I always add a dash of love for all those who'll eat mine. Hope you thought to do the same."

"Since everyone is here, let's dish up some chili," West suggested. "We've got beer and bottled waters in the fridge. Iced tea for anyone who wants a glass of that."

While West and Kelby took drink orders, the others moved to the pots of chili. Darby ladled a good amount into her bowl, hoping she would be able to get it down. As of now, her mouth and throat were bone dry, while her stomach had turned sour.

She returned to the island and sprinkled some green onions, blended cheeses, and topped it with a dollop of sour cream.

"I also have some chips and guac over here." Kelby

pointed to another counter. "And there's Spanish rice on the stove if anyone wants some of that."

Darby focused on getting everything she needed. West directed her to the patio outside, and she set her bowl and plate on the large table. Eli and Autumn were the next to join her, sitting across from her.

Then Jace appeared. She held her breath as he came and took the seat next to her. She got a whiff of his familiar cologne, and images of the two of them in bed together flooded her. She glanced at her bowl of chili, hoping no one was looking at her and the blush filling her cheeks.

As others joined them, Jace quietly said, "When did you arrive in Hawthorne?"

"A little over an hour ago," she said stiffly. She started to leave it at that but then added, "Once my boss realized she couldn't talk me into staying, I was pretty much dismissed. Packed up my office. Shut down my email account. Handed over my lanyard and keys. After that, it was running down my to-do list to wrap up my time in KC."

He didn't ask her any more questions, and Darby couldn't think of anything else to say to him. She decided that she had read far too much into what had passed between them. That all along, it was what she had thought it would be at the beginning. A fling. Nothing more. He probably had even regretted asking her to text him when she landed. His brief response should have been the heads up to her that things were done between them.

Darby told herself to move on. That Jace Tanner didn't live in Hawthorne, and she would only see him on rare occasions, if at all, in the future. This was her homecoming party —and she was determined to enjoy it.

She asked West a question about the high school, and the conversation turned to what her new job would be like. She explained to Chance how she was being hired to coach the cheerleading squads, as well as handle the two publications.

"Well, you were the editor-in-chief of the *Hawthorne Herald*. You'll know exactly how to run that. You weren't on yearbook, though, were you?" he asked.

"No, I wasn't, but Kay Timmons told me that she's leaving me copious notes. Kay said the kids are so good that both the yearbook and newspaper almost run themselves. I need to give her a call and let her know I'm here early. We're supposed to get together."

"Kay is well thought of at HHS," West said. "You've got big shoes to fill, Cuz, but if anyone can do it, you're the one."

The next hour passed by quickly. Darby began to relax, mostly because Jace didn't utter a word. It was almost as if he weren't there, so she ignored the heat coming off him and concentrated on enjoying her friends and family.

When it came time for dessert, she and Kelby went inside to gather a few cartons of Blue Bell. Sawyer followed them, and while Kelby returned outside with bowls and spoons, he asked, "Are you all right? You and Jace seemed pretty cold toward one another. It wasn't what I was expecting. I thought you'd both be happy to see one another."

"It's complicated," she said. "I think that maybe I read things into the relationship which weren't there."

"No, you didn't."

They both turned to see Jace standing in the kitchen. Sawyer glanced at the two of them.

"I'll give you the room."

Her brother picked up two cartons of ice cream and left the kitchen. Darby knew Sawyer would make sure they weren't disturbed.

Jace closed the distance between them. "What did you

read into our time together, Darby?" he asked, his voice low, laden with emotion.

She crossed her arms defensively. "At first, I thought it was just going to be a fun fling. I've never had one of those before. To be transparent with you, Jace, I haven't had a lot of experience in the dating department. I've always been more of a guy's girl. One of those girls guys liked to hang out with, but not the kind they asked out. I could talk sports all day with them, but I've never been considered relationship material. In fact, my sexual experiences are pretty limited for someone my age."

Taking a deep breath, she expelled it. "I began feeling more for you, though. More than I should have. It made me realize that it was just a quick little thing between us. I'm sure you found me lacking, and by—"

Darby never finished her thought because Jace's mouth was on hers. He yanked her to him and devoured her. She struggled against him, her arms still folded in front of her, but he wasn't letting her loose. Her resolve weakened, and she gave in to the demanding kiss.

She had no idea how long the kiss went on, only that it touched her very soul.

Jace broke the kiss, gazing deeply into her eyes. "You weren't wrong about anything," he said, his voice raw with emotion.

This time, she pushed him way, needing distance from him to think clearly.

"Then I would say you have an odd way of how you think a relationship should unfold."

He frowned. "What do you mean?"

Anger sizzled through her now. Darby wasn't ready to give in and forget the hurt of the past few days.

"You ghosted me," she told him. "I texted you as you

asked me to do. And then I never really heard anything from you."

"I responded," he said defensively. "I was busy at the time. I didn't have time for a full-blown conversation."

She arched her brows. "And you've been busy every moment since then?"

A guilty flush filled his cheeks. "I wasn't sure what to say to you."

"The first thing you do is pick up the phone and call," she said testily.

He stepped toward her, and her heart began beating wildly in her chest. His hand cupped her cheek, and all Darby wanted to do was to lean into it.

"I'm no good at this, Darby. I've never done it."

"No good at what?" she pressed, wanting to get to the bottom of whatever was going on.

His hand fell away. "This. Us. Doing an us," he said, clearly frustrated.

Jace began pacing the kitchen, raking a hand through his hair. She watched him as he tried to sort things out within himself. Her heart began softening.

Finally, he came to a halt in front of her again. She made the first move, reaching out and taking his hands. His eyes filled with tears, and she saw the pain and uncertainty in them.

"You know my past. I haven't been shy about sharing anything with you. I think losing my mom, even though she was a terrible one, marked me more than I know. Plus, I lost Eli, who loved me and protected me from everything bad. Yes, I was adopted, but the Tanners only wanted a substitute for their dead son. When they saw I couldn't replace their Jason, they grew cold and distant. I did me, and they did them. We lived in the same house, but we were worlds apart.

They never came to anything at school to support me. They left me alone summers, going on digs all around the world. I never felt close to them, much less loved."

Darby squeezed his hands encouragingly.

"Because of my screwed up past, I never want to be close to anyone. I never share my feelings. The closest people to me are Mark, my partner, and Elena. Even then, it took finding Eli and meeting him before I even mentioned to Elena that I had a brother. I haven't even said anything to Mark about it yet."

Jace looked at her. "I don't date. I don't have relationships. Yes, I'm seen with women. A lot. It's part of my business. I'm invited to a ton of events, and it's expected that I take a plus-one. So I do. I rarely escort the same woman twice. Most of the time, whoever goes with me wants to be there for reasons of her own. She has a business she's pushing or she has someone she wants to meet who'll be in attendance. She's not there for me, just like I'm not there for her. It's a business arrangement."

He paused. "And yes, sometimes it ends with sex." His hands tightened on hers. "But it's never meant anything to me. It's just a physical act where I can let off a little steam. No strings attached."

Jace released her hands. His came up, framing her face, his thumbs caressing her cheeks.

"Everything with you was different, Darby. *Is* different. With you, I relax. Let down my guard. We had real conversations, about all kinds of things. When I kiss you, I'm kissing you because I want to. Because it's an expression of how I feel about you. When I make love to you, it's more than sex. It's real."

He kissed her softly, and she reveled in the feel of his lips brushing against hers.

"I won't try to pretend to understand why everything is different with you. It just is. Yes, I was a jerk not to reach out to you. I didn't want you to feel smothered by me, like I was coming on too strong. And then the rest of the day passed, and the doubts crept in. What if you didn't want to hear from me? What if you'd thought everything was casual—and I wanted to push for more?"

A look of anguish crossed his face. "You say you're inexperienced. Well, so I am. At least at this us kind of thing. I don't know how to be in a relationship. I don't want to push too hard." He gave her a crooked grin. "I feel a little like Jon Snow. You know, from *Game of Thrones*. He cleared his throat. "You know *nothing*, Jon Snow!"

Darby couldn't help but laugh, even as tears misted her eyes. They had discussed their mutual love for the HBO series, just one of many things they had in common.

This time, she took the initiative. She slipped a hand around his nape and pulled him down, their lips touching in a sweet kiss. Jace was a strong, confident man in his professional life.

And she wanted him to feel confident in his personal life.

Darby broke the kiss and gazed up at him. "I like you, Jace. A lot. More than a lot. I think every couple goes through growing pains, trying to understand what being an us means to them. It's different for different couples. I know we have some difficulties to get through. The biggest is not living in the same town and having crazy busy schedules." She paused. "But I'm willing to make an effort to be an us. If that's what you want," she added.

He grinned at her, looking so boyish and innocent that her heart burst with love.

Love?

She wouldn't dare throw out that word. Not when they

were just finding their way back to one another. If Jace even knew she was thinking about the L-word, he would flee.

Instead, she waited for his answer.

"It's definitely what I want," he told her. "I want us to *be* an us. You're right. It won't be easy, but you're the first woman I've wanted to try this with."

Darby only hoped that she would also be the last.

Jace kissed Darby a final time, his heart singing. A euphoria filled him, a natural high that surpassed every achievement he'd ever accomplished. It didn't matter how many clients he'd signed. How many millions of dollars he had helped them to claim. While he was peerless in business, he was a neophyte at being in a relationship.

But it's all he wanted now. To be with Darby.

She was right. They had a tough road ahead of them. He didn't know how it would work because of the jobs they held, but he was willing to do whatever it took, make compromises and sacrifices, all to be with this one woman.

Ending the kiss, he said, "I guess we better go back outside. I'm sure everyone is wondering about us." He hesitated and then said, "I was jealous when I walked in."

"Why?" she asked, clearly perplexed.

"You were laughing. You put your hand on Chance's arm. I almost went ballistic, Darby."

She laughed, stroking his cheek. "Chance is like a brother to me. He's West's best friend and has been since kindergarten. I've known him forever. He's a longtime friend, Jace. Someone I trust. But nothing romantic has ever gone on between us." She shook her head. "I can't even imagine that."

"I realize that now. Listening to you talk with him at dinner tonight. But I was ready to knock off his head when I first got here."

Darby wrapped her arms around his neck, pressing her body to his. "You don't have any reason to be jealous of any other guy, Jace. I've told you how guys treat me like another guy." She kissed him lightly. "I would never give you any reason to be jealous. No other man has ever caught my eye the way you have."

"Good. Let's keep it that way."

"I guess I shouldn't google you then and see all those beautiful women on your arm over the years."

"Definitely not. Come on."

He threaded his fingers through hers, leading her through the back door to where the others were gathered. Their laughter died as the two of them approached. His gaze met Eli's, and his brother nodded approvingly.

They took a seat at the table, and West asked, "Do you have some room for dessert?"

"None for me," Darby said. "The chili was enough."

"I'll take some," Jace said, pushing a carton of Blue Bell toward him.

Kelby pushed a bowl and spoon over to him and then handed him the ice cream scoop. He filled the bowl, suddenly ravenous. But not just for food.

For Darby.

Hopefully, the ice cream would occupy his attention and help him keep his hands off Darby because all he wanted to do was touch her.

Taking the spoon in one hand, he ate a bite while his other hand found hers under the table.

"Anything you two would like to share with us?" Kelby inquired. "Especially with me being your best friend, Darby?"

Everyone laughed, and Darby looked to him. Jace nodded encouragingly.

"We're a couple," she informed them. "We know it's going to be rough, especially with me starting a new job that will be time consuming, and Jace in Dallas, busy with his client list."

"We'll handle it," he said confidently. Glancing around at those seated at the table, he added, "We also hope that we have your support."

West said, "I know the kind of guy you are, Jace. Your character speaks for itself. You're a decent man who treats others fairly. If you and Darby want to pursue a relationship, I'm all for it."

Kelby added, "Darby has been my best friend forever. I trust her judgment. If she is invested in your relationship, then so am I."

Eli cleared his throat. "All I know is that this is a loving family, Jace. They've treated me with nothing but kindness, and I'm proud to be a part of them now." He paused, his eyes glimmering with tears. "I'm also so proud of you. Of all you've accomplished. I know we're both still trying to overcome things from our past, things we had no control over, which affected us more than we'd like to admit. With Darby by your side, though, I think you're capable of doing whatever you want to achieve."

"Thanks, Eli," Jace said, moved by his brother's words. "I haven't had much of a personal life. I've been laser-focused on the agency I started and serving our clientele. But I'm eager to work on having more balance in my life. I want to spend time with you and get to know the brother I missed for all those years."

He glanced to Darby, bringing their joined hands up and kissing her fingers tenderly.

"And I want to be with this woman, whenever our schedules allow."

"If you set your mind on a goal, something you really want, you'll move heaven and earth to achieve it," Chance said. "Darby's worth every second you invest in her."

Sawyer met Jace's gaze. "I look forward to being around you more, Jace. Darby's special. We all know that. And we'll protect her because we love her."

He understood Sawyer's warning. He was her big brother, her protector, just as Eli had been his protector.

"I assure you I will always put Darby first," he told Sawyer solemnly.

"Then we should get along just fine," the attorney replied.

"That's enough serious talk," Autumn said. "I'm happy for the two of you. Let's clear the dishes and relax. Finish your ice cream, Jace. Darby can keep you company."

Everyone stood, picking up dishes and beer bottles and glasses, filing into the kitchen.

"Your family loves you a lot," he said, taking another bite of ice cream. "I received the warnings, loud and clear."

"This is as new for them as it is me," she said. "They're not used to seeing me in a relationship. Hey, *I'm* not used to it. Yes, I've dated here and there. I told you about the last guy I was seeing in Kansas City, we'd probably gone out three or four months."

Darby's fingers ran through his hair, causing tingles to dance long his spine.

"But we were better off as friends. I didn't feel close to him the way I feel about you."

He grinned wickedly. "And how exactly is that, Montgomery?"

She returned the grin. "Like I want to lick you all over, like you were an ice cream cone."

His body flashed hot in an instant. "What's good for the goose is surely good for the gander," he said seductively. "And maybe a little chocolate sauce would add some more fun."

"Maybe." She leaned over and kissed him. "I like kissing you, Tanner. I've never been someone who initiated kisses, but I'm changing. Because of you. In a good way."

He placed his hand on her thigh and squeezed it. "Same."

"This is going to be awkward," she said. "Sawyer's house is tiny. Plus, the two bedrooms are right next to one another."

"We could stay at Eli's," he suggested. "The primary bedroom is downstairs. My guestroom is upstairs."

Darby nodded. "I like that idea better. The thought of Sawyer hearing some of the sounds I make when you touch me?" She grimaced. "Not good. Not good at all."

"Do you feel a little weird?" he asked. "Everyone knowing about us. I mean, I wanted to share it. That we're in a committed relationship. But with neither of us having a place here, it's awkward."

"I don't care," she told him. "I'm just so happy that you're here this weekend. That we can spend tonight together. I know you came up to see Eli and had no idea I'd be here. I want you to spend tomorrow with him."

He started to protest, but she placed a finger over his lips. "No. You're just getting to know Eli. You have a lot of catching up to do. I'll see if I can get with Kay tomorrow. I have so much to learn and figure out before I start my new teaching position."

"When will that happen?"

"Not this week. The job is still posted. Uncle Joe told me that probably the next Wednesday would be my first day. I still need to confirm that with him. My preference would be to still have Kay come and have both of us present with the students for a couple of days before she takes off for Chicago. I know Todd is flying up tomorrow. He's going to take a couple of days and see some of the places they've been looking at online, and then he starts his new job on Wednesday."

Jace smoothed her hair, simply needing to touch her. "Once you meet with Kay this week, what else do you have planned?"

"Other than prepping and becoming familiar with everything she gives me, nothing. I'd love to look for a place to live, but Sawyer's already done that legwork for me. Right now, listings in Hawthorne are sparse, thanks to all the employees at Triple H moving to town."

"Why don't you come to Dallas and stay with me before you start at HHS?" he offered. "You could do whatever you need to during the day while I'm at work." He smiled. "And we'd have the nights together."

She smiled shyly at him. "I'd like that."

He ate the last bite of his ice cream. "Let's go inside and visit with everyone. At least for a little while. Then I want you all to myself."

* * *

DARBY PULLED into the Hawthorne High School teacher's parking lot. A few scattered cars were present, and she realized some teachers came in even on a Sunday to catch up with work. The thought depressed her, knowing how she would already be busy Friday nights this fall with football games, both home and away. That would mean no driving down to Dallas to see Jace after school let out for the weekend.

That didn't even include basketball season, much less take into account the newspaper and yearbook. She recalled on more than one occasion, when she was top dog of the newspaper, coming up on weekends to finish laying out the pages before filling them with stories she had proofread several times, not wanting a single typo to be associated with any edition under her watch. Her journalism teacher was always present, with regulations in place for students to always have supervision and not be in the school alone. That meant she would most likely be putting in overtime, both nights and weekends, with the two publications' staffs.

She pushed these thoughts aside as she got out of her car and saw Kay waving at her. They greeted one another, and then Kay took Darby inside HHS, swiping her employee badge to gain admittance.

"I'm so glad you could meet on a Sunday," she told Kay.

"Once I dropped Todd off at DFW, I had the rest of the day free. I do need to start packing, though. I've already hired movers, knowing we may have to put our things in storage if Todd can't find anything quick to rent or buy."

"Will you live in the city or head to the suburbs?" she asked.

"I have a friend from college who lives in Highland Park, which is just north of Chicago. She says it's one of the nicer suburbs, with a great school district. I've already applied there and to a few other districts nearby. I doubt I'll land a teaching position, what with the year already underway. I'll probably ask to get on the sub list. Subbing is a great way to see the inner workings of various schools. But to answer your question, I'm hoping we'll do a short-term rental in the city. Chicago's supposed to be fantastic, with lots of restaurants and shopping that's walkable. If we can do a six-month lease on an apartment, we can take our time finding a house during that time. Since I'm hoping to be pregnant in the next few months, it would be ideal to find the house and then move in and get settled before the baby comes."

Kay laughed. "I'm trying not to put my cart before the horse, but I'm so excited to be able to move with Todd and keep trying for a baby."

"I'm grateful you're vacating your spot here at HHS. And really appreciative of you taking the time to put things in good working order for me."

They walked through the familiar halls, which didn't seem to have changed much since her own days as a Hawk. A certain smell permeated the halls, the smell of a school and its books. It was one she liked.

In Kay's room, she looked over the posters on the walls and the way the bulletin board was decorated.

"Because I handle both publications, I have more than one room," Kay informed her. "This is the room where I teach the intro class. It's also where I start off the beginning of each class. Make any announcements. Pass out story assignments and assign deadlines. Then the students move into the next two rooms, which are connected to this one."

Kay led her into the first and gave Darby time to look over the layout and equipment which the newspaper staff used.

"You see a few computers in here. All staff members are assigned a tablet, though, and that's where most of their work is done. They submit their stories and features via email to both their section editor, the editor-in-chief, and me."

Kay went to one of the computers and called up the upcoming edition of the *Hawthorne Herald*. Together, they went through it, page by page, discussing the layout. Kay had lists of reporters and photographers, which noted their specialties and preferences. Some students focused solely on news. Other on sports. She was glad to be seeing everything and getting a feel for the way the newspaper worked.

"Let's go next door to yearbook," Kay said, leading Darby into a huge room. "In the corner is a small darkroom. While we do most everything digitally these days, I do teach the photographers on both staffs how to develop film the old-fashioned way."

For the next hour, the sponsor went over the timeline for the yearbook. How assignments had been made and how pages were drawn up and filled. There were enough similarities to the way the newspaper worked that Darby didn't feel utterly lost.

"You'll come to depend upon the editor and associate editor of *Horizon*. Once again, having moved to digital has been a true lifesaver from the way they did things years ago."

"You're very organized."

"You have to be, teaching so many different things and sponsoring various organizations. Again, you'll be working with some of the cream of the crop in the school, Darby. These are good kids. They won't test you as many other teachers find they are. It's easy to engage these students because they're doing something they have a passion for."

They returned to the main classroom, where Kay handed over a notebook.

"These are my lesson plans for the year for Intro to Journalism, newspaper, and yearbook." She pulled a second notebook. "And this one is exclusively for cheerleading. It's got everything you need to step in and seamlessly run the squads. Vendors I've ordered uniforms and pompoms from. Timelines on when to teach new dances or paint signs for the upcoming football game. When to start preparing for nationals."

Kay paused. "You do want to take the girls to nationals, don't you? With them being held in Dallas this year, the girls are really excited, and we're expecting a good turnout."

"I definitely want to go to nationals," she assured Kay.

They talked shop for another hour, and she realized the afternoon had flown by.

"May I take these notebooks with me?"

"You sure can. Blanche said that my job is still posted now, but you'll be able to start not this Wednesday, but the next."

"Would you consider staying a day or so with me?" she asked.

Kay smiled. "I was hoping you would say that. I'd be happy to finish the week out. Mentor you a little. Let you get to know the kids and see if they have any last-minute questions for me. When I walk out that door, though, I'm done here. The kids will know you're in charge, not me. I'm going to get a new email address and dump my old one. I'm afraid if I make myself available to them for questions, they'll continually turn to me and not to you."

"I appreciate that. I'd hate for them to be torn in two directions."

"Their loyalty will lie with you," Kay assured her.

Kay reached for a yearbook and handed it to Darby. "This is last year's. Honestly, very few students order a hard copy these days. Most of our sales are for the online edition of *Horizon*. I've tucked a list inside of each group. The varsity cheerleaders, etc. This way, you can look up pictures and be a little bit familiar with the students. Some of the girls have changed their hair and all the kids have a year's maturity, but it beats walking in the first day and not knowing what a single soul looks like."

Excitement filled her. "This is terrific, Kay. Boy, I've got a lot of homework to do."

"Text me if you have any questions. We have a home game this coming Friday. The dreaded Dragons. You're welcome to come down to the field again like you and Kelby did before. In fact, bring her. That way, I won't have to explain just yet that you have the job before you're supposed to have the job."

"Thanks so much. I'll be there. You're really making things easy for me, Kay."

"Back at you. With you stepping in, I'm able to join Todd in Chicago, something I thought would be impossible."

They returned to their cars, and Darby hugged Kay. "Do you like Starbucks?"

"Love it. What teacher doesn't live for caffeine?" Kay sighed. "Of course, I'll have to go the decaf route once I'm pregnant."

"Then I'll make sure I bring a gift card to you when I see you on Friday. It's the least I can do."

Darby texted Jace that she had finished her meeting with Kay and that she was going home now. Her phone rang almost as soon as she sent the text.

"Hey," Jace said. "Everything go okay?"

"Better than okay. I wish Kay were staying at HHS and that we could teach together. She's really a great gal."

"Kay is the reason you got to leave Kansas City," he reminded her. "Are you packed for Dallas?"

"Yes. I'll go home and grab my things. Tell Sawyer goodbye if he's there. Then I'll leave. If you're ready to head back that way, maybe I can follow you there."

"Or maybe you can just ride with me."

"I hate to disappoint you, but Kay asked me to stop by and visit with her and the cheerleaders on Friday night. It's another home game. That means I need to be back in Hawthorne."

"I'll have you back in plenty of time for the game."

"But you'll have to leave the office really early to get through Friday traffic and up to Hawthorne," she protested.

"Remember, I'm the boss. We can leave at noon. Or whenever you like."

"I know you wanted me to spend the weekend with you."

"Hey, I'm getting you for the entire week. I'm happy with that."

She relented. "Okay. Meet me at Sawyer's."

Darby drove to her brother's. He already knew she was going to spend the week in Dallas, but she let him know that she'd be back on Friday for the football game.

"Jace can stay here," Sawyer told her. "I know I'll hear all kinds of sexy sounds through the walls, but I don't want you to think that you can't bring him here."

He dropped a kiss on the top of her head. She wrapped her arms around his waist.

"Thank you, Big Brother. You know I love you."

"Of course. I'm the great Sawyer Montgomery. Everyone loves me," he teased.

Jace arrived five minutes later and took her suitcase to the car. She told Sawyer goodbye and got into the passenger seat. Jace started the car, and they made their way back to Dallas.

Darby had high hopes for what the week together would bring.

CHAPTER
Twenty~One

Jace felt more grounded with Darby around. Even if she wasn't at work with him, he knew she was at his condo, prepping for her new job. He'd taken time to read over the lesson plans Kay had shared with Darby, as well as gotten online and looked at examples of the *Hawthorne Herald* and *Horizon*. Both the newspaper and yearbook were far more sophisticated than his own high school's publications from a dozen years ago when he'd graduated. Darby's enthusiasm was catching, and he was eager to see what her students would produce, glad that he now had a handle on what she would be doing.

She was already working on choreography for her cheerleading squads. She explained how the national competition worked. Several cheer organizations existed, and her former one, Cheer USA, would be the competition she would take the group she coached to. Kay had planned for the Hawthorne JV and varsity squads to compete in Dallas, and Darby was holding to that plan.

He had two meetings he could not put off, and Darby had

said she understood. One was with a prospective client who quarterbacked the SMU Mustangs in Dallas. Jace had followed Boyd's career in high school and continued to do so once he signed a letter of intent with SMU. He had meet with Boyd on three previous occasions, and the senior had asked to meet in person with Jace tonight. It was SMU's off-week, so he was eager to visit with Boyd, who'd told Jace he was bringing his girlfriend to the meeting at Fondren, one of the libraries on campus.

Jace had decided to bring Darby with him. Not only would she be able to see him in action, he thought it would help relax Boyd and his girlfriend to have Darby present. He pulled up to his building, and Darby bounded out the front doors, dressed casually in black leggings and a red tunic top. She got into the car.

"I wore red for SMU," she said, accepting a quick kiss from him. "Anything to help convince Boyd that you're the best agent for him."

"He can't decide tonight," he explained. "Legally, he wants to maintain his amateur status and finish out play this year. I've met with Boyd a few times over the years. Had my eye on him since he was a sophomore in high school."

"That long?" she asked.

"Yes. A good agent is always keeping an eye out for talent. Some of the student athletes burn brightly in high school and then fizzle out in college. Others see their potential rewarded with a college scholarship, but they don't have that It Factor that pushes them to the NFL level. Only a handful of college athletes are drafted by the NFL. Even then, many of them don't see much play or are cut from their team in the first year or two. I think Boyd has what it takes to be successful in the NFL."

"Has he met with other agents?"

"If he's smart, yes. Some agents will make promises they know they can't keep. Lie to an athlete about everything from their client list to how much their clients rose in draft rankings after they started repping an athlete. A smart athlete will do his homework and meet with a variety of agents before making his decision regarding representation. I'm just glad I'm still in the running with Boyd."

They drove to the SMU campus and parked in a visitor lot, walking to Fondren Library.

"Do you always meet an athlete on campus?" she asked. "I would think you'd want to get them away."

"It's better to meet here," he explained. "Because I cannot buy them a meal. I can't even give them a cup of Starbucks I've bought. The same applies to their parents. I can't take Mr. and Mrs. Thompson out to a meal and pitch myself to them. The NCAA has strict rules regarding agents and their relationship to potential clients. I'm careful to always stay on my side of the line and not dance anywhere close to it."

"Has it cost you a client in the past, you playing strictly by the rules?"

He nodded. "It doesn't matter. I'd rather retain my integrity and know I did the right thing. If an athlete is meant to sign with me, he will at the right time, of his own free will."

Jace glanced around and saw Boyd stand and wave.

"There they are," he said.

As they moved toward Boyd, Darby asked, "Are you certain you want me here for this?"

"I do," he assured her.

They reached the grouping of chairs, and Jace shook hands with Boyd.

"Thanks for agreeing to come to campus mid-week, Mr. Tanner." He turned and indicated the young woman who'd come to her feet. "This is my girlfriend, Kacie Kennedy. She's an accounting major and will graduate next spring when I do."

Jace shook hands with her and then said, "And this is my girlfriend, Darby Montgomery. She coaches the cheer squad at Hawthorne High School."

Darby shook hands with Boyd and Kacie, and they all took a seat.

Boyd kicked things off. "I asked Kacie to come and meet you because she's a good judge of people. Plus, she knows numbers."

Kacie leaned forward. "Boyd told me he's met with you several times now because he feels comfortable with you. You're here tonight more for me than Boyd, Mr. Tanner."

"Kacie and I are going to get married," Boyd added. "We're not officially engaged yet, but we're a team. Whichever agent I decide to go with, it'll be a team decision."

"Good to know," he said easily. "I'll direct much of what I say to Kacie then. Feel free to chime in if you have any question, though, Boyd."

"Yes, sir."

He liked how polite Boyd was. Though many of the athletes he tried to recruit immediately called him by his first name, Boyd had always been respectful and addressed him as Mr. Tanner. Jace didn't correct him. If that's what Boyd wanted at this point, he was happy to keep with the more formal title.

"Before I ask anything of you, Mr. Tanner, I'd like to ask your girlfriend a few questions," Kacie said.

"Fire away," Darby told the young woman.

"Why would you go with Jace Tanner as your sports agent if you were Boyd?" Kacie bluntly asked.

"First, let me say I don't know much about the specifics of

Jace's job. What I do know is his character. I would say trust is the single-most important factor in a relationship between a professional athlete and his agent. Boyd needs someone he can rely on. Jace will always tell Boyd the truth, not what he thinks Boyd wants to hear. Jace won't make false promises to you, telling you that you'll be drafted by a certain team. At the same time, he's an active agent. He'll be at the Senior Bowl or East-West Shrine game if Boyd earns an invitation to those all-star games. He'll show up at the NFL combine and give you a truthful, accurate read on your performance."

Jace saw Darby was just getting warmed up. The fact that she knew football was definitely a plus.

"Jace has a proven track record. A sterling reputation in the industry. He might not be the largest sports agency, but he is hands-on. I've met his staff. They're first-class professionals who know their jobs. He will network for you. Negotiate the best contract as if he were a hungry dog with a bone. If Jace believes in you, then he goes one hundred percent. He will stick by you through thick and thin."

Darby paused. "He'll also present you with other opportunities, those beyond football. Some might involve endorsements. Others could be linked to charity work. He will always be transparent and open about whatever he's doing on your behalf." She smiled at him. "And he's a wonderful communicator. That's another key factor."

Darby braced her elbows on her knees, leaning forward. "You both seem like smart individuals. You've already educated yourselves about what's to come down the road. Jace will be there every step of the way with you. He doesn't brag. He simply gets things done."

She paused a moment. "I know what you're thinking. It's his girlfriend talking. Of course, she's going to sing his praises. Even before I knew Jace personally, I knew of him. Probably the most important thing I can share with you is that West Sutherland, my cousin, is one of Jace's clients. If West decided to sign with Jace, I can assure you that he vetted him properly. And Jace wasn't West's first sports agent. He signed with someone else out of A&M. My cousin saw something in Jace. He trusts Jace. West is comfortable with him. He's even convinced a few of his teammates to sign with Jace."

Leaning back, she concluded with, "I would say that's a satisfied client, one who is willing to pitch his agent to others."

"West Sutherland?" Boyd asked. "From the Cowboys?"

"Yes, West is my cousin. We grew up together in Hawthorne. He's retired from the NFL now, but Jace still reps West in various endorsement deals."

Darby fell silent, and Jace could see the wheels spinning with both Boyd and Kacie. He let them think for a good minute before he spoke.

"Do you have any other questions for Darby, or can I say something?"

"Please, go ahead," Kacie encouraged.

"The one thing I want to emphasize is that if Boyd signs with me, he doesn't put all his eggs in one basket. Yes, there are many agents who simply tell their clients that they'll handle everything for them." He paused. "I don't work that way. It's sometimes called bundling."

Kacie nodded. "Yes. We've met with two agents who referenced that. Why don't you utilize that, Mr. Tanner?" She looked to Boyd. "To us, it seemed to streamline things. Give fewer people we have to deal with and lets Boyd focus on football."

"I stand with Boyd and will represent him in any contract he wishes to sign, be it with a team or to endorse a certain product. I'll work my ass off to get him the most favorable deal. But I firmly believe that Boyd should have other professionals who are independent of me, simply because it provides a system of checks and balances, much like the way our government is run."

Jace saw Darby was listening as intently as the two seniors were.

"No one person should be in charge of everything for you," he continued. "No matter how great your relationship is with your agent, you need to bring in others. Preferably, a team of others. I can make those recommendations to you, but my recs are not in any way a part of Touchdown Talent Management. For example, you'll need insurance. Good insurance because playing professional sports can be a dangerous occupation. You'll need an accountant. A financial advisor. An attorney. You'll probably want to have a nutritionist. Maybe even a chef. A personal trainer beyond what your team provides to you. I can even recommend a masseuse to help handle the trauma to your body after a game, as well as an acupuncturist.

"All these people are independent of TTM, however. I'll handle all negotiations, and my partner Mark draws everything up into a nice, legal document. My office can also handle marketing and social media for you. Beyond that, I *want* you to have a team of other professionals you can rely on. No one person should have that much power over you." He paused. "Too many athletes have let one agent do everything—and they've been taken advantage of financially."

Boyd nodded thoughtfully, absorbing what Jace had detailed. He slipped a hand around Kacie's.

"I get it. Especially if you're too trusting and make a mistake in your representation, your agent could really screw you over and leave you with nothing."

"Exactly," Jace said. "I'm never going to do that, Boyd. I

will always look out for your best interests, and that means finding you expert representation in other fields, as well as repping you in negotiations with your future team's management or endorsement deals."

The couple looked at one another, and then Kacie said, "You've given us a lot to think about, Mr. Tanner."

He handed his card to her. "Feel free to call me anytime, Kacie. Boyd already knows that. If you'd like to stop by TTM and see our offices and meet our staff, we'd be happy to accommodate you."

Darby spoke up. "I know West wouldn't mind speaking with you regarding anything from the client's perspective."

"That's a very generous offer, Ms. Montgomery," Boyd said. He grinned sheepishly. "West is a real idol of mine."

"This is your off week," Darby pointed out. "Maybe you'd like to come to the Hawks game on Friday night. I could arrange for you to meet West before the game."

Boyd's face lit up. "That would be incredible."

"Let me check just to be sure."

Darby took out her phone and tapped a few buttons.

"Hey, West. Got a favor. Boyd Thompson, SMU's quarterback, is thinking about signing with Jace. He knows you're a client. Could he and his girlfriend stop by the game Friday night and talk with you beforehand?"

She paused, listening and nodding. "Yes. That's good. Okay. Thanks, Cuz."

Darby hung up. "West said you could come by about two and meet with him in his office. Then he's got the pep rally and a ton of prep work with his staff and the players before the game. That would give you about thirty minutes to pick his brain. Would that work?"

"Yes," Boyd said enthusiastically. "Definitely, yes. Where's Hawthorne?"

Darby laughed. "About half an hour past Decatur. Say, ninety minutes or so from here."

"I'd have to cut my last class," Kacie said. "But the prof is a Dallas Cowboys fanatic. If I tell him I'm meeting with West Sutherland—and maybe bring back an autograph—it wouldn't be a problem for me to miss it."

Darby sent a quick text and received an even quicker reply. "Okay. West said go straight to the field house. It's between the high school and the stadium. He's looking forward to meeting you."

"We should stay for the game," Kacie said. "That would be the polite thing to do."

Jace stood. "You two can work that out. If you're at the game, we'll see you there." He offered them each his hand. "You've still got plenty of time to decide on an agent," he assured them. "My biggest advice is don't rush into anything. You won't miss out. A competent agent will take care of you, no matter how early or late you sign."

The couple exchanged a glance, and Boyd said, "We've felt some pressure from other agents to do that. You saying this really alleviates some of our worries."

Darby also wished the couple good luck, and Jace led her back to the car.

"They're a sweet couple," she said after they were both in the car. "And you were terrific with them. I believe they've already decided to sign with you. West is just a little icing they're indulging in."

"Hey, you were the big salesperson. You said a lot of nice things about me."

"I believe in you, Jace," she told him, her eyes shining with sincerity.

"I believe in us," he replied. "Let's go grab pizza from

Campisi's and bring it home. It's the best in Dallas and only five minutes from campus."

She pulled out her phone. "I'll call in our order to make things go faster." Grinning, she added, "You know, so we can put in some quality time in the bedroom after dinner."

Jace kissed her, hard, and said, "Pizza is always something that we can stick in the oven and keep warm. I like the idea of working up an appetite. For you *and* pizza."

He drove away from the SMU campus, feeling good about his meeting with Boyd and Kacie.

And even better about the night ahead with Darby.

CHAPTER
Twenty~Two

Jace woke Darby, making love to her slowly, savoring every moment. All his reluctance at settling down with one woman for life seemed ridiculous now. Though he had remained closed-off his entire life, rarely showing emotion, he was openly affectionate with her now.

Even those at TTM had noticed the change in him, though Elena was the only one to comment about it to his face. She had told Jace that while she admired his integrity and work ethic, she had always thought him a chameleon, as if he were an actor playing different roles when he interacted with various people. Elena said that Jace always was himself —yet he morphed into different aspects of himself, depending upon the client he dealt with. She praised the new openness he displayed and threatened to turn in her resignation if he did anything to chase Darby away.

As he dressed, Darby watching him from the bed, he said, "We've got a charity casino party to attend tonight. It also has a silent auction."

She frowned. "What's the dress code? I only brought one dress with me."

"Wear a cocktail dress," he responded. "I'll wear black tie. Some women may wear a full-length gown, but the younger crowd will go cocktail." He grinned. "And with your toned legs, you need to go short so everyone can see them."

"Why don't you go without me?" she suggested. "Do your see and be seen bit and then come home. We can have a late dinner."

He went to the bed and leaned down, kissing her.

"I want you on my arm tonight," he insisted. "This is the first time in my life that I'm part of a couple. I want to show you off to everyone in Dallas."

"I can't go," she said flatly. "The dress I brought won't pass muster. I do own one cocktail dress which is back in Hawthorne, but I don't have a way to get it here and back since I rode with you."

"Silly, just go buy one today."

She looked at him, her gaze steely. "I'm not going to do that, Jace. As a teacher, I'm not invited to these kinds of dressy events. The one black dress I have is fine for the few occasions I do receive an invitation to something really nice. I'm not going to spend money on something I don't need."

"Hey, you'll be going to lots of things with me, so you'll need to buy several dresses. You've got free time today, plus you're in one of the best shopping towns in America. You can pick up a half-dozen or so dresses today."

Her lips thinned. If the set of her jaw told him anything, Jace knew Darby was more than upset.

"*This* is what I've tried to tell you," she said. "I can't be driving down to Dallas at the drop of a hat to attend some gala or charity event. I'll have obligations in Hawthorne which can't be ignored. I'll have practices which run late with the cheer squad. There may be some nights I'll be up at school, helping put the paper to bed."

She paused, her eyes filling with tears. "My life is in Hawthorne, Jace. Not here."

He sat on the edge of the bed, cupping her cheeks. "Your life is with me. We're going to work it out."

Darby shook her head. "You can't just say that and expect a magic wand to be waved, making it come true. You're being bullheaded, Jace. I don't like that."

"Hey, we knew we were going to have to compromise about some things. Social events will be one of those things." He kissed her lightly. "We'll work this out. I promise."

He rose. "Use your time wisely today. Get your shopping done."

Shaking her head, she said, "That's another part of what you don't get."

Confused, he asked, "What are you talking about?"

She huffed. "You just want me to run out and buy a dress. Or dresses. The kind of dress you're talking about costs money, Jace. Lots of money. I don't earn the salary you do. I can't afford to blow a month's wages on a single dress, much less several of them."

"You don't have to do that. Sorry, I didn't even think of that."

He pulled out his wallet and handed her a credit card. "Use this. Buy whatever you like. Some cocktail dresses. A few nice suits. Even some long gowns."

"I can't do that," she said, pushing the card back at him.

"Why not?" he asked, his frustration growing. "I have the money. I'm the one who's asking you to attend these events with me. I don't mind paying so you'll look nice and fit in."

"But I *do* mind you paying," she said. "I've always provided for myself. My parents didn't have a lot of disposable income. We were all thrilled when I earned the cheer scholarship to UT. Then I traveled all summer, going from cheer camps across the country. I was paid to teach at the workshops, plus I had all my travel comped, from hotels to meals. I saved every penny from that job and bought what I needed in college, from clothes to makeup to paying for haircuts."

Shaking her head, she said, "I won't take your money."

Jace worried they were at an impasse.

Relenting, Darby said, "I will buy one dress today using your credit card. One. That's it. And I will wear it more than one time, which I'm sure is taboo, but that's what I plan to do. And I won't be able to come to Dallas often, Jace. You've got to understand that."

He was just realizing what living in two different places meant. Darby couldn't be at his beck and call when he wanted to attend places he'd been invited to. Especially Friday nights, when she would be with her cheerleaders at games. Suddenly, the gulf between them seemed to widen, and he didn't have a clue how to keep it from growing.

"The casino party starts at eight," he finally said. "There's a cocktail hour prior to that. Can you be ready at six-thirty? I keep some clothes at the office to change into, so I won't need to come back here to dress."

"Yes. I'll be downstairs," she said, her voice neutral.

"Good. I'll see you then."

He walked out the bedroom door and only got a few steps before turning around, stopping in the doorway.

"I know we have a lot to work out. More than I want to think about. I've been spoiled, having you here with me all week." Determination filled him. "But we will work things out, Darby. I promise you that. I'm used to getting things done. I'll make this happen."

Jace left, afraid to stay any longer and have to confront the differences between them and their careers. His gut told him that Darby would never willingly move to Dallas, and there was no way he could move to Hawthorne.

He drove to the office, trying to put their mounting problems aside, and concentrate on his clients.

* * *

DARBY TRIED to shake off her mounting depression as she showered and dressed for the day. She put on a nice blouse and pair of black slacks, knowing she would need to shop in stores which catered to a certain kind of customer.

Reality was catching up to them. This week together at Jace's condo had been magical, full of time together. Dinners out. Walks after dinner. Late-night talks, with plenty of love-making tossed in. It had all been like a house of cards, though, and it was starting to fall. As a teacher and sponsor of extracurricular activities, she would need to be in Hawthorne a majority of the time. Jace, on the other hand, had a life he'd built in Dallas. His business was here. His social commitments were numerous. While he had made adjustments in his calendar this week because of her presence, he couldn't afford to continue skipping out on the glittering events.

Glumly, she picked up her cell phone and called Kelby.

"Hey. How are things going this week?" her friend asked brightly.

Suddenly, Darby didn't want to share with anyone, not even Kelby, how uncertain she was about Jace. How she doubted they had a future together. Yes, she loved him, but love couldn't solve every problem. It was a good thing she'd kept her feelings to herself. If they had exchanged those three little words, then things would be even more complicated than they already were.

"Got a question for you. Jace is taking me to a big casino party tonight. It's probably for some charity. I need to pick up a cocktail dress to wear. I don't know where I should go shopping for one."

"I wish you were a few inches taller because I have a ton I could loan you," Kelby said. "But you definitely want to go to NorthPark."

"Isn't that where Wyndham & Warren is located?" Darby asked, referring to the last place Kelby had worked before she'd been let go, thanks to a scandal which was not of her own making.

"Yes. You don't have to be loyal to me. They've got some great dressy clothes."

"I wouldn't put a dime in their pockets after the way they treated you," she declared.

"That's sweet. I appreciate hearing you say that. North-Park has a ton of great stores, though."

Kelby then named half a dozen, with Darby jotting down the names.

"I'm on a budget," she admitted. "Can you steer me toward the one which might be the most reasonable?"

"NorthPark isn't about budget clothing," her friend said. "My best advice is to try and shop the sale racks. How are you set for shoes? And a purse?"

"I brought a dress and some black pumps. The dress isn't dressy enough. The pumps will have to do. I only have a crossbody purse. I'm afraid adding an evening bag would break my bank."

"Then go without one," Kelby suggested. "Just give Jace a lipstick to carry for you. If it's a casino party, they give you fake money to play with. Frankly, they can get boring after a while. Since Jace is so hot for you, you probably won't even be there that long. You can get by with just a lipstick."

"Good advice. Thanks, Kel."

"How is everything else going?"

She swallowed. "Every day has been better the one before," she shared. "I know Cinderella will be leaving this ball soon, however. Reality awaits me in Hawthorne."

"You don't sound excited."

"Honestly, I can't wait to meet my students and begin a new career. I'm just wondering how I can keep things going with Jace while I'm doing it."

"I'm here if you need an ear."

"I know. We'll be back late Friday afternoon to go to the game. Kay asked if I could stop by with you again and visit with the cheerleaders before the game."

"We can do that," Kelby said. "We'll send Jace down to stand with Eli to keep him busy. Text me a picture of which dress you decide on. Or if you're having trouble deciding, send me some from the dressing room. You know I'm always happy to give my opinion."

"You have great taste, Kel. Champagne tastes. Probably a little too rich for my blood."

"You'll find something. I know it."

"Okay. I'll send you a picture."

Darby checked to see where NorthPark was. Way too far to walk from Jace's condo, so she brought up her rideshare app and scheduled a ride to the mall. Once she arrived, she walked the entire mall, consulting the list of stores Kelby had provided to her. The windows displayed models in chic clothing.

She decided she would buy something classic. Elegant. Timeless. That way, she could wear it for years to come and justify whatever price the dress was.

Entering the first store, she strolled through, eventually finding a sales rack which was picked over. Finding nothing there, she perused the rest of the store, pulling two dresses to try on. She was afraid to look at the price tag at this point. A salesclerk escorted her to the dressing room. She tried on both, taking a picture of herself in each outfit, then glancing at the tags and wincing.

Changing back into her own clothes, she left the dressing room. A salesclerk approached her.

"Would you like these two?"

"I may be back," she said coolly. "I'd like to try a few other places before I make up my mind."

After going to four other dress shops, she took a seat on a bench by a fountain and pulled up her pictures. She texted four to Kelby. Her friend texted that she liked the first and third one. Darby liked those the best, as well. While all four dresses cost far more than she could spend, those two were the most expensive. Then again, she knew Jace would be introducing her to the crème de la crème of Dallas society. She didn't want to embarrass him.

She returned to the first store and went to the salesclerk. "I'm back. I'd like to purchase one of the dresses I tried on earlier."

"I put them aside, hoping you'd be back," the woman said, smiling at her. "Let me get them."

When she returned, Darby indicated which one she wanted and handed over her credit card. She paid her balance in full each month in order not to ever have to pay the exorbitant interest fees. She'd also practiced only charging what she could pay for at the end of each month. It was a good thing Sawyer was letting her live with him for a few months. Though she'd offered to pay rent to him, he'd waved her away. Now, she was grateful to have a cushion so she could build up her bank account.

"You will look spectacular in this dress," the salesclerk assured Darby. "It's something you can wear today and ten years from now, as well."

"I hope so," she said.

Once she'd paid for the dress, she walked through Neiman Marcus and requested a rideshare for pickup there. She figured it was the best known store at NorthPark and that a driver would easily be able to find her outside its doors.

Back at Jace's condo, she tried on the dress again, liking how well it fit her. She unzipped it and hung it in the closet, spending a couple of hours going over ideas for future stories and columns for the *Hawthorne Herald* and looking through the yearbooks again, trying to match names and faces. She knew almost everyone at this point. Even though these students' appearance would have changed some in a year, it filled her with confidence to enter her new teaching position knowing most of their names.

Darby took her time doing her hair and makeup, knowing she would be scrutinized being with Jace. She donned the black cocktail dress and slipped into her pumps, wishing she had brought her single pair of sky-high black stilettos. They hurt her feet after an hour, but they would've been killer with this dress. Maybe the next time she wore it, she could wear the stilettos.

Jace texted that he was leaving the office. It usually took him ten to fifteen minutes to make it back to the condo, but she decided to go downstairs anyway. Darby chose a lipstick and took it with her, keying in the code to lock the door behind her.

When she saw his car pull up in front, she walked outside. He quickly got out of the car, and for a moment, he took her breath away in his black tux. To think a man this handsome and smart cared about her almost made her grow dizzy.

"Wow!" he said. "Just ... wow. You look amazing, Darby. I don't deserve to be seen with you."

Trying to make light of things because feelings of love were swelling within her, she said, "Chris Hemsworth and Ryan Gosling were busy tonight. I suppose you'll do."

Jace laughed and opened the passenger door for her. She handed him the lipstick, saying, "Tuck this into your pocket for me, okay?"

He did so. "I want to kiss you so badly, but I don't want to mess you up."

She got into the sports car as he came around and slid behind the wheel. She caught a whiff of his cologne.

"Seriously, no actor in Hollywood has anything on you, Tanner. You clean up nicely."

Taking her hand, he brought it to his lips for a tender kiss. "Back at you, Montgomery. I'm going to be the envy of every guy there tonight."

"I doubt that."

"Doubt all you want, but just remember that you're mine —and I'm proud of you."

Darby hoped everything would go well tonight and that Jace would be happy that he had brought her.

CHAPTER
Twenty~Three

As they drove to the charity event, Darby said, "You never mentioned what tonight is about. Who's sponsoring it. What they're raising funds for."

"It's being held by one of the Texas sportswriters' associations," Jace told her. "The funds raised tonight will go to juvenile diabetes research. About fifteen years ago, one of the leading sports columnists for a Houston newspaper had a son diagnosed with juvenile diabetes. The idea for this event started with him and in Houston. It's grown exponentially over the years. The main fundraising event occurs in Houston one year. San Antonio the next. Then Austin, Ft. Worth, and Dallas before it rotates back to Houston."

Because she was a huge sports fan, Darby was excited that she might be meeting reporters she was familiar with. Though she had lived out of state for over a decade, she had a digital subscription to the *Dallas Morning News* and kept up with the sports scene in Texas that way, especially her beloved Texas Longhorns and the Cowboys since West had played for them for so many years.

Jace added, "They hold the event in the middle of the week since all these sportswriters are busiest on the weekends covering games. Because of that, it'll be an early night. We should be out of here no later than ten o'clock. Probably sooner."

They pulled up to a well-known hotel, and a valet met them. Another opened Darby's car door for her and assisted her in getting out. Jace handed over his valet key, and they entered the hotel's lobby. Suddenly, panic washed over her, and she looked at him.

"Do I have lipstick on my teeth?" she asked, baring her teeth at him.

He laughed. "No. You look beautiful. Besides, I would've told you if I had seen any."

"I just want everything to be perfect this evening. This is the first time I'll be mingling with people you see socially, as well as do business with."

They rode an escalator up to the mezzanine level where the ballrooms were located and stopped at a table where Jace gave their names. They were given wristbands to wear to show they were a part of tonight's event, as well as a stack of pretend money to play various games of chance.

The woman who registered them said, "If you don't know how to play any of the games of chance, you can use this QR code to download the rules." She pointed to a placard on the table. "We also have volunteers scattered around the ballroom who can also help guide you. Or you can simply watch a game for a round or two before deciding to jump right in."

"Where is the silent auction being held?" Jace asked. "I saw an item on the website I want to bid on."

"It's in the adjacent ballroom. Doors are open so guests can flow freely from the casino games to the auction without having to come outside and around. Restrooms are to your left. Enjoy your evening."

Jace's fingers threaded through hers, giving Darby a boost of confidence as they walked into the large ballroom. It was already about half full, and gameplay was already in progress. Food and drink stations were set up around the ballroom, and a passing server stopped to allow them to take a flute of champagne.

"Let's make a loop around the room," he suggested. "That way, I can introduce you to a few people, and we can see which games are available and what we want to do."

"Good idea," she agreed.

It took almost forty-five minutes to circulate around the room. It seemed that Jace knew everyone—and everyone knew him. Darby was thrilled to meet sportswriters from various newspapers and magazines, as well as a few major online sites, recognizing almost all of them from their pictures, which appeared next to the columns and news stories they wrote. There were also sports anchors from various TV stations in Dallas, and she got into a lively discussion with two of them about next month's Texas/OU game, which was traditionally played during the State Fair each year at the Cotton Bowl on the fairgrounds.

One argued with her that it was the OU/Texas game and not the other way around.

Shaking her head, Darby said, "You're a traitor to the state if you refer to it that way."

He laughed easily. "Let's just say that my daughter—and my money—went to OU. I try to stay neutral in most sports contests, but I like to support my little girl when I can. She graduated magna cum laude, and she's now in her second year of med school here in Dallas at UT Southwestern."

The sports anchor pulled out his phone, showing Darby a picture of him with his daughter.

"Smart and beautiful," she said. "Obviously, she takes after her mother."

Everyone laughed, and Darby realized that she was relaxed and thoroughly enjoying herself. Though she had dreaded attending tonight's event, it was turning out to be far different from what she had anticipated. Then again, it revolved around the world of sports, something she knew and loved. A different event or gala might be a far cry from what she was experiencing tonight.

They continued moving through the room, and she met a few professional athletes who were also in attendance. Some played for the Dallas Mavericks, while others played for the Texas Rangers or Dallas Stars. A handful were on the Dallas Cowboys roster, and Jace represented two of them. She sensed the pride he felt in her when he introduced her to the players.

Immediately, Darby began asking questions about a defensive scheme and some of the play calling which had occurred in last weekend's game. The two players spent a lot of time with her, answering her questions in detail. She suggested a coverage the Cowboys weren't using, and one player agreed with her that they should implement it.

When they got ready to move on, one of them even said, "Tanner, you better hold on to this one. She knows her stuff." He grinned. "Maybe even more than you do."

Jace laughed. "Maybe I should hire Darby. She could be my new shark."

They moved away, his hand on the small of her back, causing those familiar tingles to dance along her spine.

"You're doing great tonight," he praised. "I knew you would. You're definitely in your element, talking sports."

"It's something I've loved since I was young. It's going to be so good, being back in Texas, rooting for all my home teams."

"Shall we try our luck at the tables now?"

"Sure," she responded.

They started at the roulette table. Jace had a few winning spins, while Darby lost money twice and decided to quit betting and merely watch him. They moved on to a poker table and stayed for a while. She had better luck there, almost doubling her money.

He leaned over and whispered into her ear, "Remind me never to play poker with you. Talk about being a shark. You definitely know how to move in for the kill."

They opened up their spots for new players after a few more hands and continued to try other tables. She had already drunk one glass of champagne and now sipped on a glass of Moscato. She wasn't a big drinker and decided this glass of wine needed to last her the rest of the evening.

Jace said, "I see someone I've got to talk to. It's business. It's confidential, so would you mind if I leave you alone for a few minutes?"

"I think I'll go check out the silent auction. You can find me there when you're done."

He leaned over and kissed her lightly on the lips, and Darby knew he was staking his claim publicly.

She entered the other ballroom, which was much smaller than the one she'd left. Perusing some of the auction items, she found that most of them pertained to sports, whether it was tickets to a future game or memorabilia, such as a player's jersey or a baseball mitt or hockey stick. Every now and then, some vacation trip was thrown in, usually to an exotic locale such as Fiji or Greece.

A sports columnist from Ft. Worth whom she'd met

earlier in the evening came up to her and said, "I find everything here a little rich for my blood. Then again, we're trying to raise money for juvenile diabetes."

She nodded. "I'm a teacher, so I'm definitely on a limited budget. I'm afraid I won't be bidding on anything."

For a few minutes, they discussed the Cowboys chances for winning their division and moving into the playoffs, and then the writer said, "I'm glad to see Jace is finally with a woman who has a brain between her ears. I see him frequently throughout the year, and it's a different woman on his arm each time. You've got substance, Darby, and I can tell that Jace is really interested in you."

His phone buzzed, and he looked at the screen. "If you'll excuse me, I need to take this."

"Of course," she said, glowing from his words. She knew Jace had been good for her, but she was also wanted to be good for him, too.

Moving to the next item in the silent auction, she began reading the description when the scent of heavy perfume invaded her space. Darby looked to her right and saw a stunning brunette, one with flawless skin and a slinky dress that would cost her three month's salary. Intense brown eyes assessed her.

"You have made quite the splash this evening," the woman said, sounding both judgmental and a bit envious at the same time.

Since the woman didn't introduce herself, Darby said, "We haven't met. I'm Darby Montgomery."

She did not offer the stranger her hand.

The woman sniffed. "Penelope Rossi. I am a jewelry designer in Dallas. My clientele is quite exclusive." She paused. "So, you are the flavor of the week."

"I beg your pardon?"

"Jace's new toy," Penelope clarified, causing Darby's temper to flare. "He changes women frequently, so don't get used to him being by your side. Tonight might be the only time you are seen with him. I believe they call it a one and done in the sports world."

A sick feeling washed through her. Darby started to turn away, but Penelope put a hand on Darby's forearm.

"You won't hold his interest long," Penelope said confidently. "I know. I was his flavor of the week last week."

The words startled her. *She* had spent most of last week with Jace before flying back to Kansas City on Thursday morning.

Penelope gave her a knowing smile. "You are replaceable. We all are. Jace Tanner is as handsome as a Greek god, but he doesn't have a soul. This time last Thursday night, *I* was the one on his arm. We dined at The Mansion. He fawned over me, and yet here I am this evening without him. And *you* have taken my place, just as another will take yours soon."

Nausea now filled Darby. She had gotten on a plane, and Jace had gone out with this woman the very day she left Dallas. No wonder he hadn't had time to text her back. He had been with Penelope Rossi. She dropped her arm, causing Penelope's hold to break.

Coolly, she said, "It was nice meeting you."

Turning away, Darby walked out the doors of the small ballroom and headed to the nearest restroom. She locked herself inside a stall, breathing deeply in and out, trying not to give into the tears which threatened to fall.

How could Jace make her feel as if she were the only woman in the world, all the while stringing along other women? Penelope might not be the only one. Doubt filled her, and Darby was certain there were others. And once she returned to Hawthorne, Jace would be left on his own. A lot.

Relationships had to be based upon trust, else they eroded quickly. Her heart told her that while she thought Jace was the only man for her, he was nothing more than a player. He knew what to say. What to do to make a woman feel as if she were the center of his universe. With her in Hawthorne and him in Dallas, it would take a lot to keep their relationship going. Knowing what she did now, Darby believed she better cut ties with him before she was hurt more than she already was.

She already loved him. She was thankful that she hadn't spoken those words aloud to him because she would have felt incredibly foolish if she would have done so. Most likely, Jace would have parroted them back to her, not meaning any of it.

She was stuck without a car. She couldn't go back to Jace's condo and sleep in the same bed with him, not after what she had learned this evening.

Darby decided she would call Sawyer. Her brother would come and get her.

But it struck her. She didn't have her phone with her. She hadn't brought a purse. By the time they got back to Jace's condo, it would be too late to call Sawyer and have him drive down to Dallas to get her and go back to Hawthorne. She had talked to him yesterday and learned he would be in court tomorrow morning, and she didn't want to drag him away from Hawthorne when he needed to get his sleep in order to be fresh for his client.

Leaving the restroom stall, she studied herself in the mirror. Then Darby steeled herself, knowing she would need to put on the performance of a lifetime. It would be wrong to cause a scene here in front of so many people. She had been determined not to embarrass Jace in any fashion, and she would hold to that. A public breakup would be humiliating for them both, and it might also affect his business.

She returned to the silent auction room, finding him in conversation with someone she didn't know.

Coming up to them, she slipped her arm through his. He turned and smiled at her, causing her heart to shatter into a thousand pieces. Still, she returned his smile. Once he finished his conversation, they moved away.

"Where were you?" he asked.

"I went to the ladies' room," she replied evenly.

"I still have a bunch of money of yours in my pocket for you to gamble with."

"Then let me go see how fast I can lose it."

It wouldn't be the only thing she had lost this night.

They returned to the casino party, and as Darby had expected, she lost of the rest of her money quickly because she couldn't concentrate on the games in front of her.

"Have you lost your magic touch, Montgomery?" Jace whispered into her ear.

The touch of his lips grazing her earlobe almost had her coming undone. She gave him a tight smile.

"I guess my luck finally ran out."

He glanced at his watch. "It's almost a quarter until ten. Want to call it a night?"

"Yes. I would."

Jace took her hand, lacing his fingers through hers. As they headed toward the ballroom doors, Darby caught sight of Penelope Rossi watching them. The woman lifted her wineglass in a mock toast as they passed by her.

Darby's heart ached. What was going to happen in the next hour would be the most painful thing she had ever gone through. Her gut told her that she would be spending many a miserable night after this, yearning for Jace. She would need to remind herself that he wasn't the man she had fallen in love with. That had been an illusion. The Jace she loved was kind. Considerate. And only had eyes for her. Then again, it was probably how he treated every woman. Every flavor of the week, according to Penelope Rossi.

As they waited for the valet to bring the Porsche around, Jace said, "You're awfully quiet."

"I suppose I'm all talked out," she told him.

"Well, you were definitely a hit. Dallas loves Darby Montgomery."

His car arrived, and she got into it, nausea bubbling up inside her again, knowing what lay ahead.

They reached his parking garage and exited the vehicle, using the elevator to go up to his penthouse.

Once inside, Jace arms enveloped her, and he kissed her.

Darby didn't kiss him back.

Quickly, he pulled his lips from hers, studying her anxiously. "What's wrong?"

"I can't do this anymore, Jace. I don't want to do this anymore."

Confusion filled his hazel eyes. "Do what, Darby? I don't understand."

She pushed away from him, freeing herself. "That's the problem. You've never understood. I thought this might have a chance to work. I let my guard down—and let you in. I should have listened to that nagging voice I kept hearing."

Darby's gaze met his. "*We* aren't working. We are too different, Jace. We live such different lives. We don't even reside in the same place. I can tell now that long distance would kill this, what we have between us." She sighed. "I want to cut my losses while I can."

She saw the hurt spring to his eyes, but anger quickly replaced it.

"That's it?" he demanded. "You think we're too different

and that a little distance will be hard, so you're going to cut and run?'

His words felt like a knife, piercing her heart. Dully, she said, "We've been like a couple on *The Bachelor*. We've had some phenomenal dates. Yes, we have amazing chemistry, but just like those couples, the fantasy ends and reality sets in. The track record for that show is abysmal."

"We aren't on some TV show, Darby," Jace said bluntly. "This is real life."

"Yes, it is. And I'm saying that our two worlds don't mix. We both have careers that we aren't giving up any time soon. We simply don't mesh, Jace. I am grateful for the time I spent with you, but I want to go back to Hawthorne. To life in a sleepy town where not much of anything happens. You belong here in the big city, cutting deals and hitting up social affairs. You're a mover and a shaker. You thrive on pressure. That's the last thing I want."

She shook her head. "I don't want to be where you are, and you certainly don't want to be stuck in a place like Hawthorne."

Her temples throbbed painfully. "I'll sleep in your guestroom tonight."

No, if she did, he would come to her. Cajole and wheedle and make love to her until she couldn't think straight.

"On second thought, I think I'll check into a hotel."

Jace took a step for her, and Darby held up a hand. "Don't try to change my mind," she said firmly. "Stay here. Give me a minute to pack my things."

She turned quickly, praying that he wouldn't follow her. As fast as possible, she slipped clothes from hangars and from inside dresser drawers, tossing them into her suitcase. She removed her toiletry bag from the bathroom and collected her chargers, tablet, and phone. Giving the room a final look, she didn't find anything that belonged to her in sight.

Exiting his bedroom, she returned to where he still stood. It didn't look as if he had taken one step.

"I'll go now."

Darby couldn't help herself. She leaned up and brushed her lips against his cheek.

"Take care, Jace."

He didn't reply.

She let herself out of the condo and took the elevator downstairs, feeling numb inside.

Was she wrong to walk away from the man she loved?

She couldn't be completely sure of anything, but she knew she didn't belong in this big city, going to fancy parties and making small talk with people she didn't care to be around. If she stayed with Jace, it would boil down to her needing to quit her new job and move to Dallas.

And that was if he really cared for her and wasn't seeing other women on the side.

"Better safe than sorry, Darb," she said under her breath. "Protect your heart."

In the lobby, she asked the concierge for a reasonably priced chain hotel nearby. The woman gave her a sympathetic look and suggested one.

"Yes, that'll do. Where is it located?"

"Let me make a reservation for you, Miss Montgomery."

She didn't realize the concierge knew her name. "Please. Thank you. One night."

While the woman made the call, Darby opened her ride share app and arranged for transportation. When she finished, the concierge told her that they were holding the room for her.

"I appreciate your help."

As if sleepwalking, she went outside and waited for her driver. The trip to the hotel took less than ten minutes. The clerk at the desk asked for her credit card, and Darby handed it over. She signed for the room and was given a key.

When she went inside the hotel room, she locked it securely behind her. Like a zombie, she removed her expensive new cocktail dress and let it drop to the floor. She stepped from her shoes and then removed her underwear and bra. Naked, she pulled back the covers and climbed into bed. Immediately, she turned her face into the pillow

So that no one would hear her loud sobs.

Twenty~Four

"We finished painting all the signs, Ms. Montgomery," Carrie, the captain for the varsity cheer, said.

"Make sure all the brushes are rinsed and the paints are put away," Darby replied, shutting down her tablet. She would finish reviewing the final layout for the rest of the year-book pages tomorrow.

"We always do. Do you want to come look them over?"

"Sure," she said, accompanying Carrie to where her cheerleading squads were already cleaning up.

Kay had been right. These girls were organized and oper-ated as a well-oiled machine. Slipping into the role as their cheer coach had been a breeze, as well as fun. She moved among the signs, laughing at a few, praising the girls for their efforts.

"Once the brushes are rinsed and the paints stored, let's go ahead and walk over and hang them in the stadium." The cheerleaders used a quick-drying paint, which would make this possible.

Over the next hour, the signs were affixed to various points around Hawks Stadium, where they would face their arch enemy, the Eagles, tomorrow night for the school's homecoming game. Darby was glad her life was so busy now.

Because it gave her very little time to mope over Jace.

The last six weeks had flown by as she had acclimated herself to her new teaching position. The cheerleading squads were cooperative and ready to learn from her. She had worked on choreographing new dances for them to perform at pep rallies and had beamed with pride as she'd watched the dances brought to life in front of the entire school. She had also worked with the cheerleaders on the cheers they knew, some from her days as a Hawks cheerleader, and others new to the repertoire. Once football season ended, they would began in earnest in working on their performance in nationals. Already, Darby and Carrie had mapped out their overall routine and would refine it in the weeks to come.

She had enjoyed teaching the Intro to Journalism course, too. Those students were eager to please and decent writers. As far as the newspaper and yearbook staffs went, they practically ran themselves, just as Kay had predicted they would. Both staffs were led by students who exhibited strong leadership skills and talent and got the best out of their fellow staff members.

"Gather around, ladies," she called, and the cheer squads moved closer to her.

"I want to thank you for how welcomed you've made me feel over these last six weeks. I know many of you were very close to Mrs. Timmons, and she would be proud of how open you've been in accepting me and the small changes I've asked for from you. You make me proud to be a life-long Hawk. Now, let's go and change into your uniforms so that we can get ready for the homecoming parade."

Darby followed the teenagers from the stadium to the high school, seeing the parking lot already frilling with the various floats. Homecoming was a big deal in Hawthorne, and the town supported this parade. She saw floats from various school clubs and organizations and walked passed ones representing the community, as well. The bank. A local dentist's office. Even Triple H had decide to participate, their float being the largest on the parking lot.

She had survived these last few weeks because of her family and friends. Sawyer and Kelby had been her rocks. Her brother had continued to let Darby live with him, and she was now on the list to rent an apartment when the new complex opened the week after Thanksgiving. Kelby had spent many hours in Darby's company, helping with the cheerleaders and commiserating over a glass of wine. She saw West at school every day, and he had smoothed the way for her, introducing her to various faculty members. Some had even been teachers when Darby attended HHS, and she was proud to join their ranks.

The hardest had been being around Autumn and Eli. She knew her cousin was torn, not wanting to take sides, but still wanting to support Darby. Eli had simply given her a hug and told her that he would help in any way he could. She did know that Autumn and Eli had gone down to Dallas for a weekend, spending it with Jace. Eli had also gone a different weekend to spend time alone with his brother.

Jace had yet to visit Hawthorne again.

Darby still loved him. She yearned to be with him, but she had resigned herself to the fact that their lifestyles were too different. If their jobs had been more compatible, she believed they would have been able to compromise and stay together. Instead, she was glad she had been the one to make the decision to walk away from their relationship. Giving herself permission to do so gave her the power to heal more quickly. Unfortunately, that healing process was crawling along. She knew she couldn't flip a switch and stop loving Jace. When she had a moment to herself, all she did was think about him, the hurt twisting in her gut painfully.

West had even offered to end his professional relationship with Jace, but Darby had forbid him from doing so, telling her cousin that Jace was the best sports agent in the business and that her past involvement with him shouldn't influence West's dealings with Jace.

She entered the high school and once the cheerleaders had changed from their paint-splattered T-shirts and into their uniforms, she helped them take the large bags of candy for them to toss from their float to the children in the crowd back to the parking lot.

Darby went over to Carrie's dad, who would be driving the float the girls rode on.

"Thank you again for letting the cheerleaders work on building the float at your place, Mr. Johnson."

"Happy to let them do so, Ms. Montgomery. We have plenty of land, and half the girls are at our place most of the time anyway. It was enjoyable to see the float come to life from scratch."

"Carrie is a wonderful young lady," Darby praised. "A real go-getter. She's an excellent student and a terrific role model for all the girls on the squad."

"I'm really proud of her. I didn't know what I was going to do with myself after her mom and I divorced and Janie left the state. Carrie was only three at the time. We struggled a bit, but she's been an easy kid to raise. I learned all about how to do French braids, and I pretty much know the lyrics to every Taylor Swift song written." He sighed. "I'm going to be pretty lonely once she leaves for college next year."

Darby gave him a hug. "You can FaceTime with her. Send her encouraging texts. You'll get through it."

She climbed aboard the float, having the cheerleaders set the bags of candy at intervals so each had access to one.

"Remember, don't throw big handfuls. We need to make the candy last all the way from here to the square and back. Plus, we don't want any little kids to be hit and hurt, so toss one piece at a time. Gently."

The parade would move along its traditional route, from the high school to the center of Hawthorne. It would loop around the town square and then head back to HHS on a parallel street. She wanted to make certain that the children on the return route had just as much a chance to claim candy as those on the first half.

Darby climbed down from the float, West giving her a hand.

"You've done a great job with the cheer squads, Darby. Their float looks amazing." He chuckled. "Unlike the football team's."

She glanced over to the flatbed, where the football team was gathering. Two pathetic, handmade signs adorned it, one on each side. The rest was completely bare.

"Your players have had more on their minds than decorating a float. We just need you to get out on the field tomorrow night and claim a win over the Eagles. After all these years, they're still our number one enemy. They'll be gunning for you and your team, West."

He grinned. "We may have a trick or two up our sleeves tomorrow night. Just keep your eyes open at the beginning of the third quarter."

She smiled. "I'll do that. Something tells me I might see a halfback pass. Or Statue of Liberty play."

Her cousin shrugged, laughing. "Just watch. That's all I'm saying."

Kelby appeared. She kissed her husband and hugged Darby as West waved goodbye, ambling toward his team.

"The float looks terrific!" she exclaimed. "I'll be at the pep rally tomorrow."

The homecoming pep rally always moved from the high school's gym outdoors to the stadium. The entire town was invited to attend. Darby hoped there would be a good turnout.

"Are you ready to hear all the tinkling of cowbells in the halls tomorrow?" Kelby asked, referring to the mums girls would be wearing. Many times, these symbols of a Texas homecoming had cowbells of all sizes attached to the dozens of ribbons which flowed from the flowers.

"I've heard mums have grown even larger than when we were in high school," she said. "They used to cover the entire front of us. I remember not even being able to sit behind a desk when I was wearing one."

They both laughed, remembering good times, and then Kelby grew serious.

"How are you doing, Darby?"

"I'm content," she said. "I'm busy as all get out, which really helps. The newspaper staff has been a joy to work with. Things have changed quite a bit since my time running the *Herald*. It's so much easier now with everything created digitally. And *Horizon* is really beginning to take shape," she said, referring to the yearbook. "In fact, I need to go and meet with photographers from both staffs."

Kelby hugged her again. "See you at the pep rally in the morning."

Darby sent a group text to the photographers she knew were scattered about the parking lot, taking candids, and she went over their final game plan, as far as shots to be captured. Two left after their meeting, heading to the town square so they could take photographs in a different setting and from different angles, as well as capturing crowd shots of the town's residents as they watched the parade.

She saw Eli and Autumn near the Triple H float and made her way over to them.

"Hey!" she called.

Eli climbed from the bed of the float and helped Autumn down. They both greeted her warmly.

"What do you think so far about homecoming in Hawthorne?" she asked Eli.

"Obviously, I missed out on a lot when I was in high school." He slipped an arm about his wife's shoulder. "But Autumn is helping me make up for lost time." He glanced over. "Your cheerleaders' float is one of the best ones in the parking lot."

"They're hoping they'll win in their division. I think Triple H will walk away the winner in the community division."

"We have Kelby to thank for that," Autumn told her. "She helped design the float for us."

"I followed the progress of it being built on Instagram," Darby said. "That was clever of her to capture volunteers for the hospital taking the float from nothing to something."

"Kelby is brilliant when it comes to social media," Eli praised. "Hogan Health has decided to follow the beta program she began here in Hawthorne. Kelby will run the Hogan corporate account, as well as continue to post for Triple H here in Hawthorne, while being responsible for hiring locals to manage social media in the various small towns where Hogan Health has hospitals and medical facilities."

"Kelby is going to need to hire some help," she said. "Her company is growing. It's becoming more than a one-woman job. Especially since they're trying for a baby."

Someone called Eli's name, and he excused himself. Autumn reached out and took Darby's hand.

"How are you doing?" she asked quietly.

She swallowed. "Okay. Some days are harder than others, but the job is keeping me very busy. For that, I'm grateful."

Darby wanted to ask if Jace had asked about her but was too proud to do so.

"I don't know if I should say this to you or not, but Jace seems very unhappy," Autumn shared.

She shook her head. "It's none of my business, Autumn. We're already dancing a fine line with Jace being your brother-in-law. I hope that both you and Eli will continue to have a close relationship with him. I just don't care to hear anything about him."

Autumn squeezed Darby's hand. "All right. I'll see you at the game tomorrow night. Go, Hawks!"

"Go, Hawks!" she echoed, her heart suddenly not into any of the hoopla going on about her.

Darby told herself to fight off the sinking feeling. To focus on what she had—and not what she didn't. This was the life she had chosen for herself, and she knew she would only be as happy as she allowed herself to be. She did not regret leaving Cheer USA. Already, she was forming friendships with other staff members at HHS, and she enjoyed the variety that each day brought.

Blanche Biggerstaff began barking orders over a megaphone, saying, "It's time to head out. You've done a great job lining up in the order you're supposed to be in," the principal praised. "Now, let's go out and celebrate with the town of Hawthorne. Go, Hawks!"

"Go, Hawks!" thundered the crowd.

Darby had her cheer squads climb onto their float, and one of them asked, "Aren't you coming with us, Ms. Montgomery?"

She recalled from her own cheering days that the cheer coach had never ridden in the float.

"No. It's your night to shine. Soak up every minute of it. I'll be waiting for you here when you get back."

The cheerleaders began protesting, and Carrie said, "We want you to ride with us, Ms. Montgomery. You've done so much for us since you arrived. We want you to share in this moment with us."

Touched, Darby's eyes misted with tears. "Okay," she said, climbing onto the float.

She joined the girls, looking out over the parking lot as Blanche gave instructions, signaling for the next float to depart, trying to space them out evenly. She glanced over to the football team, and West caught her eye and waved to her. For a moment, she was taken back to her own days in high school, when she and West, along with Kelby and Chance, were a tight foursome. Darby said a quick prayer of thanks, glad to be back in her hometown, among family and friends. Her heart still hurt, but she knew with time—and distance from Jace—that she would slowly began to heal.

Twenty-Five

Jace disembarked from his plane, having been gone ten days. He'd visited five cities, meeting with three current clients and four potential new ones. The trip had also included attending two different college games and two NFL ones. He was bone tired.

And liked it that way.

He had found that keeping busy was the only remedy for missing Darby, knowing he was patching a bullet hole with a Band-Aid. Consequently, he doubled down, working even longer hours than usual. When he left work, it was to attend meetings related to business or social affairs where he could talk business. No one had accompanied him as a plus-one. His interest in women had come to a standstill. The thought of sex with anyone other than Darby had kept him celibate.

The driver dropped him at his office, and Jace carried his suitcase and briefcase to his office. No one greeted him when he entered. He would like to think it was because everyone was too busy to even realize he was passing through. Instead, he knew it was because he had bitten off heads left and right after Darby abandoned him. Pride had kept him from apologizing to anyone.

Darby would've been angry at him for that.

Hell, he was angry at himself. All the time. But he didn't have a clue how to fix things. She'd been right. Though their sexual chemistry was off the charts, their lifestyles and professions were utterly incompatible. Her life revolved around the small town of Hawthorne, while his was continually on the go, a fast pace that thrived in a big city. Compromise was out of the question. Neither of them would budge from what they did or where they lived. Jace just needed to get past it.

But damn, his heart was heavy.

He blamed himself for having gotten involved with her. He should have known not to do so. Work was his drug, and he was addicted to it. Being personable around clients and at high society affairs while keeping an emotional distance was his trademark. It was only when he veered from that and let Darby into his heart that all the trouble had erupted.

Jace had learned his lesson, all too well. In the future, he would not become emotionally involved with a woman. Enjoy being seen with her. Enjoy the sex. And then move on.

The fact that the moving on from Darby was causing him trouble stuck in his craw.

Elena wasn't at her desk as he went inside his office. He closed the door, and that would be indication enough to her that he had arrived since it always remained open while he was gone.

Rolling his suitcase into a corner, he took his briefcase to his desk and found several neat piles atop it. Phone messages. Documents which needed his review. A list of items every employee had been working on during his absence from the office. While he'd checked in a few times a day with Elena, it was nice to get an overall picture of what had happened while he'd been on the road.

A light tap sounded, and Mark came in. "Good to have you back. I think."

He sighed. "Good to be back. It's nice to be in the office and become grounded again."

Mark crossed the room and handed Jace a few file folders, saying, "Contracts for you to review." He named the clients involved, and Jace nodded.

"I'll look them over tomorrow," he said, rubbing his eyes. "I haven't gotten much sleep lately. I'll put fresh eyes on them tomorrow."

"That's fine," his partner assured him. "Anything you'd like to talk about?"

While they had known one another in college and Mark was the closest thing to a friend Jace had, he never spoke of personal matters with Mark. His partner had married five years ago and was the father to a three-year-old and a baby. Mark came to work and did a fantastic job, and then he went home and devoted himself to his family. He let Jace attend the bevy of social events, saying he was now a homebody.

Now wasn't the time to dump his sorrows. Jace would keep his heartache to himself. No one knew he had loved Darby, much less that he still did.

And always would.

"No, I'm good. I've got an art auction to attend in Deep Ellum tonight."

"Why don't you give the social scene a break and just go home and get some sleep?" Mark suggested.

Giving his partner a devilish smile, he said, "That ain't me."

Mark shook his head. "I'll see you tomorrow."

Half an hour later, Jace decided to leave the office. It was almost six anyway. He could go home and relax an hour before he headed back out.

Elena was at her desk again, furiously tapping at her computer's keys. She glanced up and nodded to him, saying, "You see everything I left for you?"

"I did. Anything else I need to be filled in on?"

She paused, looking as if she were contemplating telling him something. Then she began typing again. "Nope. You've got the art auction tonight. I'll see you tomorrow."

Her tone was dismissive, and it bothered him. Jace was used to enjoying being around Elena. She didn't let him get away with anything, and she kept the office and his life running smoothly. He probably should give her another bonus. Or a raise. Darby would approve of that. He winced as he headed to the elevator, telling himself to stop thinking about her, knowing it was impossible. They said time healed all wounds, and he wondered how much time it would take to get Darby Montgomery out of his head and heart.

He drove home and dumped everything from his suitcase in a pile for his housekeeper to deal with. She came in on Tuesdays and Fridays, doing his laundry and cleaning the condo until it sparkled, as well as running errands for him. She dropped off clothes at the cleaners and picked them up. Kept his fridge and liquor cabinet stocked. Even collected his mail, something he usually forget to pick up in the lobby. Since tomorrow was Friday, she could deal with the dirty clothes then.

It didn't feel right, though. He returned to the pile, separating the clothes which could be washed from those needing to go to the cleaners. He placed the dirty clothes in his hamper and draped the rest over the chair in his bedroom. Jace had found himself doing little things such as this, and he knew Darby's influence on him would last for a long time.

Going downstairs to his Porsche, he drove to the Deep Ellum art gallery where the auction would take place. It would display works in numerous mediums and was featuring up and coming artists on the Dallas scene. He snagged a glass of champagne and quickly downed it, then picked up a few canapés. The last time he'd eaten had been on the plane hours ago, and he realized he was hungry.

He moved through the art gallery, speaking to a few people but mostly avoiding the crowd, pretending to study the various pieces of art without conversation. Paintings hanging on the wall were part of the auction, as well as pottery, sculptures, and even jewelry. He paused in front of a display of turquoise jewelry, his mind, wandering, when he heard his name. Coming out of his reverie, he saw Penelope Rossi had joined him. She was the last person he wished to see this evening.

"Ah, Jace Tanner. Our paths cross again," she said, smiling mischievously. "It must be fate."

Shrugging, he said, "We attend some of the same events." Glancing at the card next to the jewelry, he said, "I see this is your work. Nice."

Her brows arched. "Are you saying that to be kind, or do you really like it?"

Jace remained silent. Actually, he didn't like it at all, finding it too clunky. Darby never would have worn anything so bold and in your face. She was petite. He could see her wearing a delicate necklace on a thin chain. Simple diamond studs.

"Jace?"

He looked at Penelope, realizing he'd gone off on another tangent. "I was thinking of the type of woman who might wear a design this bold."

"I noticed you aren't here with anyone tonight. I haven't

seen you with any woman in a while." Pausing, she studied him. "Not since you brought that short, average-looking woman to the casino party."

Jace knew she was trying to provoke a response from him, so he kept his temper under control.

"I don't think Darby is average-looking at all. She's striking."

Again, Penelope assessed him. "Then why isn't she here with you if you are so enamored with her?"

"She doesn't live in Dallas," he said coolly, ready to end their conversation and move on.

"I knew she was just another woman passing through your life," Penelope said. "I told her so."

Shock filled him. Jace clasped Penelope's elbow. "What did you tell her?" he asked, his words quiet but filled with rage.

Penelope tossed her hair and leaned into him, her heavy musk perfume overwhelming him.

"I believe my exact words were that she was your latest flavor of the week. I told her that I knew all about that because *I* had been your choice the week before. That you had wined and dined me at Dallas' most exclusive restaurant, only to drop me without warning."

Sudden clarity filled Jace. Darby had already struggled with doubts about how their lives might mesh. With Penelope telling Darby about the dinner he had shared with her at The Mansion, Jace could only imagine the spin Penelope had put upon it. He feared Darby would have totally misinterpreted what Penelope had shared. After all, the optics didn't look good, with him spending a few days in Darby's company, only to escort Penelope to dinner the very same day Darby had left town.

Had that been the catalyst which had caused Darby to

reevaluate their relationship? Did she believe he had been unfaithful to her the moment she had left Dallas?

His gut told him that's exactly what Darby had thought. Out of context, it did sound bad. Jace knew he had only fulfilled an obligation to Penelope, since he had been the one to cancel their date so that he could take Darby to dinner and spend time with her.

He released Penelope's arm. "You deliberately tried to poison what I had with Darby," he accused.

Her satisfied smile told him all he needed to know, but she said, "If I couldn't have you, why should she?"

"You are vile, Penelope. You knew when we arranged to go to the charity event together that it was a one-time situation. I felt bad that I had to cancel, and that was the only reason I took you to dinner. Do not speak to me again. Do not even come within my field of vision."

"Are you threatening me, Jace?" she asked indignantly.

"No. I'm making it clear that I want nothing to do with you. Ever."

He walked out of the art gallery without purchasing anything or even saying goodbye to the host. Jace walked the streets of Deep Ellum for over an hour, turning everything over in his mind. He knew now that Darby had been spooked by whatever Penelope Rossi had said to her. She had been enjoying herself at the casino party, and then she'd done an about-face.

Whether they made it or not as a couple should have been between them, without Penelope's intervention.

Jace was ready to do something about that now.

He looked around, trying to figure out where he was, and then headed back to where he'd parked his car. Driving home, he decided to call Eli.

"Hey," his brother said. "How was your road trip?"

He'd shared with Eli about his upcoming trip but hadn't called him during it.

"Productive," he replied. "What have you been up to?"

"Autumn and I went to the high school's homecoming parade tonight. They hold one every year the night before the big game. This year they're playing the Eagles, and I've learned that that's their longtime rival. Hawthorne leads the series by two games now."

"What was the parade like?" Jace asked. "I've never been to one."

Eli described some of the floats to him, including the one Triple H's staff had put together. He explained how the building had been documented on their Instagram page. As they spoke, Jace pulled up the account and was surprised at how elaborate the float was. Guilt filled him. Eli was always asking about his work. He should reciprocate more. Follow this account. Be a better brother.

Be a better man.

"How's Darby doing?" he asked, softly.

"Whoa. Outta left field question." Eli went silent a moment. "Do you really want to know?"

"Yes."

"She's doing okay. Busy with teaching and the activities she's sponsoring. Her cheerleaders won first place among the school floats tonight. You could probably see it on the HHS website or on Instagram."

Jace was already typing into his phone, pulling up the Hawthorne Hawks' account and seeing floats and other pictures from the parade this evening. Darby was in one, and his heart skipped a beat catching sight of her.

"I miss her," he admitted. "I screwed up, Eli. Royally."

"I gathered you did. Darby hasn't said a word to me about what went down between the two of you. She's not a person who would badmouth someone. She's kept details of your breakup to herself. Maybe Kelby knows the truth. Or at least some of it. They're tight."

"My question is, what are you going to do about it, Jace? Are you going to make things right?"

He thought for a minute—and decided that life with Darby was better than life without her. Whatever he had to do. Whatever it took.

"I'm coming to Hawthorne to see if she'll take me back," Jace declared.

CHAPTER

Twenty-Six

Darby was glad the day was cool and crisp, exactly what an outdoor pep rally just before Halloween should be. No rain was in the forecast, so the game would not be affected by weather tonight. Her cheerleaders were setting up their megaphones and pompoms as the band and drill team took their places in the stands on the home side.

She glanced across the field and saw the visitor side was almost full. Knowing she had time before Blanche began dismissing students over the PA by class, she wandered across the field and went into the stands, finding Aunt Meg and Uncle Joe in the center of things at the fifty-yard line. Autumn and Eli sat next to them.

Aunt Meg hugged her, and Darby said, "I see you're all decked out in your Hawks paraphernalia."

"This is my lucky shirt," her aunt said. Fingering the button she wore, she added, "And I've worn West's button since he played quarterback here. But only on homecoming since he graduated."

Uncle Joe laughed. "Meg is so superstitious. Me? I just put on whatever."

"I hope you'll lose the suit and tie tonight and wear something more casual to the game," she told him, looking to her cousin and Eli. "You two are playing hooky from Triple H."

Eli laughed easily. "Autumn said we simply had to come to the pep rally. That everyone would be here." He glanced around. "I see other doctors. My banker. Atticus' vet. The guy who owns the hardware store. Homecoming really is a big deal in Hawthorne."

They chatted a few minutes, and then she saw the senior class arriving.

"I better get back to the other side so I can supervise the cheer squads."

On her way down to the field, Dizzy waved to her, and she asked, "Is the diner closed?"

"For two hours," he said, beaming at her. "I always shut it down so the staff can come to the pep rally. Your girls look good this year, Darby."

"I'm very proud of them," she said, happiness swelling within her. Though her personal life was in freefall, she was thriving professionally, knowing the change in careers had been the right move.

It still didn't make her miss Jace any less, though.

As she walked across the turf, she held in the urge to turn a few cartwheels. She still worked out with her squad daily, stretching and teaching them new moves for cheers, even turning a few backflips every now and then. It was hard to walk across this football field, though, without remembering her own days as a cheerleader.

Her phone buzzed in her pocket, and she saw she had a text from Kelby.

> Surly client. Won't be able to make the pep rally. See you tonight at the tailgate!

Darby knew Kelby was disappointed not to be here, but her friend was dedicated to her business. Kelby had a way of keeping others calm around her, so Darby hoped she could iron out the problems with the grumpy client.

She had the varsity squad set up where the junior and senior sections met in the stands, with the JV squad on the border of the sophomores and freshmen classes.

West stopped by. "Just checking in, Cuz."

"Got your pep rally speech prepared?" she teased, knowing he loved to speak off the cuff. West was so charming that Hawks fans gobbled up whatever he said. "I remember how when we were given a project to complete and a choice to do something written or oral, you always went for the oral presentation."

He grinned. "It's easy for me to get up and talk. That gift of gab Mom passed along to Summer and me."

"Well, you're doing an amazing job with the team, West," Darby praised. "You were born to coach."

Nodding, he said, "I really feel I'm in my element. Especially being able to come back and coach in Hawthorne."

Darby went to the cheer squads, having them gather around in a large circle.

"Homecoming is a special time of year, especially for you seniors. The parade. This pep rally. The game and tomorrow night's dance. These will be events you will look back on in the years to come and cherish these memories. I'm so proud of all of you, but especially my seniors. You've been true leaders, both to the other cheerleaders and the entire school. Let's go out and give our best today. Hawks on three. One, two, three."

"Hawks!" shouted the girls, joy on their faces.

By now, all the students had arrived, and the band was playing a catchy pop tune. The drill team was doing a hand routine in the stands, while her cheerleaders were doing a dance they'd learned in camp to the music. When it ended, the student council president stepped to the microphone to lead the school in the Pledge of Allegiance.

From there, the pep rally resembled ones from Darby's own days as a student. The band played. The drill team performed. Both cheer squads did a new dance they'd been working. Classes chanted competing for the spirit stick, which always seemed to go to the seniors during the home-coming pep rally, though the freshman displayed a lot of vocal energy.

Then West took the microphone, addressing the crowd. He displayed the perfect balance of humor blended with a more serious tone. Those present in the stadium ate up his anecdotes, and everyone, including his players, were inspired by his words. By the time West finished speaking, the crowd was even more enthusiastic than before. The two football captains, one from offense and the other from the defense, spoke after their coach, and the students were on a natural high, ready to trounce the Eagles at tonight's game.

By then, it was time for the school song. Darby stood a little taller, pride swelling within her, at being an alum of HHS and now a part of its faculty. Then the band began playing the school fight song, as the football team was the first to exit the stadium. Blanche took over the microphone, directing the freshmen to return to second period, followed by the other classes and groups.

"Let's take everything inside," she told the cheerleaders, who gathered their equipment and headed to the gym and locker room.

Darby spent the next fifteen minutes helping girls put on their mums. She recalled seeing pictures of her mom and Aunt Meg back in the day, their mums the size of a corsage, pinned to their shoulders, with ribbons streaming past their waists. By the time Darby reached high school, though, mums had taken on a life of their own, taking up the entire front of her cheer uniform, the braided ribbons falling to her ankles.

That tradition lived on, and her cheerleaders were smart enough to have create a harness, which lifted over their heads and fastened on the side and in back. It helped hold the mum to its wearer without using dozens of large hatpins to keep it in place.

After all mums were attached to their owners, Darby said, "Remember, you can bring your mum to the game tonight and rest it against your megaphone. No wearing of mums during the game, though. It would be impossible to do your cheers and flips and build a pyramid."

The girls left for class, and Darby went to her own classroom, finding her newspaper staff hard at work. The homecoming edition of the *Hawthorne Herald* would be available in the cafeteria today during lunchtime, and students were busy gathering up hard copies to take to the lunchroom.

"Don't forget to drop some off in the faculty lounge and at the front office," she reminded them. "The rest can be taken over to the stadium. Fans tonight will want copies to read, as well."

While those deliveries were being made, Darby met with the editor-in-chief and photography editor, along with two photographers who had covered this morning's pep rally. The pictures taken this morning would appear in the next newspaper.

After they decided which photographs the *Herald* would use, she said, "Be sure to send copies of these to *Horizon*. You both got some great shots. I'll see what the yearbook photographers got once I meet with them, but they may want to use some of your pictures, as well."

She found herself too busy to go to the lounge for lunch, which usually happened once or twice a week. Thankfully, Kay had left a small fridge for Darby, saying it would be too much trouble to move the fridge to Chicago. Darby always kept it stocked with bottled waters, yogurts, and fruit. She pulled out a carton of yogurt and an apple now and ate while she input grades and then checked her emails.

A student she recognized as one of West's offensive lineman entered her room. He wore a lanyard with an office aide ID card and carried one of the old-fashioned mums with the single mum and mostly short ribbons a foot long hanging from it.

"Ms. Montgomery, this is for you." He handed it to her, along with a small box.

Darby looked at it. "Do you know where it came from?"

He shrugged. "Nope. I just deliver whatever they tell me to."

"Thank you."

Darby studied it. It had one long ribbon spelling out *Homecoming* and an even longer braid woven together with the school's colors. It also had a ribbon with *Hawthorne High School* and the year. Trinkets attached to the center of the mum itself included a tiny, plastic football and a small, stuffed Hawk. She was touched by the gesture and supposed one or more of the cheerleaders had made it for her.

Opening the box, she found several hatpins and used them to attach the mum to her left shoulder. She retrieved her cell phone and took a selfie, sending it to Kelby.

Look what I got! Must be from my cheerleaders. Maybe you should've talked West into getting you a mum! Hope you worked your magic and the irritable client is happy now. See you soon.

She didn't get an immediate reply from Kelby and knew her friend must still be putting out fires.

Darby finished up the school day, with varsity cheer being her last class of the day. When she asked if they had been the ones to make the mum for her, all she saw were blank faces.

"It would've been a good idea," one said. "Sorry we didn't think of it, Ms. Montgomery. But it really looks nice."

Now, her curiosity was growing. She didn't think any student on the newspaper or yearbook staff would have spent the time making a mum for her. Maybe it was one of the JV cheerleaders or a cheerleader mom who had done so. She would figure it out so she could send a thank you note.

The squad members helped one another out of their mum harnesses, and they practiced their newest dance, one which they had performed at the pep rally today and would continue to do during the remainder of the football season.

"You look really sharp," she complimented once they had repeated it three times in a row. Carrie had fallen out of line after the first time and watched with a critical eye.

"I think we can incorporate some of these dance steps into our competition routine," Carrie told the others.

They spent a few minutes discussing what they wanted to do for nationals. Varsity and JV would perform together since the competition required a certain number of cheerleaders to participate, but Darby had agreed that it would be up to varsity to agree to the moves of the routine.

"We need to nail down the choreography," Carrie said.

"Starting next week. We've got down our chants and dances for the rest of football season. Let's begin on Monday creating our routine. Ms. Montgomery and I have already worked on a lot of it, trying to get an overall idea of what structures we want to create and the music we'll use. We'll talk about that on Monday."

She let the squad go a few minutes early. They already spent early mornings, after school, and nights working on things. The gift of getting out of the parking lot just as the bell rang and not having to be stuck in after-school traffic was a reward she could easily manage.

Darby stayed at school, working on lesson plans and some ideas for nationals, until it was time to walk over to the tailgate. She was greeted by so many people on her way over, making her feel good. She didn't just fit in Hawthorne.

She belonged here.

"Hey, Darby," Autumn said when she arrived. "Wow—you've got a mum!" She looked to her husband. "This is what guys give their dates." Autumn laughed. "Actually, the size of the one Darby is wearing is about the size girls give their guys. They wear them on an elastic band around their biceps. Who gave it to you, the cheerleaders?"

"I don't know," she said. "None of them said they did. I have a feeling one of their moms made it for me."

"Made what?"

She turned and saw Kelby. "I'm talking about my very cool mum. Thank goodness it's not ginormous." She played with one of the ribbons. "It's the perfect size and a thoughtful gift. I just need to track down the giver."

"I'm glad you like it," Kelby said. "It's only right that you should have one since I'm sure all your cheerleaders did."

Darby explained to Eli about how large mums now were

and the harnesses the girls had developed in order to keep their mums on.

"That's insane," he said. "How much would something like that even cost?"

"I've heard guys spending up to three hundred dollars," she said.

Eli shook his head and slung an arm around Autumn. "Sorry, babe. I'd rather spend that kind of money on a weekend getaway with you."

Autumn slipped her arm around his waist. "I don't need a mum. All I need is you." She kissed him.

"Love is in the air," Uncle Joe sang, flipping a burger.

Darby ate quickly, wanting to get over to the stadium. Kelby accompanied her, asking, "How did the pep rally go?"

"Actually, it was like going back in time," she shared. "They still do so many of the same traditions we did when we were students."

She talked about the jalapeño eating contest. The skit. The competition for the spirit stick. How the entire visitor side had been filled with supportive Hawks fans from the town.

As they went through the turnstile, Kelby said, "You sound really happy."

Darby stopped. "I'd say contented. I feel like Dorothy, having come home after going to Oz, and realizing that there really is no place like home. I'm a part of Hawthorne, and I like that."

She paused, her throat thickening with emotion. "Am I a little wistful that I couldn't make things work with Jace? Absolutely. But Hawthorne and his glitzy world in Dallas just didn't mesh."

Taking Kelby's hands in hers, Darby added, "I like what I'm doing. I like being here with you and my family. I'm enjoying my job and working with so many different kinds of students." She sighed. "And hopefully, I'll find someone I can share my life with one day. Not anytime soon. Because I did love Jace. Those feelings didn't go away when I made the decision to stick to a life here. I hope they'll eventually fade, though."

Kelby squeezed her hands. "Everything is going to work out the way it should," her friend said optimistically. "Let's go down to the track."

They entered the stands, which were only beginning to fill. In the next forty-five minutes before kickoff, they would be packed. Players from both teams were going through stretching and would soon begin their pre-game drills. She saw the band and drill team had already claimed their spots in the bleachers and would make their way to the field in half an hour for their pregame show.

Making their way down to the bottom of the stairs, they went through the gate and started along the track. Then Darby froze.

Jace was talking to the three cheerleaders already there. As she and Kelby approached, he turned. If she thought her heart had been racing before, it went into triple-time now, thumping so hard that she felt the mum she wore shaking.

"Hey, Darby," he said, making her want to slap him—and kiss him—at the same time.

"Jace," she said evenly. "What are you doing here?"

"We've got a lot to talk about. Either before or after the game. Your call."

She couldn't talk to him now. She'd be a mess if she did. Mascara running down her cheeks and violent trembling wouldn't be a great look in front of her students and the entire town of Hawthorne.

"After," she said curtly.

"Okay," he said, no emotion in his voice, making him hard to read. Then he approached her, picking up her hand and placing something in it. "I'll see you after the Hawks win."

As he walked away, she forced down the lump in her throat by swallowing hard. Then she opened her hand. Inside it was a folded ribbon. She let it drop open in the slight breeze.

Darby & Jace

She looked at it, dumbfounded, and then realized Jace had been the one to send the mum to her.

"It goes here," Kelby said softly, taking the ribbon from Darby's hand and attaching it to the mum.

"*You* made this?" she asked, her voice breaking.

"Jace asked me to. That's what I was working on this morning. He wanted you to have it to wear. At school today and the game tonight."

Darby glanced down at the ribbon bearing their names and then looked blankly at her best friend.

"Why?"

"I think that's something you'll need to take up with Jace," Kelby said firmly. "I'll see you later. Call if you want to talk. No matter how late it is."

"Okay," she said softly.

Kelby walked away, and Darby looked down at the mum again. Yes, it was just a stupid corsage. It didn't mean anything.

Or did it?

Twenty~Seven

Jace returned to the gate and mounted all the concrete steps until he'd reached the top row. Everything below him was starting to fill in quickly. He'd never bothered going to a game when he was a high school student. Usually, he had a cross country meet the next morning, so he didn't want to be out late. He always wanted to be rested and fully hydrated before a race. Staying out late to watch a game by himself had never appealed to him.

He sat, making certain he was not directly in front of the cheerleaders, not wanting Darby to feel as if he'd deliberately sat in her line of vision. Turning his eyes to the playing field, he watched as the football team broke into groups for their drills.

Suddenly, he noticed Autumn headed his way. She took a seat next to him.

"Did Eli send you?" he asked.

"No. I came on my own." She hesitated a moment. "I like you, Jace. I'm thrilled that you and Eli have reconnected after so many years of being apart."

"But you're also worried about your cousin."

Autumn nodded. "You really hurt Darby. She's keeping quiet about your breakup, but I understand that it was her choice to walk away from your relationship."

He smiled ruefully. "And here I've turned up again, like a bad penny. You think I'm going to hurt her again. Let me say this, Autumn. I was plenty hurt when Darby left. It came out of the blue. She really didn't want to talk things over. I understand more about that decision now."

Briefly, he told her about running into Penelope Rossi and learning about the conversation Darby and the jewelry designer had the night of the casino party.

"I'm upset that Darby believed everything Penelope said and didn't let us talk things over."

Autumn frowned. "Can it really work between the two of you, Jace? Don't get me wrong. I think you're really good together, but you have completely different lifestyles. Darby wants a life in Hawthorne. You're firmly entrenched in Dallas. If I don't think it can work between you, just think of what Darby would say."

"It'll work," he said stubbornly. "It has to. Because I'm crazy about her. Crazy in love with her."

"Oh!" Autumn looked taken aback.

"I should have told her first. Not you," he apologized. "But I plan to say those words tonight. Don't worry, Autumn. I have a plan. I'm just hoping that it works."

She patted his knee. "If it does, I'll be so happy for you. If it doesn't?" She bit her lip. "I don't want to take sides."

"You won't need to," Jace insisted. "Darby's been your cousin your entire life. I've only been your brother-in-law a couple of months. Let's be positive and know everything will work out so that you aren't pulled in opposite directions."

"Eli and I are here for you, Jace. Good luck."

Autumn returned to her seat. He saw Eli give him a thumbs up, and Jace returned the gesture.

The halftime show was held before the game. The Hawks' opponents were allowed to have their band play, and their drill team performed. Then the home team's band took the field, playing a medley of patriotic songs. The drill team did their thing, and Jace thought both groups outperformed the other school.

Then it was time for the football team to make their appearance, and they came crashing through the large banner the cheerleaders held high. The fight song played, with everyone in the stands singing along. Jace knew the words. He'd been on the HHS website daily since Darby had left. He had read copies of the *Hawthorne Herald* online. Watched videos of previous pep rallies. Kept up with West's team and knew they were predicted to be tonight's victors.

The first quarter was close, but the Hawks scored twice in the second quarter to go up by ten points. Halftime came, and the band took the field again. Three girls were named over the PA, escorted to the Hawks logo on the fifty-yard line by their parents. He noted one was the varsity cheerleader captain. Jace had avoided looking at Darby during the first half, but he found her in the crowd now, seeing how she eagerly awaited the results of the homecoming vote.

The fans erupted when Carrie Johnson was named as the new homecoming queen. Even from a distance, he saw how proud Darby was.

The homecoming king was announced next, with two of the nominees being football players. The third was a guard on the basketball team, and it was this teenager who was named king. He joined Carrie Johnson in a convertible, which was then driven slowly around the track as the rest of the homecoming court was announced. He saw it included a couple from the freshman, sophomore, and junior classes.

The rest of the game passed in a blur. Jace looked at the field, but his thoughts were a mile away as he tried to decide exactly what he wanted to say to Darby.

He became aware that the game had ended when not only did a loud, sustained cheer break out, but the stands vibrated from students stomping their feet. Quickly, he located Darby again, seeing that she headed down to the track. She hugged Carrie, obviously congratulating her captain, and then went to speak to several of the other girls, embracing them, as well. He figured they must be the seniors on the squad.

As the players left the field and bystanders began leaving the stands, the PA announcer reminded students of the homecoming dance tomorrow night in the high school's gym, starting at eight o'clock.

Jace let the stands thin before making his way down the concrete stairs. He stopped on the last row and took a seat, waiting for Darby. The last cheerleader left, and Darby looked into the stands, seeing him. She made her way toward him.

"Believe it or not, all the lights will go out inside the stadium in about ten minutes. We probably need to find somewhere else to talk. I don't want to get caught in the dark."

He rose and followed her up the steps, dying to touch her but afraid if he did, she'd flee. They saw a few stragglers as they made their way out the gates, Jace still on Darby's heels.

"I'm parked over there," she said, pointing.

Jace continued to trail after her, his mouth going dry, his heart hammering against his ribs uncomfortably.

They reached her car, and she unlocked it, tossing in

what she carried. Then she shut the door and leaned against the vehicle's door, crossing her arms.

"Talk."

"I feel like a nervous schoolboy, called to the principal's office," he told her. "For something I didn't even do."

Darby didn't say anything. Her brows arched, as if she were bored and wanting him to get on with things.

"Let me speak first, and then you can ask me anything. Or say whatever you want. Can you do that?"

"Of course," she said crisply.

"I had planned to attend a charity event with a woman named Penelope Rossi."

Jace looked to see if Darby would react hearing the name, and he saw she stiffened slightly.

"Instead, I told Penelope something had come up. I broke the date with her—to be with you. We went to Adelina's that night. That was the start of everything for me. I was already attracted to you. Had enjoyed flirting with you at the wedding. But I fell for you that night, Montgomery. Hard."

Her eyes widened, but she kept silent.

"You were—are—all I can think about. I'm in love with you. I was afraid to say those words to you because I thought it was too soon. Hell, I've never been in love. I thought maybe I was misreading my own feelings. The situation. But with every beat of my heart, it cries out your name, Darby. I decided that it was love, something I've never experienced in my life. I've locked away my emotions and have always been stoic for as long as I can remember. While I come alive and act a part as an agent, the outgoing, affable professional, it's as if no one's ever known the true me.

"Until you came along."

He watched her blink several times and knew she was not immune to what he was telling her.

"I did arrange to take Penelope to dinner after you flew back to Kansas City. After all, I was the one who'd broken the date. I felt I owed her. She's an up and coming jewelry designer, and she was counting on going to that event with me and having me introduce her to some high profile people." He shook his head. "But I didn't really want to be seen with her. My heart already belonged to you, Darby. I took Penelope to dinner at a place where she'd be happy being seen. It was an early night. Dinner and nothing else. I never saw the inside of her apartment. Whatever she told you about that night, it was a lie."

"I see," she said, her voice shaking.

He took a step toward her, the need to touch her too great. Jace cupped her cheek for a moment, inhaling her floral perfume. Then he took her hands, forcing her to uncross her arms.

"I love you, Darby Montgomery. I will do whatever it takes to be with you. I know you're happy here in Hawthorne, teaching at HHS. I wouldn't ask you to move closer to me."

"But—"

"Nope. No interruptions. I said I would say my piece, and you agreed not to speak until I was finished. "

She nodded, looking contrite.

"I'm the boss, or at least I'm an equal partner with Mark. I own Total Touchdown Management. I can run it any way I see fit. Because of that, I met with Mark first thing this morning and laid out my plans for the future. He agreed to everything I wanted. I then met with my entire staff."

Jace slowed down, taking a deep breath. Darby squeezed his hands encouragingly, giving him the courage to continue.

"I told them that I was moving to Hawthorne because the woman I loved lives there and without her, I don't have any kind of life worth living. I will go to the office two days a week for meetings and check-ins, which means staying in town overnight. I'll still have to do some traveling. That can't be avoided. Some of that will be on weekends, and I can't change that. But the rest of the time, I told the staff that I'd work remotely from Hawthorne. Why not? They can text me. Email me. Zoom with me. Technology has made it easy for many people to work from home. Hell, I already do a lot of Zooming or FaceTiming with clients as it is. They won't care if I'm sitting in my office in Dallas or one here."

Jace gazed deeply into Darby's eyes. "The point is, I can try and be here as much as possible. Not one hundred percent of the time, but I can arrange my schedule to be here more than I'm gone." He smiled. "I also told Elena that she's being promoted. She knows sports. She's gotten plenty of experience working at TTM. She's got a few hoops to jump through to gain her sports agent license and registration, but that won't take long. Our clients already love her. And having another agent in the office is ideal. We're growing. It was only a matter of time before I promoted her anyway. She's already got someone in mind to replace her, and that interview is lined up for Monday. An interview I'll do from here."

He looked at her, hope in his heart. "I've said my piece. I love you. I want a life with you. I want us to be an us here in Hawthorne. So, what do you say? I mean, you don't have to give me an answer right away. I know you'll need to—"

Jace never finished his sentence because Darby was suddenly kissing him hungrily. All the strain and worries from the last few months melted away. There was only her. Him. Them.

Wrapping his arms about her, he crushed her to him. The kiss went from hungry to hot to wild. And it went on for a long, long time.

Finally, she ended it, staring up at him.

"I say yes. Yes, to us. Yes, to our life together," she said, her breathing still as ragged as his.

Joy filled him. "Good. Yes, to us. I hope that means yes to marriage. Babies. A house and a dog and a cat and a hamster and whatever else you might want."

She smiled at him, stroking his cheek tenderly. "All I've truly ever wanted, Jace, is you. I've loved you for what seems like forever. And I'll always love you. Until you turn gray. Or go bald."

He laughed and kissed her again, his heart bursting with love for this woman. This place.

And everything they would build.

Together ...

J ace said, "It's out of your hands now. The girls have practiced for hours. Muscle memory will take over. That, and adrenaline. They'll probably come off the stage and not even remember being out there."

"I know you're right," Darby said. "I just want this for them so badly."

The Hawthorne combined cheerleading squads had performed both Thursday night and Friday afternoon and night. They had made it to the finals and were currently ranked second in their division. This final outing would include everything they had prepared for. It would start with a cheer. Continue with a dance which she and the seniors on varsity had created. From there, they would begin a chant, segueing into various stunts, from one-handed cartwheels to backflips to two large human pyramids.

She wanted this more than anything, especially since Peggy Mortimer, her former boss at Cheer USA, was here.

"I'm sorry Kay didn't come down for the competition."

Jace had offered to fly the former cheer coach from

Chicago to Dallas, but Kay had turned down the generous offer for two reasons. First, she said this was Darby's group now, not hers. Kay didn't want to be a distraction to the girls. Second, she was eight weeks pregnant and nauseous for about four hours in the mornings. She told Darby that even the thought of being on an airplane made her stomach queasy.

"One more group, and then HHS is up," Kelby told them. Her friend sported a baby bump and was five months along. She glowed even more than she usually did.

"I'll go out to my seat now," her husband said, giving Darby a sweet kiss. "Whatever happens, you're the best cheer coach ever, and HHS is lucky to have you."

She watched him leave, and Kelby said, "Get that goofy, lovestruck smile off your face and go give your squad a final pep talk."

Darby laughed, heading toward where her girls were gathering. She looked at this group, and they grew quiet.

"You have heart," she told them, bumping her fist against her chest. "Each of you loves the sport of cheerleading. You put your heart and soul into it. You are selfless. You put the group first. Always. I am so proud to be the coach of such a loving, caring, compassionate group of young women. Such dedication is rare.

"Take a look around you. These girls will most likely be lifelong friends to you. And you will all remember this moment when you went out in front of that audience and competed for a national title. If you win it, we'll certainly celebrate." Darby paused. "But I believe in our hearts, we are already winners. Do your best. Have fun out there. We'll be the last group to compete. Good luck. Hawks on three. One, two, three."

"Hawks!" cried the group.

Carrie motioned for the girls to line up. From the music, Darby knew the group performing still had about ninety seconds to go. She took a deep breath and closed her eyes.

Coming home to Hawthorne had been the best decision of her life. She had found her place at HHS, teaching and coaching. More importantly, returning to Texas had allowed Jace into her life. He'd been good to his word, finding temporary office space with Sawyer in his office on the town square. Jace had kept his Dallas condo for the times he was working in town, and they had rented an apartment to live in while their home was being constructed, their property adjacent to Kelby and West. They had wed in a small, intimate wedding over the Christmas break, and Jace had promised to take her on a honeymoon over spring break next month. She had no idea where they would go, but it didn't matter.

All that mattered was that they were together.

The audience cheered as the group on stage finished, and Darby flashed a thumbs up at her cheerleaders, her gaze meeting Carrie's. They had talked several times about Carrie's future, but their focus the past few weeks had been on nationals. Carrie wanted to bring home the grand prize trophy, just as Darby and Kelby had done during their own days of cheering for the Hawks.

She winked at Carrie, and the captain signaled for the team to follow her to the floor. Darby heard cheers erupt from the crowd, knowing so many she loved had turned out to support her. Sawyer was there, along with West. Autumn and Eli had come with her aunt and uncle. Many of her students and residents of Hawthorne had also made the trek to Dallas to watch the competition.

Glancing over, she saw one of her photographers snapping pictures from backstage. Another one would be out front, capturing pictures. Carrie's dad was going to video the finals, so the girls would be able to watch their own performance and see how it stacked up against their fellow competitors.

Darby's lips moved silently, mouthing the words to the cheers and chants. The music was loud, and she could see much of the crowd was on its feet, clapping along as her girls moved to the beat. She watched, bursting with pride, as the stunt portion played out. Darby had been a flyer, one of the girls lifted into the air for stunts, and she knew how much rode on a flyer's performance. The HHS flyers moved from thigh stands to split-lifts to liberty and single base stunts flawlessly.

Holding her breath, she waited for the grand finale, a double, two-high pyramid. Both pyramids had the flyers connecting with other flyers, with half holding another flyer's hand and the other half holding a different flyer's extended leg. Darby held her breath, watching the girls get into place—and holding their positions for the required amount of time.

The flyers dismounted, and all the HHS cheerleaders beamed as they jumped, doing pikes, herkies, and toe touches, while others did choreographed backflips and round-offs in unison. The girls finished in one long, straight line, their fists raised in triumph.

"Yes!" Darby and Kelby squealed, grabbing one another, jumping up and down, tears streaming down their faces.

She could hear the enthusiasm of the crowd and then the sound of 'Hawks, Hawks, Hawks' began echoing throughout the arena.

Dean Baker, who had been standing backstage supervising, looked at Darby. "I don't need to see the scores. I think we already know which team just claimed the national title."

Her squads poured backstage, joy on their faces,

breathing heavily from all the exertion. They were falling into one another's arms, laughing, crying, babbling.

Carrie found her and hugged Darby tightly.

"Thank you, Mrs. Tanner. Whatever happens, we feel like winners."

More girls came over, hugging both her and Kelby, and Darby steered them to some steps which led from the stage to the floor of the arena. They huddled in a group on the side, waiting for the results to be tabulated.

When Peggy came onto the stage, a hush fell over the crowd. Darby's girls all held hands—and their breaths—as Peggy began to speak.

"Cheer USA is thrilled at the turnout for this year's national competition. It's been the best year yet, and we hope to see you next year in Phoenix. Now, here's what you've been waiting for."

Peggy announced fifth, fourth, and third place. It came down to Hawthorne and Ezby, a team from West Texas. The moment Ezby came from Peggy's mouth, her team broke out in shouts, bouncing up and down, knowing they had been named national champions.

In the pandemonium, Peggy motioned for Darby to come to the stage, and she waved for her entire group to follow her. Peggy handed over a large trophy, and Darby held it in one hand, balancing the base against her hip.

At the microphone, Darby said, "I have been so blessed to work with these cheerleaders from Hawthorne High School. They were originally coached by Kay Timmons, and she deserves to share in this success."

She turned and looked at the glowing faces of the combined JV and varsity squads and said, "I have never seen a squad which works so diligently, one which is dedicated to being the best they can be. I also have never known another group which loves one another the way these young ladies do."

Raising the trophy high, she concluded with, "Here's to the Hawthorne Hawks cheerleading squad, your national champions!"

The girls mobbed her while the raucous crowd shouted their support at the top of their lungs.

Jace found her, pulling her from the sea surrounding her. He captured her face in his hands.

"I am so proud of you," he said.

Smiling, she told him, "I just followed my heart to Hawthorne. And you."

Her husband kissed her, and Darby knew that they had so much to look forward to as their lives unfolded in Hawthorne, the place of her heart.

Also by Alexa Aston

HEARTS IN HAWTHORNE

Heartstrings and Helmets

Heartbeat Harmony

Agent of the Heart

Hearts and Hooves

Hoops and Hearts

LOST CREEK, TEXAS HILL COUNTRY

The Perfect Blend

Painted Melodies

Script of Love

Love in Every Bite

Whispered Melodies

SUGAR SPRINGS

Shadows of the Past

Learning to Trust Again

A Perfect Match

A Fresh Start

Recipe for Love

MAPLE COVE

Another Chance at Love

A New Beginning

Coming Home

The Lyrics of Love

Finding Home

HOLLYWOOD NAME GAME

Hollywood Heartbreaker

Hollywood Flirt

Hollywood Player

Hollywood Double

Hollywood Enigma

LAWMEN OF THE WEST

Runaway Hearts

Blind Faith

Love and the Lawman

Ballad Beauty

SAGEBRUSH BRIDES

A Game of Chance

Written in the Cards

Outlaw Muse

KNIGHTS OF REDEMPTION

A Bit of Heaven on Earth

A Knight for Kallen

SUDDENLY A DUKE

Portrait of the Duke

Music for the Duke

Polishing the Duke

Designs on the Duke

Fashioning the Duke

Love Blooms with the Duke

Training the Duke

Investigating the Duke

SECOND SONS OF LONDON

Educated by the Earl

Debating with the Duke

Empowered by the Earl

Made for the Marquess

Dubious about the Duke

Valued by the Viscount

Meant for the Marquess

DUKES DONE WRONG

Discouraging the Duke

Deflecting the Duke

Disrupting the Duke

Delighting the Duke

Destiny with a Duke

DUKES OF DISTINCTION

Duke of Renown

Duke of Charm

Duke of Disrepute

Duke of Arrogance

Duke of Honor

About the Author

USA Today and Amazon Top 100 bestselling author Alexa Aston lives with her husband in a Dallas suburb, where she eats her fair share of dark chocolate and plots out stories while she walks every morning. She enjoys travel, sports, and binge-watching—and never misses an episode of *Survivor*.

Alexa brings her characters to life in steamy historicals, contemporary romances, and romantic suspense novels that resonate with passion, intensity, and heart.

KEEP UP WITH ALEXA
Visit her website
Newsletter Sign-Up

MORE WAYS TO CONNECT WITH ALEXA